I0662779

Imperfect Promises

ELIZABETH NOYES

W

Write Integrity Press

Imperfect Promises
© 2018 Elizabeth Noyes

ISBN-13: 978-1-944120-70-2

All rights reserved. No part of this publication may be reproduced or transmitted in any form or by any means without written permission from the publisher.

This book is a work of fiction. Names, characters, places, and incidents are either products of the author's imagination or used fictitiously. Any similarity to actual people and/or events is purely coincidental.

Scripture references are taken from The New International Version ®NIV ®. Copyright © 1973, 1978, 1984, 2011 by Biblica, Inc. ™ Used by permission of Zondervan. All rights reserved worldwide. www.zondervan.com.

Published by Write Integrity Press, 4475 Trinity Mills Road, PO Box 702852, Dallas, TX 75370
Find out more about the author, **Elizabeth Noyes,** at her website: **www.ElizabethNoyesWrites.com** or on her author page at
www.WriteIntegrity.com.

Printed in the United States of America.

Contents

Dedication

Imperfect Promises is dedicated to all the men and women who serve and defend the United States of America. Whether military, police, fire fighter, or any other uniformed worker, your dedication and willingness to endure hardship is recognized and appreciated, for you represent the very heart of our great country. A huge shout of appreciation is also extended to your families for, like me, they know firsthand the sacrifices involved with sharing a loved one with five million other people. Thank you all for your service.

Chapter One

He'd landed in hell—a place of eternal waiting, fiery heat, despair, regret, and weariness.

And bugs. Lots of bugs. Both the flying kind and the creepers. Mosquitoes, ants, sandflies, roaches, no-see-ums, and tarantulas so scary-looking and lightning-fast they made nightmares seem like sweet dreams.

Jonas swiped at the perspiration pooling in the hollows under his eyes. His beard had grown long and thick over the past few months. Now, after parboiling in his own sweat for days on end, he itched like a flea-bitten mongrel and stank to high heaven. No wonder the old timers called August the dog days of summer.

What would the prim and proper Miss Townsend say if she could see him now? Worse, if she could smell him. Knowing Shea, she'd pinch her nose, make a face, and laugh.

A rough expletive erupted over the headset.

"Problem?" Jonas asked.

"Nasty little biters are eating me alive," John Archer, his friend and long-time partner in these two-man missions growled and swore again.

Jonas couldn't hold back a chuckle. "You're getting soft in your old age, Arch."

"I'm two months older than you, Ghost-man. Tougher, too.

"Riiiight."

"Our target is way past late." Archer changed the subject. "We're losing daylight."

Jonas shot a quick glance skyward where the fierce sun had passed its zenith. With each tick of the clock their hope of getting out of this accursed land tonight faded. "Patience, grasshopper. Toure will come. If not today, then tomorrow. His ego demands it."

They'd both learned the art of patience long ago, but Sebastian Toure had proven more unpredictable than anticipated. The man never took the same route, never rode in the same vehicle, and never went anywhere without his baker's dozen—twelve armed-to-the-teeth bodyguards plus a driver.

Jonas and Archer had spent the last nine weeks tracking Toure. Two long months they'd watched and waited in the sweltering heat, taking notes and making

plans until three days ago their patience paid off. Toure's very randomness had yielded a pattern in his movements. It seemed even the wiliest of men remained creatures of habit.

"What makes you think that narcissist has an ego?" Archer asked.

"Because according to all the dots you connected, celebrating his successes feeds his sense of self-worth. Adulation is oxygen to him."

"I hope I connected those dots the right way."

"I hope so, too."

Toure, like most psychopaths, didn't believe the rules applied to him. Instead of falling into anonymity after the Nigerian government rebuked and dismissed him for his involvement with a human trafficking organization while on a diplomatic mission to the United States, he'd thumbed his nose at them and formed his own militia.

Toure's *Mayakan 'yanci,* his freedom fighters, worked under the radar, one more splinter group of the much larger Ansaru militants and therefore off limits to the governmental powers—at least until Toure started picking off the other leaders. To add insult to injury, he absorbed the members of the defeated factions into his band. The Mayakan's numbers swelled to a significant amount with no sign of slowdown which created a problem for everyone.

Jonas stared at his grip on the Canadian-made

McMillan TAC-50 LRSW. Calloused hands, strong, and more than capable of doing terrible, but necessary things. His skin pigment was fading. If the mission didn't end today, tomorrow latest, he'd have no choice but to reapply the reddish-brown stain made from walnuts.

His spirits sank. A new application of dye would last at minimum four weeks, which meant another month waiting for the stain to fade enough to avoid questions from the folks back home. How much more of his life did he have to give?

An hour passed before Archer spoke again, this time with urgency. "Movement."

Jonas snapped to attention. Every detail jumped into sharper focus. His pulse spiked with an adrenaline rush and the fierce need to finish what he'd come here to do and end this waiting game. He'd promised himself once before to never return. This time he intended to keep his pledge. "Location?"

"One o'clock. Treeline."

Dust plumes drew his eye. He could hear the faint whine of engines.

Peering through the Schmidt & Bender telescopic sight atop his rifle, he spotted several vehicles as they rolled into the clearing. "This is it. You called it."

"I'm always right," Archer declared. "I count three trucks, two jeeps, and a—huh, would you look at that. Looks like Toure got himself a Benz. Wonder if it's bulletproof?"

Jonas studied the souped-up SUV with the chrome Mercedes emblem on the front. An armored car out here in the middle of nowhere? Could Toure announce any more clearly his self-importance? "That would be my bet. You know what it means."

"He's on the verge of making a move. Something big."

Jonas kept his eyes trained on the cadre of men pouring from the vehicle as they herded a group of bound captives before them. In the clearing, they surrounded the now kneeling prisoners and raised longneck bottles and aluminum cans high to salute the sky. The Mayakan fought like demons, but afterward, they drank themselves stupid at these celebrations while shouting obscenities at the world.

"You know, for a guy who's leery of his own shadow," Archer said. "This part of Toure's circus never changes."

"Foolish, but lucky for us," Jonas answered. "Wait for it ... wait ...."

The rear door of the SUV opened. Toure stepped out and, right on cue, the Mayakan flew into a frenzy. A few of the more zealous ones fired their weapons in the air.

"Target confirmed," Archer said.

"Target acquired."

"I count thirty armed, including Toure and his goons, plus another eight unarmed prisoners."

"Roger." Jonas settled a little deeper into his prone

position.

Next, the Mayakan would issue a ceremonial invitation to the prisoners to join their ranks. Not like they had a choice. The first one to refuse got a bullet in the back of his head, which made the decision easier for the rest.

Two of Toure's guards unloaded a couple of wooden pallets and stacked them in the center of the clearing in front of the prisoners.

"They're setting up a stand," Archer added.

Toure smoothed his hair and brushed at his starched fatigues.

"Distance to target?" Jonas asked.

He'd already made the calculations using a Vectronix rangefinder, estimating the distance to the center of the clearing at 7,400 feet, a cool one-and-a-quarter-mile shot. While it didn't come close to the longest shot on record, it beat his longest attempt. So be it. They hadn't gotten this close since arriving in the country.

"Distance is 2,251 meters," Archer answered. "I have eyes on the zone."

A good spotter validated data and kept a constant eye on the surroundings, taking on the preponderance of situational awareness. This allowed the sniper to zero in on the target while maintaining an advantage of a wider vision field, all of which translated to greater accuracy.

Jonas slowed his breathing. With his feet splayed out, body relaxed, and finger light on the trigger, he settled the

crosshairs on the target. They had one shot at success, two at most. "Wind?"

"Negligible," Archer replied. The Kestrel mobile weather station had long been a sniper's best friend.

"After the shot, call for evac in sixty."

"Don't you think that's cutting it a little close?" Archer asked.

Jonas did the math again while keeping a bead on the target. Fifteen minutes to low-crawl to the wooded area behind them followed by a five-mile sprint to the landing zone. Maybe a little aggressive given their full packs, but he didn't want to stick around here any longer than necessary. "What do you suggest, old man?"

"Watch it, Flash. I don't want to get stuck here any more than you do, but the chopper won't wait if we don't make the LZ at the appointed time, *fahimta*?"

"Yes, I understand." When Archer tossed out Hausa words, he'd reached his limit. "You decide. Clock starts when I pull the trigger."

The long, drawn-out sigh in his ear almost brought a smile to Jonas's face. He made up the edgier half of their team, whereas Archer erred on the safe side. The balance worked well for them and was, no doubt, the key to their success over the years.

"He's stepping up." Archer wouldn't speak again until the deed was done.

Toure hopped onto the makeshift podium and made a

Hollywood-worthy gesture with his hands outstretched in the air.

His followers roared with pleasure.

Jonas caressed the stock of his weapon. The McMillan's 0.5 minute of angle would prove its worth today. He'd wanted the shoulder-launched, laser-guided Judas missile, a can't miss weapon system with advanced bio targeting technology. The new stuff afforded much greater accuracy at longer distances, but the sheer weight of the thing in addition to the other gear he and Archer had to lug around proved the tipping point. Instead, Jonas had opted for the standard .50 caliber long range sniper system, one he knew in intimate detail.

The telescopic sight framed the group of terrorists congregated in the clearing with Toure in the middle.

Jonas's gut clenched even as he sought the void, a place of quiet calm where nothing but the target existed. He settled the crosshairs on the target's forehead.

Toure's skin color fell somewhere between black and darkest brown. His blinding-white teeth made a dramatic contrast when he grinned and, of all things, he wore a huge diamond stud in his left earlobe. The leader of the Mayakan stood there exposed for the longest moment before he pumped a fist in the air and threw his head back in a laugh.

The diamond flared, dazzling in the sunlight.

Jonas dipped the crosshairs lower, seeking the largest target area. This shot demanded a center mass hit. Given the vital organs in the human torso, the bullet's caliber, the lack of a medic, and the distance from any medical center, Toure's odds of surviving such a wound were improbable.

Jonas's index finger curled around the trigger, his touch feather-light, steady as a neurosurgeon's. His heartbeat slowed. Time stopped. Another deep breath. Exhale and—

Toure's head exploded.

"What—?"

"Another sniper," Archer yelled. He'd pushed up on his elbows, head above the brush line, and scanned the area with binoculars. "There. West."

Disbelieving, Jonas watched Toure collapse. His face—heck, most of his head was gone.

The Mayakan remained frozen for three ticks of the clock before bedlam erupted. A few of the men rushed to form a barricade around Toure's fallen body. Too little, too late. Several others invoked a death blossom, spraying indiscriminate fire in all directions before they scurried for cover.

"Someone took my shot!"

"I know. The question is who?" Archer, on his knees now, still looking through the binoculars, pointed toward the west. "Got him. Eleven o'clock. He's good."

Jonas turned his rifle where Archer indicated. Through the scope, he spotted the faint movement of swaying brush. Someone every bit as proficient in the art of concealment as them.

A quick sweep back to the Mayaƙan showed them regrouping, scanning the area. They had no idea from which direction the shot had come, but it wouldn't stop the panicked soldiers from searching.

"No time," Jonas said. "We gotta go. Now."

"Already on it. Evac in sixty. Pack up."

Jonas almost smiled. Archer had changed his earlier assessment of how much time they needed to reach the LZ. When a mission went south, you didn't hang around. Nothing was more dangerous than unharnessed fear and chaos.

Still wearing his camouflage covering, Jonas packed up his rifle and gear, shrugged on his pack, and started a double-time crawl toward the stand of corkwood trees behind them.

Archer followed close on his heels.

Quarter of a mile later, they'd used up twelve of their precious minutes. Still, they took time to shimmy out of the straw and brush covered ghillie suits before setting off in a sprint to the rendezvous point.

Forty-two minutes later, calves burning and lungs sucking air, he turned to Archer

"Chopper ETA in six," his pal yelled. "Almost there."

The distinctive whup-whup-whup of the helo's blades sliced through the air a few minutes later, announcing the aircraft's arrival. Jonas burst into the clearing but stopped

to stare at the all-black chopper coming in low over the treetops. "What in the name of Moses?" Sure wasn't anything he'd seen in the Army. Marines either. What all did Fowler have his fingers in?

"Don't know, don't care as long as it flies." Archer blew past him.

Jonas reached the helicopter a step behind Archer as the skids touched the ground.

"Looks like you boys stirred up a hornet's nest," one of the helicopter's crew members said as he offered Archer a hand up.

"Go, go, go," Jonas yelled scrambling in behind him. Time to vacate the premises. They could figure out later the puzzle of the covert blackbird without markings and the identity of the sniper who'd stolen their thunder.

Chapter Two

With the addition of another log, the campfire quickened, shooting sparks high into the air. The snap-crackle sounds and dancing flames lulled the group huddled around it into quiet tranquility.

Shea shook off the enchantment to glance at her charges on this last campout. Twelve this trip, the youngest a nine-year-old girl, the oldest a boy who turned twelve today. Their largest number yet. Too bad Jonas wasn't here to enjoy the campout with them.

"You plan on eating that, son, or turning it to ash?" Rascal, the grizzled old foreman, called to one of the boys.

Bobby jerked the stick out of the fire.

"Sorry, pal. You got the last marshmallow," Shea told him. Since their camping expedition ended tomorrow, they had just enough foodstuff remaining for breakfast and a mid-morning snack before they got back to the ranch. She'd planned well, maybe too well.

Unperturbed, Bobby examined the charred goo for a second and popped it in his mouth, using his teeth to scrape it off the stick. He made a blech face but swallowed. The boy hadn't shied away from eating anything put in front of him these last three days, not the tea they'd brewed using spruce needles and river water, not even the gnarly, brain-like morel mushrooms with stumpy stems they'd scored earlier today.

"Time to turn in," Shea called out. "Tomorrow we head home. Don't forget, you guys are in charge of breakfast, cleanup, packing, and leading us back to the ranch. Anybody want to guess which direction we go?"

All twelve kids looked up at the heavens where a multitude of stars twinkled against the clear night sky. One-by-one, they all pointed toward the southwest. "That way," Trish, the youngest shouted.

"Good work." Shea grinned at them. These kids had soaked up every scrap of knowledge she and Rascal had thrown at them along the way. They'd have lots to share when they returned for the new school year in another week.

"Vern, you got first watch. Clint, you take second," Rascal instructed the two ranch hands he'd brought along to help. "I'll take over at four."

Rascal Sutcliff had ruled as foreman of the Triple C since forever, but how he managed to wake up for his early morning turn boggled her mind. The man didn't even wear a watch. Still, he insisted on posting a look-out each night. Cameron land might provide the safest campground in all of Idaho, but, as he put it, a smart person stayed extra vigilant when they took responsibility for someone else's kids.

Vernon Beauchamp, the older of the two hands Rascal had enlisted, looked to be in his mid-to-late forties. He'd come to the Triple C Ranch back in May, rugged and worn, with fifteen dollars in his pocket and a wealth of experience. Jonas had hired him on the spot. Vern, a man of few words, nodded to Rascal, tossed the rest of his coffee out, and disappeared into the night.

"Miss Shea?"

She looked up from where she knelt on the ground to spread her bedroll and found Clint Loomis, the younger of the two ranch hands, standing over her. Good-looking in a boyish kind of way. He seemed like a good sort from what she'd seen of him, though he barely looked old enough to shave.

Clint snatched his hat off, looked at the sleeping bag she'd spread, at the campfire, at his boots, and at last took a quick peek at her face. "I, uh ...."

Shea groaned in silence when he looked away yet again. Normally, she could spot the first signs of attraction from a mile away, which gave her ample time to head the guy off. Clint hadn't thrown a lick of interest her way the entire outing. Until now.

His hands worked their way around the brim of his hat, curling the edges with ruthless fidgeting. "I, uh, wanted to thank you for, uh, letting me come along. And, uh, I wondered if, uh, you and me, if we—"

"Sorry, Clint. I didn't have anything to do with who got the job." She cut him off before he could embarrass himself. "You and Vern have been a great help, but you need to thank Rascal for picking you."

Shea gave him her polite I'm-not-interested smile, turned her back, and made a show of checking on each of the girls. Some people had called her cold, and even rude at times, but in her experience, nipping a man's interest in her at the start more often than not prevented a later need for outright rejection. Not something she enjoyed.

"Uh, yeah. Right. Okay," Clint mumbled.

"You got them horses bedded down yet, Clint?" Rascal called from the other side of the fire.

"Yes, sir. I'll go check on them again," he called back.

Shea breathed a quiet sigh when the thud of his boots faded. She'd have to thank Rascal herself.

Her shoulders drooped with relief, but the familiar feeling of guilt crept in. She didn't like hurting anyone's feelings, but neither did she want any man's attention. The good Lord knew she tried to make herself unattractive.

Frumpy clothes, no makeup, hair pulled back in a messy ponytail did the trick most times. Still, some guys had no taste. Others took her standoffishness as a personal challenge, and then there were the ones who didn't understand "no" and got angry when she got blunt. Thankfully, Clint seemed quiet, painfully shy, nothing like other guys his age.

On the far side of the fire, Rascal spread his blanket roll near where the boys would sleep. He had to be in his seventies, but other than a little creakiness in the mornings, nothing seemed to slow him down. Even now, he squatted on his haunches to bank the fire for the night. Why hadn't she realized before how much comfort Rascal's steady presence brought?

Funny, Jonas made her feel the same way. She pushed the image of him away, tired of how he invaded her thoughts.

With the girls curled up in their sleeping bags, Shea crawled inside her own. Another outing done. Another summer gone. Only the second year since she and Jonas had launched this idea of making his father's land an outdoor camping experience for kids.

With everyone settled, the night noises crept in. Soft crackles from the dying embers, a whinny from one of the horses, insects buzzing. Off in the distance, an owl hooted.

"Miss Shea, can I ask you something?" Ella, the ten-year-old in the sleeping bag next to her whispered. She lay curled on her side with her head propped on her hand.

"Of course, sweetie. What do you want to know?"

"Last year's camp was so much fun with Mr. Jonas." The little girl had been the man's constant shadow during the campout last summer. "I missed him this year. Do you think he'll come back?"

Were her thoughts so loud? And what kind of answer could she give when she had no idea where he'd gone, why, or even if he would return? His family didn't even talk about it.

"I don't know, but I'm sure he'll come back when he's ready."

Ella gave a solemn nod before rolling onto her back. "I hope so. I mean, I like Mr. Rascal and all, but ... he's not Jonas."

Rascal had a lifetime of knowledge and the patience of an angel. He liked the kids, and they liked him. But Ella had the right of it. Rascal wasn't Jonas.

"Tell you what, let's look for a shooting star and make a wish for him to come back, okay?" Tired after a long three days, little Ella would fall asleep in no time.

Shea stared up at the stars, watching for meteors. Bone weary from the long days in the saddle, she'd developed a healthy respect for those who came before without any of the modern conveniences. Still, her mind refused to turn off. Jonas seemed to dominate her thoughts lately. He had a permanent gleam in his eyes and a ready smile for the

crankiest man, woman, or child. Kids gravitated to him. Shoot, most people did. Women in particular.

She hated the thought, hated the way it made her feel disappointed and irritable.

All the Cameron men won the lottery with the handsome gene, but Jonas took good-looking to a whole new level. And yet, behind all the lighthearted fun and wicked banter, she'd noticed a darkness behind his smile, a shadow that seemed to touch his soul.

No, she didn't need a star to wish upon. She might not know what her future held but she knew it didn't include Jonas Cameron. She had no time or interest for a man in her life, definitely not one with commitment issues. And especially not now, with the mountain of debt she owed for school. She rolled onto her side and closed her eyes, determined to rest. Come Monday, her life at the diner would resume, her days filled with a different kind of hard work.

There in the dark, though, behind her closed lids, a pair of twinkling blue eyes laughed at her lies.

Chapter Three

"This better be the last time," Jonas snarled at the young assistant sent to fetch him for yet another meeting. He'd already gone through seven days of grueling debriefs, long hours of interrogation, medical examinations, lab work, and psychiatric testing, both with Archer and alone. He'd repeated every detail he could recall of the hunt for Toure at least a hundred times, and Agent Kevin Fowler, the man in charge of this wreck of a mission, hadn't shown his face once.

Until today. Now Fowler wanted to hear it for himself.

Jonas tamped his anger down. Getting ticked off, even as a civilian, wouldn't get him what he wanted—a ticket home. No, the most important thing any of them needed to know was Sebastian Toure, that blemish on humanity, no longer existed. His threat to Nigeria's stability, to the Cameron family, and to the bigger chess match between the United States and the terrorist world would no longer terrorize anyone. Neutralized. But not by him.

Outrage, disappointment, relief, and guilt made a heady cocktail. His mission had turned out both a failure and a success. What a conundrum.

"C'mon." Archer clapped him on the shoulder. "Let's get it over with. They have to let us out of here sooner or later."

They followed the lackey through a maze of hallways in the underground building to a small conference room.

On the far side of the table, Fowler flipped through a file folder. "Good morning, gentlemen. Come in and have a seat."

Jonas took one of the chairs across from Fowler and somehow kept his mouth shut. What he wanted to say wouldn't endear him to the powers in charge and might even extend his stay.

Archer took the seat beside him. "Honestly, Agent Fowler, much as I love your facility and gracious as your staff has been, I do believe we've overstayed our welcome. I'm not sure what more we can give you, except blood. Oh, wait. We already did."

Apparently, Archer didn't have the same qualms as Jonas.

Fowler's smile didn't match the dead, shark-like look

of his eyes. He leaned back in his chair, fingers interlaced over his abdomen, and ignored Archer's gibe. "I know this has gone on longer than you like, and I appreciate your patience. The lab tests ensure the two of you don't take any hitchhikers home. The psych tests reassure our legal eagles that you won't go postal the moment you step onto U.S. soil. And I've been waiting for confirmation of something I think will interest you. Once we finish here, there's a jet waiting to take you home."

Jonas leaned forward and rested his forearms on the table. He wanted out of here in the worst way, wanted to see his family, to sleep in his own bed without keeping one eye open, and yet curiosity got the best of him. "Confirmation of what?"

"Would you care for some coffee? Water?" Fowler made a careless gesture toward a nearby cart.

Archer's eyes rolled up.

Agent Kevin Fowler, once a director with the Bureau of International Intelligence, now worked as a BII contract agent on cases of his choosing, typically those involving human trafficking across international lines. He liked to play mind games but never diddled around like this. He had something to tell them, something he didn't want to say.

"No," Jonas snarled. "No coffee. No more tests. No more delays. Spit it out."

"Very well." Fowler opened the file folder, sorted through several papers, and chose one sheet. After studying it a moment, he slid it across the table.

Jonas and Archer looked at the grainy photo of a man in native garb with a dark blue scarf around his neck. A *keffiyeh*. Many Islamic terrorists wore specific colors and patterns of the traditional headwear, symbolic of their rebellion and unity. This one resembled nothing like Jonas had seen before. To make matters more interesting, the man held what looked to be a Dragunov SVD, a Russian-made sniper rifle.

Jonas didn't recognize the man. He pushed the paper closer to Archer, who studied the photo a few moments longer and gave a shrug. He didn't know him either. Taken from a distance and under poor lighting, the grainy image offered little identifiable information.

They both looked at Fowler.

"That, my friends," Fowler said. "Is the new Ghost."

"What?" Jonas growled.

"He the one who took out Toure?" Archer asked.

"Yes."

"You fed him our intel. You set him up, didn't you?" Jonas accused.

Fowler nodded this time.

"Why?" Jonas asked.

"That single word holds a multitude of questions and twice as many answers. For the sake of time and getting you on your way, I'll try to simplify my answer." Sitting forward, Fowler laid his arms on the table mirroring

Jonas's posture.

"I've been in this business a long time, long enough to recognize when the two of you came along I had stumbled onto something special. Individually you appeared brash, arrogant, competitive to a fault, and more confident than any man has a right to be. All your hero juice would have gotten you killed in the field your first year—if your own teammates didn't get rid of you first. I took a chance pairing you together. It was your good fortune and mine that the tactic paid off. Against all odds, the two of you bonded in a way no one could have foreseen. Working as a team, you recorded more mission successes in your three years together than the next four teams combined. Impressive."

Archer stared somewhere over Fowler's left shoulder, his features made of stone. Neither of them considered praise appropriate to their line of work. Their job wasn't about medals or accolades.

"I've also hung around long enough to know when one of my men hits the invisible wall," Fowler went on. "The one proclaiming he's done. You both hit it on your last mission. Goodbye Superman complex, hello mortality. The good news is I didn't have to fire either of you. You opted out and walked away."

"None of that means jack now. You gave away our mission." Jonas pounded the table with his fist and rose to his feet. His anger had risen to a dangerous level. On one hand, what Fowler had done seemed like betrayal. On the other hand, he felt almost grateful. "Why'd you set us up? Why not let us finish the job?"

"The little girl."

The ten-by-ten room blurred for Jonas. Everything froze—his body, his lungs. Time. But not his heart. That organ shredded into a million pieces when the images from the hateful day rushed in, memories he hadn't allowed since ....

Madenu. The little girl with the dirty face and huge, snaggle-toothed grin. Her fascination with the big, burly American soldiers. The dingy yellow, too big dress she wore. The bright blue headscarf he'd given her. And the ever-present dolly in her arms, a gift from Archer. She came to their camp every day for the sweets and treats the soldiers gave so freely. Men who missed their families, who needed to know there was something here worth fighting for. Worth dying for. Madenu's laughter would bubble out whenever they picked her up, swung her around, or gave her rides on their shoulders. A bright spot in a desolate place.

Archer gripped his arm. "Sit down, buddy. You're about to keel over."

Jonas's legs grew weak. He collapsed back into the chair but couldn't stem the memories.

Madenu running toward their camp. Short legs pumping hard. Terror stamped on her face. Tears streaking

down her cheeks. Her screams. Arms waving. The man at the edge of the village. The rusty rifle aimed at her. Archer pointing. The CO yelling. Another man running toward their camp. Allah Akbar! Explosives. Suicide bomber. Shoot ... shoot ... shoot ....

Jonas wiped sweat from his brow and noticed how badly his hands trembled.

Blood. So much blood. The gaping wounds in her chest.

Sheer force of will and a deep, ragged breath helped banish the memories. No good could come of reliving such nightmares. "I followed orders," he rasped. "I took the shot."

"Yes, you did," Fowler continued. "You neutralized a man who would have killed your entire squad, including Sergeant Archer here. In your mind, you did the right thing, but your heart still thinks you should have saved the girl."

His voice stronger now, Jonas said, "Doesn't have squat to do with you replacing me with a new Ghost."

"Actually, it does. The incident with the girl messed with your head. It still does. Tell me you don't have nightmares after all this time."

Jonas had to look away.

"I couldn't stop you and your brothers from coming after your sister, so I did everything I could to make your mission a success. My mistake came when I asked you and Archer to stay on and finish Toure. You and your family have done enough. Since I couldn't send you home in the middle of a mission, I used the intelligence you provided instead to create a new Ghost, one who would increase the chances of success for this mission, and who will never lead back to you or your family.

"You're done, Sergeant. Now, go home and find a good woman who'll have you, settle down, make some babies, and enjoy life. Both of you. You've earned it. Gentlemen, your work is done. The United States government thanks you for your service. There's an aircraft on the tarmac ready to take you home."

Fowler gathered the photo, stuffed it in his folder, and started toward the door. At the threshold, he paused. "One more question, Cameron. I had doubts whether you'd pull the trigger on Toure. Would you?"

Jonas didn't hesitate. "Yes, sir. I would have."

"Good to know, but I'm still glad you didn't have to. For what it's worth, three days after you and your unit pulled out of the little girl's village, another terrorist group swept in and killed every man, woman, and child in the village as a warning to others. Your little Madenu never had a chance. Now, I have to caution you about something you already know. Nothing of what we discussed here today leaves this room. Understand?"

"Understood," Jonas and Archer chorused.

The door closed behind Fowler with a click, but his words lingered in the air. *Go find a good woman who'll*

have you, settle down, make some babies, and enjoy life. Whether he'd earned the right or not remained debatable, but for the first time in his life Jonas didn't break out in hives at the thought of a relationship. With a woman. One woman.

He turned to look at Archer, one eyebrow lifted. "What do you think?"

"About what? The new Ghost? Fowler throwing all our work to someone else? His psychoanalysis of you, or us going home? Cause I'm all for any of it."

"No. I mean all his drivel about settling down."

Archer rubbed his beard-roughened jaw with one hand and took his own sweet time with an answer. He never once broke eye contact. "Guess it depends on what you want."

"I asked what you think."

"Seems like good advice. Me? I'm tired of dirt, sweat, rancid coffee, mosquitos, and blood. I kind of like the idea of waking up to a sweet-smelling, warm body every morning. Of the female persuasion, mind you. Hot showers, clean clothes, steak, and hamburgers. And not getting shot at. I mean, what's not to like? Your brothers seem happy enough. James and Derek, too. Has to be something to this marriage stuff. Why? You considering it?"

Jonas considered Archer's last question. "Yeah, had it rolling around in the back of my mind for a while. I think maybe I'm getting too old for frolicking like an alley cat.

Simple sounds real good about now."

Archer stared hard at him. "Got somebody in mind, don't you?"

"Maybe."

"Hoo-wee," Archer grinned. "So, tigers can change their stripes. Never thought I'd see the day Jonas Cameron settled down. I mean, you're a legend, man."

Jonas answered with his own grin and a punch to his friend's arm. "Says the guy who hooked up with the bearded lady at the circus."

"Doesn't count. It was a bet and you know it. Won me fifty bucks, too. Now, tell me about your girl."

A picture formed in Jonas's mind of long, blonde, wavy hair begging for his fingers to tangle in it. Her soft, brown eyes drew him in like a Star Wars tractor beam, while her voice put fire in his veins. Her smell—all of sudden he couldn't wait to see her again. "Let's go home. I'm done here."

Chapter Four

"Order up." Shea slid the plate of food onto the serving counter—three eggs over easy, hash browns, sausage, bacon, ham, a biscuit, sausage gravy, and a five-stack of silver dollar pancakes on the side topped with a big glob of huckleberry jam. The Rodeo Roundup, a heart attack in the making, remained a crowd favorite of the heartier appetites at the Calico Diner.

The breakfast rush seemed extra heavy for a Monday, but now they had a lull in the storm of hungry diners.

Shea stepped into the staff bathroom, wet a paper towel, and wiped her sweaty face. Three weeks had passed since the campout on the range with the kids. She missed them, missed riding Cinnamon, the horse loaned to her by the Camerons. The pretty little brown mare with her four white stockings reminded her of Kit-Kat, the horse she'd had while growing up on the Cornerstone Cattle Ranch. Steady and calm as a sunny day, and sweet-tempered to boot.

Leaving her horse behind still hurt.

Wistful brown eyes stared back from the mirror. From idyllic childhood to child laborer, student to full-time caregiver, and now minimum wage drudge. How had her life gotten so mucked up?

Not a drudge. She made more than minimum wage with the tips she earned, and she loved the diner. "At least Mama taught me how to cook before she took off," she murmured to her reflection. She'd had to do lots of that, feeding the ranch hands.

"I made a fresh pot of coffee," Dee Dee hollered from the kitchen. Just what she needed. Dee Dee's coffee was tons better than the concoction Shea'd had to dream up when her father expected her, at age twelve, to take over the household duties and even homeschool herself.

The breakfast crowd disappeared every morning around this time, leaving them a good half-hour or so before they had to start prepping for lunch.

Shea headed out front and sat on one of the stools at the counter where a steaming cup waited for her. A generous splash of cream and a spoonful of sugar later, "Mmmm" was the only sound she could manage.

The bell over the front door tinkled and turned her

moan into a groan. Instead of looking, Shea took another sip. It wouldn't hurt for the customer to wait while she drank her coffee.

A man took the stool two down from her.

Shea glanced up but didn't recognize him. A good-looking man, she pegged him to be in his late twenties.

"Coffee?" Dee Dee asked him as she placed a menu on the counter.

"Yes, please." He had a beautiful smile and used it to his advantage. "What's good?"

Dee Dee leaned an elbow on the counter. "Depends on your hunger level and what day you come in. Today, the Rodeo Roundup is guaranteed to fill a hollow leg or you could opt for the loaded oatmeal. It's thick and rich, with walnuts, raisins, apples, bananas, and a generous splash of cream."

Shea choked on a too-hot gulp of coffee, wincing as it scalded her throat going down. Her friend and boss had developed an immunity over the years to charming scalawags who thought they could sweet-talk their way through life, yet Dee Dee tucked a wayward salt and pepper curl behind her ear and turned her spotlight smile on this guy. What made him different?

The man studied his choices. "I don't suppose you could do a simple ham and cheese omelet? With wheat toast on the side?"

"Yeah, I can do an omelet," Shea replied when Dee

Dee looked her way. Taking a final sip of her coffee, Shea took her cup and returned to the kitchen, all too aware of masculine eyes following her.

Dee Dee wrote the stranger's order on a ticket and hung it on a clip in the grill window. "That's Shea. She's why everything on the menu is good today. Come in tomorrow and you get Cecil Delacroix. All bets are off then."

"This Cecil?" The man asked. "He's not a good cook?"

"Oh, Cecil's a great cook," Dee Dee answered. "Don't get me wrong. He worked at the Dixie Diner here in town before it closed, but he hails from somewhere down south—Louisiana, I think—which means he likes his spices. He can get a little heavy-handed with Cajun seasonings."

"Heavy is an understatement," Shea hollered through the window.

"Yeah, but some folks like the heat," Dee Dee continued, head shaking. "Those with cast iron stomachs, that is."

The conversation out front continued as Shea washed her hands and rounded up what she needed for the omelet. Her boss and dear friend had curiosity enough to kill a dozen cats, and a knack for ferreting out bits of information and best kept secrets. Any minute now, the interrogation would start. All Shea had to do was listen.

"So, I haven't seen you in here before," Dee Dee said.

"New in town, or passing through?"

Shea smiled, set the pan on the stove to heat, and cracked three eggs into a bowl. Adding a splash of water, she whisked them with a fork and made a mental reminder to check on the egg delivery due this morning.

"New," the stranger answered with a laugh. "But since I'm only here temporarily, I think I might qualify as passing through, as well."

He had a nice voice and a nicer laugh. Seemed pleasant enough. With the omelet pan on medium heat, Shea added a pat of butter, swirled it around until it melted, and poured in the egg mixture. After sprinkling in a little salt, pepper, and a generous pinch of fresh, chopped thyme, she set about dicing up some country ham and grating a handful of sharp cheddar.

"Well, welcome to Hastings Bluff. I'm Dee Dee Guthrie. I own this joint. And you are?"

"Wes Grainger. Stranger in town and connoisseur of fine diners. Pleased to meet you."

"So, tell me, Wes Grainger, what brings a good-looking young man like you to the backend of nowhere?"

Shea grabbed a plate, spooned huckleberry jam into a small ramekin and a dollop of whipped butter into another, placed them on one side of the plate, and dropped two slices of bread in the toaster.

Wes laughed again. "I work for Lost River Development in Idaho Falls. They're interested in developing some land along Route 93 for commercial use, apartments or condos, something like that. I'm here to assess locations around Challis and your fine town."

With the egg cooked, the ham added, and the cheese beginning to melt, Shea tilted the pan, folded the eggs over, slid the omelet onto the plate, added a pat of butter to make it shine, and topped it with a sprig of fresh parsley. Ta-da. The perfect fluffy omelet. She hadn't lost her touch. Maybe now Dee Dee would let her expand the diner's tired old menu.

She grabbed the plate of food and a saucer with the toast and delivered the order.

"Here you go," she set the omelet in front of the stranger with a flourish. In an aside to Dee Dee she whispered, "We're low on eggs. I thought Polly promised them first thing this morning."

As if on cue, the bell tinkled again, and Polly Prescott herself walked in with a covered basket on her arm. Oh boy. She held the title of worst gossip in four counties, had a reputation as the biggest skinflint around, and fostered the love/hate relationship between herself and Dee Dee.

"Good morning, ladies." Polly started out. "My grandboy, Seth, had a function to attend yesterday. He didn't get back until late, so I brought part of your order myself. I have thirteen eggs here, all I could manage with my arthritis. Twelve for you plus one I'll have Shea cook for me. Three dollars, please."

Turning to Wes, Polly held out a hand. "I don't believe we've met, young man. I'm Patricia Prescott. I suppose you could call me the matriarch of this town. And you are?"

Before he could respond, Dee Dee slapped a dollar and a handful of change on the counter. "He's a customer, Polly. Here's your money."

Polly stared at the money. "You owe me for twelve eggs. Do you need a calculator, dear?"

"No, I bought thirteen eggs. If Shea's cooking for you. I'm buying the extra egg and you're paying for the meal." Dee Dee laid a menu on the counter. "See, one egg scrambled, that's a buck, plus tax brings it to $1.06. I assume you'll have water as usual, and no toast?"

Polly did a good imitation of a pufferfish about to explode. "You're charging me a dollar for the same egg I sold you for twenty-five cents? That's robbery. Price gouging!"

Wes leaned forward with a worried expression and spoke in a low voice to Shea. "They always this way?"

"You have no idea," she whispered back.

"Kettle, meet pot," Dee Dee snapped. "You charge me twenty-five cents per egg, which is fifteen cents more than the going rate."

"Well, you're up charging a thousand percent," Polly barked.

"I think you're the one who needs a calculator. Let's see, there's the cost of the egg, the mortgage payment on this building, kitchen equipment, electricity, oh, and let's not forget Shea's expertise and the wages I pay her. Then there's clean-up, cost of butter, dishwasher soap, loss of revenue for late, incomplete orders ... shall I go on?"

"Fine. You can tack on another two dollars for your egg orders. Transportation costs."

Shea had to turn away before she started laughing and got both ladies ticked off at her. She fumbled for the coffee pot under the pretext of refilling Wes's cup. Not daring to meet his eyes for fear they both might burst into uncontrollable giggles, she said behind her hand, "Sorry about those two."

"I find them quite entertaining. Tell me, would it help if I paid for the old lady's breakfast?" he asked.

She looked at him, horrified by the idea. "Shhh. Merciful heavens, no! Dee Dee would ban you from the Calico Diner for life. Worse, you'd have to eat pop tarts and potato chips for the rest of your stay here, because she would contact every eatery in a fifty-mile radius and tell them what you did. Besides, it's her turn to concede."

Confusion chased his mirth away. "Her turn?"

"Yeah, they take turns one-upping each other, though they don't usually do it in front of an audience."

Now he looked plain bewildered. "They ... take turns?"

Head nodding, Shea explained. "They're both strong-willed women with a lot of influence in this town and great

respect for each other. This way, they get to test the other's mettle without fear of losing status in the community."

"So—"

"Wait. You'll see."

The argument had continued while Shea and Wes spoke, but the combatants had moved into the wind-down stage. "Because you have fresh eggs and you've been reliable with deliveries until today, I'll let this slip-up pass," Dee Dee said to her rival as she swiped the change up and laid two bills on the counter in their place. "But I still want the other two-dozen eggs that I ordered by three this afternoon. Deal?"

"All right, but you owe me a scrambled egg," Polly retorted.

"Fine. Shea, honey, would you take care of Polly's breakfast?"

"Coming right up." Shea took the basket of eggs from Polly and hurried off, hiding her grin until she reached the kitchen.

She whisked the eggs, *two* eggs, and poured them into the frying pan, scrambled, dressed up with a little cheese, a side of hash browns, and two slices of bacon, but no toast—Polly preferred a biscuit. Crazy characters, wacky stories, and never a dull moment. A typical day at the diner. And now with a newcomer to quiz and roast. One with a sense of humor and who didn't look half bad. Gosh, she loved this town.

The doorbell tinkled. Again. So much for today's slow time.

"Hello, Shea."

Her head jerked up at the sound of a man's deep baritone in her kitchen. A too familiar voice. Shea closed her eyes for a moment, squared her shoulders, and turned around.

Jonas Cameron stood in the doorway, hands in his jeans pockets, charisma turned on high.

She studied his long, lanky frame. He'd changed. More handsome than ever, but his skin looked darker now like he'd stayed out in the sun for too long. And his hair hung longer than she'd ever seen it. He wore it pulled back in a short queue and tied off with a leather cord. The biggest difference in his appearance, though—he had a beard. And not the razor-shaped two-day scruff so popular with the younger men today. Jonas wore his short and thick, which gave him an edgy, dangerous look. Not every man could grow a full beard like his. "Hello, Jonas. You came back."

Lame, but what do you say to someone who'd walked away from his commitment to dozens of kids without a second thought? Did he expect to pick up where he left off?

"Yeah, I did. Rascal says the camps went well. Said you ran the show almost singlehandedly."

"It's not like I had a choice. When did you get home?" She hadn't meant to sound so harsh, hadn't meant to ask.

"Little over three weeks ago. Had a lot of catching up

to do at the ranch. You have time to talk?"

Dee Dee looked at her through the order window, eyebrows lifted high, but for once she minded her own business.

Hurt swelled inside Shea. He'd been home a month and not given her a thought. With effort, she broke the mesmerizing pull of his dark blue eyes. Devil's eyes. Full of charm and wicked temptation. She knew better than to fall under Jonas Cameron's spell, under any man's spell. A lesson she'd already learned the hard way.

Using a cloth to wipe down the spotless work area, Shea busied herself straightening plates and saucers, and tidying up the spices on the shelf. Anything to avoid looking at him. "Nope, no time."

"When—"

"Look, why don't you have a seat out front and let Dee Dee take your order." Shea gave him her back only to discover Polly's scrambled eggs dry and crispy. Ugh. She flipped them into the garbage, wiped the pan, and started over.

"Uh, Shea?" Jonas said from the doorway.

"Yes?" She put a little extra snip in her answer but didn't bother turning to look at him.

"You mad at me?"

"Why would I be mad? I mean you left without warning or explanation. Not even a goodbye. Your family didn't know where you went, or at least that's what they said. I didn't know when or if you'd return, Jonas. Or if you were still alive. But then, it's not my business, is it?"

She whisked the two new eggs and tossed them in the pan before whirling around with her hands on her hips to confront him again. At least he looked contrite. "You got back a month ago, and *now* you want to talk? I thought we had the friend thing going on. Guess I thought wrong. You know what? I have work to do. You need to leave. Customers aren't allowed in the kitchen."

For a moment he looked affronted before a kaleidoscope of expressions played across his face— surprise, concern, hurt, annoyance, and a flare of anger.

Shea turned back to Polly's breakfast ... and tossed two more eggs in the trash.

Chapter Five

Locked in the small box, left to broil under the Afghan sun, reality faded in and out. His wrists and ankles throbbed, raw and bloody from days of struggle. His body ached from the beatings, the cuts, and burns. The thirst. No matter how hard he struggled, the shackles wouldn't give, and yet he couldn't stop trying. How much longer? These devils broke two prisoners last night. The tortured men had spilled everything. And died screaming.

Somewhere in the depths of his subconscious, Jonas struggled to break free of the nightmares, but one morphed into another and then another, jumping time and space, relentless repetitions of terrible memories.

Angry clouds churned across the Nigerian sky, suffocating what little daylight penetrated the dense jungle canopy. He moved forward one slow step at a time. Silent. Invisible. A wraith. Death tracking the men in the clearing ahead.

A small animal rustled in the nearby brush. Insects buzzed with annoying monotony. Tree frogs started up their evening chorus, all oblivious to the terrible predator stalking their habitat. He adjusted the night vision goggles and scanned the area for his target.

There. A single open-air hut. One person inside. Snoring. Three others asleep on the ground near the dying campfire. One guard to keep watch, but whose chin rested on his chest.

Foolish men. So careless. He crept forward, a thief in the night with a knife in his hand.

Jonas flailed and heard his own voice, "It's a dream, only a dream." Except it wasn't a simple dream. Not even a nightmare. He'd lived every one of these memories and would do so again and again.

The destroyed city block held danger at every turn. Too many places to hide. Every face a potential enemy. Every hand holding a weapon. He'd come as fast as possible, already knowing he was too late. The soldier, one of his own team, stood on a block, hands bound behind his back. A rope, fastened into a noose and placed around his neck, hung from a street light. Bloody and battered, the man bowed his head and awaited his fate.

One of the hajis kicked the block from under the

soldier's feet. Swift judgment. Swifter death. No soldier should die this way.

He couldn't save his brother in arms, but he could exact his own justice.

The cold, emotionless void welcomed him. He dropped to one knee, raised his rifle, and settled the crosshairs on the forehead of the insurgents' leader.

A groan brought Jonas up from the depths of hell, almost to waking, but the demons weren't finished with him yet. They resurrected yet another memory and dragged him down.

Laughter floated to him on the air. His teammates playing basketball. Foolishness in this heat, but laughter helped lighten the darkness. He smiled, envious of their ability to forget for a time.

From his position on the ridge above the camp, he scrutinized the area, rifle at the ready. His turn to keep watch. No movement outside the camp. No dust plumes in the distance that might signify unwelcome visitors. Nothing except dirt and boredom.

A prickle of tension crawled down his spine. Anyone who stayed for any length of time in the sandbox developed sensitized instincts. Below, the players stopped midstride, each one looking around. Worry etched their sweaty faces. They felt it, too, an indescribable itch. A sense of wrongness. He peered through his rifle's scope and cleared the ramshackle buildings one by one, all of his senses on high alert. Evil lurked out there somewhere. Closer now.

From his camouflaged niche on the hillside, he swept the area again in search of a threat. He spotted Madenu, the little girl who came to their camp most every day for candy. The six-year-old with her bright smile and easy laugh, who gave them back a touch of sanity in this upside-down world, who pranced, sometimes skipped, and reminded them of the reason they'd come half-way around the globe to fight.

Except today she ran, sprinting as fast as little legs could carry her.

Three men poured from another building farther down the street. Correction, not men—boys. Older than Madenu, but no more than fourteen. They ran, following in her footsteps.

Oh, crap! "Twelve o'clock. Incoming. Three boys. Take cover," he yelled into his mic. He took careful aim at the one in the lead ... and saw an old man emerge from the building Madenu had fled. He raised a rifle and pointed it at the girl.

Madenu waved her arms now, yelling, frantic.

"Shoot," his CO screamed through the headset. "Shoot those—"

The boys wore mesh vests. Explosives.

"Shoot," called his CO again.

He aimed ... spft. The kid in the lead went down. Spft ... the second boy went down.

The sound of a rifle shot jerked his attention back to Madenu. No! She lay face down in the dirt, blood pooling under her small body.

The third boy had gotten close now. Too close. Spft. He got the last shot off. A moment later, the kids' packs exploded. A second more and—

The explosion took out a portion of their fence but did no real damage to the camp itself. No injuries. Only three dead boys and one little girl. Could he have saved her? Could he have taken out the old man and still stopped the three boys?

Jonas woke with a start, heart pounding, gasping for breath. He reached for the Smith & Wesson under his mattress and leveled the weapon in a two-handed grip at his bedroom door.

The knock came again.

Disoriented but alert, his eyes moved nonstop around the room as he assessed it for threats.

Another knock, harder this time. "Jonas? Wake up, son. Rascal needs you at the big barn.

Sweat poured down his face in rivulets despite the cool night air. Blasted dream. "I'm up, Dad. Give me a second." He shoved the gun back under the mattress and reached for the jeans he'd dropped on the floor the night before. Opening the bedroom door, he asked, "Is it Sunshine?"

"Yeah. He said you wanted to be there for her first time. I'll make coffee." His father, who'd already dressed, stared at him for a long moment. "You okay?"

"Fine. Give me five minutes."

His father studied him a few seconds longer before he turned away.

As the booted footsteps receded down the stairs, Jonas walked back to his bed. Trembling like an old man with palsy, he took several deep breaths. The nightmares had stopped more than a year ago but had returned with a vengeance since he came home this time. Why?

No matter what triggered them, locking his bedroom door last night was one of the smartest decisions he'd made in a long time. What if he hadn't secured it? What if Dad had come in? Tried to wake him?

Shoving the terrible memories aside, he searched for another image, something light and positive as he headed down the hall to the bathroom he'd once shared with his two older brothers. With them both married now, he had it all to himself.

Long, blonde hair caught up in a ponytail captured his thoughts. Light brown eyes with flecks of green and gold. Shea's creamy complexion entranced him with how it turned rosy whenever he teased her. He loved the easy way she had with the kids. So sweet and caring.

And he'd hurt her feelings.

He went back to his bedroom and pulled on his boots, stamped his feet to settle them in, and reached for the gun again ... but then withdrew his hand. The last mission had

conditioned him to carry a weapon again. He'd struggled with leaving it here under the mattress since coming home, not liking the naked feeling.

Taking time to pull the covers up, he ignored the lure of the Smith & Wesson and left the room emptyhanded. Important decisions awaited. His presence put his family at risk. Intolerable.

Jonas crept down the stairs toward the kitchen in the morning darkness, taking care to avoid the squeaky third to last step. Silent movements came second nature to him.

The aroma of freshly brewed coffee chased the last of his demons away and put a smile on his face. Coffee. The Cameron family cure-all.

Illumination came from the soft, recessed lighting above the cabinets. His dad stood by the coffeemaker, two thermoses on the counter.

Jonas collected one of the thermoses. "You don't have to come, Dad. Go back to bed."

His father grunted, which triggered a persistent cough. "Not the first time I got up before the chickens. Won't be the last either. Now, tell me. You having nightmares again? I knew no good would come of you and your brothers traipsing off to Africa."

Jonas rubbed a hand against the back of his head and tried to grin. He didn't want to do this, not at oh-dark-thirty in the morning after a long restless night. "But something good did come of it, Dad. We got Mallory back."

His father's right eyebrow lifted, a sure sign he knew full well Mallory's abduction didn't explain why Jonas had remained behind after his brothers brought her home.

Jonas's grin slipped. He'd never been able to put anything over on Dad. Cody Cameron was nobody's fool, but sometimes diversion worked. "Coffee ready yet?"

"When you left after college, you thought you owned the world. Twenty-two and full of sass and vinegar. I figured the Army would toughen you up, but I never dreamed they'd take my happy-go-lucky son and send me back a ghost of the man."

Dad poured the coffee into the thermoses and handed one over. "I know you went through some difficult stuff over there, son. I've seen the scars—physical, mental, and emotional. I hoped you'd open up to Garrett since you used to stick like glue to his side as a boy. Or even Wade after Garrett moved in with TJ. Heck, I hoped you might even come to me. I can't see what's going on inside your head, but I know these nightmares are bad, worse than before. Don't keep it bottled up. Deal with it. If it means getting doctor help, do it. If you need to barricade yourself in the hunting cabin until you can work through it, go for it. But don't wait too long. Some things don't get better on their own."

"Dad, I don't think—"

He held up a hand. "Don't think. Do. Sometimes you have to lance a boil and let the bad stuff out so you can start

the healing process. Yeah, I know it's uncomfortable. Hurts like a son-of-a-gun, too."

"I don't know, Dad." Jonas couldn't meet his eyes.

"You're not in this alone, son. You hurt. We hurt. Don't lose sight that what tears you apart affects those who love you. No getting around it. Now, let's get a move on. Sunshine won't wait on us, you know. And get your jacket. Temperature dropped overnight. It might be the middle of October, but I think fall has arrived."

Nodding, Jonas took the offered thermos and grabbed his coat from the peg in the mudroom. When did his old man get so wise?

Later that afternoon, after mother and foal were cleaned up and settled in a clean stall with fresh hay, his whole family stopped by. Mom, always looking out for her brood, brought sandwiches and an urn of coffee.

"She's such a beautiful little thing, son. What will you name her?"

Jonas hadn't been able to clear his head all day. When the nightmares weren't replaying through his head, or guilt eating at him over pulling his weapon on his dad, his mind relived the encounter with Shea yesterday. Things sure hadn't turned out like he'd expected with her. She'd shot him down without a bit of remorse. Not something he was used to, and it bothered him. A lot.

"I vote for Elvira," Garrett, his oldest brother spoke up. "It's perfect with her dark coloring."

"I've got it," Garrett's wife, TJ said. She swayed side to side while rocking their newborn son in her arms. "Freckles. See all those tiny little white spots scattered across her back?"

Of course. TJ had dark, red-brown hair set off by a dusting of the same color flecks on her nose and cheeks.

Jonas shook his head. "Elvira—too goofy. Freckles is, well, too cutesy. This little filly needs something special.

"Princess."

"Flicka."

"Midnight."

"No, no, and no." He shook his head, but the names kept coming, each one wilder than the previous. "C'mon guys. You can do better than this."

"Knew a woman named Hilda once. A real sweet lady. Pretty, too." Rascal suggested.

"NO!" everyone shouted at once.

"How about you, Mom? Help me out here, will you?" Jonas pleaded.

Cate Cameron loved horses, and they loved her. His mom stood by the stall, stroking Sunshine's nose. "Interesting how the foal turned out black like the sire and not Sunshine's lighter brown color. And all those little white specks scattered over her back. It's almost like she has Appaloosa blood, except she looks nothing like an Appaloosa. More like a fairy sprinkled her with stardust."

Everyone fell silent.

"That's it," Jonas said in a reverent tone before he leaned over and kissed her cheek. "Stardust. Perfect. My mother, the genius."

Excited chatter erupted, everyone agreeing on the foal's name. When the laughter died down, Mom asked, "Okay, which one of you boys will drive my cart back home so I can snuggle up beside my husband in his big, warm truck?"

The groans began. She'd complained forever about wasting gas to run from the house to the big barn and home again. A few years back Dad bought her a little white golf cart, complete with a pink fringed top. Great for summer use, but with freezing temperatures moving in and a top speed of fifteen miles per hour, no one wanted to brave the cold. And neither of his brothers would be caught dead driving the prissy thing.

He didn't mind, though. It would give him a break from his over-cheerful and intrusive family. He'd spent too much time alone the past few years and liked it too much. His brother, Garrett teased him about winding up like old Goren Tudor, the recluse who threw rocks at anyone who came near his shack.

"I'll drive it home, Mom."

"Thank you, Jonas," his mom said, patting his cheek. "The rest of you don't dally. Dinner is still at six sharp."

"Aren't you afraid word will get around to all the ladies in town? I mean driving your mama's pink golf cart, not cool, man." Derek, his sister Cassie's fiancé teased.

Jonas waited until his mother turned away before he punched Derek's arm.

His other sister, Mallory, pulled him aside. "Have you seen Shea yet? She asked about you all the time while you were gone."

Sunshine kicking him in the head couldn't have stunned him more. If Shea had asked about him more than once, why blow him off now? "I stopped by the diner yesterday. Told her I wanted to talk, but she gave me the cold shoulder." He shrugged.

Both of Mallory's eyebrows lifted. "And here I thought you knew something about women. You disappear on her without a word and when you finally return you demand to talk? Please tell me you apologized for your unannounced disappearance or at least offered an explanation?"

He frowned. He didn't owe anyone an apology much less an explanation. Well, okay, he did kind of dump the whole kids camp thing on her, but he'd known she could handle it. No harm, no foul, right?

"Jo, you know I love you, but sometimes you're such a man. Shea thought of you as a friend. She worried about you. And what do you do? Ignore her for a month and hurt her feelings. You need to fix this."

"Not a month. Three weeks."

Mallory speared his chest with a finger. "Don't be

dense. It's not a good look for you." She left him and walked over to where James, the town's sheriff who was Mallory's almost-but-not-quite fiancé waited.

Shea had asked about him? Often? A smile tickled the corners of his mouth. Did it mean she cared about him? A little? Or had he ruined his chances? The question now was how did he get her over being mad. Or, the bigger question, did he want to?

Stupid thought. Of course, he did. Without seeing it coming, he'd fallen for the unapproachable woman who wasn't so standoffish once he got to know her.

Jonas caught his dad giving him a funny look. Banking the silly grin, he pulled a stone-like expression into place and headed toward his father. "Hey, Dad, I've been thinking. What you said makes sense, you know, about spending some time up at the cabin. Think I'll pack up a few things tomorrow and head out after I finish up with the horses. It's close enough I can still get down here every day."

"All right, son. But don't take too long working out whatever's got your head spinning on its axis. You know your mother will send me to drag you home, and these old bones don't take kindly to long hours in the saddle anymore."

The drive back to the house took longer in the cart, but he didn't mind. It gave him time to sketch out a plan of action, figure out how to get control of the nightmares, and more important, how to win Shea Townsend over.

The sun had sunk low in the sky while they'd waited for Sunshine to give birth. Five minutes into the drive home, his cell phone rang. The name on the display sent a chill through his blood which had nothing to do with the dropping temperature. "Fowler," he answered. "I thought I'd heard the last from you. What's up?"

"Cameron." The raspy voice laughed. "I thought so, too, but you remember the promise I made about the threat to you and your family? Well, turns out I was premature making such a statement."

Not a real surprise. "Details."

"The Mayakan cell working out of Idaho Falls."

"You said you had them all in custody."

"We do, but it seems they did some recruiting under the radar. We got a lead on three locals they enlisted before we shut them down. Two are in custody. We can't account for the third."

"Description?"

"White male, forty-ish, six feet, medium build, short brown hair. No distinguishing marks but wears a cowboy hat and boots."

"Your description fits ninety-five percent of the male population of Idaho, Montana, Wyoming, and both Dakotas."

"I know. I'll keep you posted. Might want to let your buddies know."

"Roger."

Fowler disconnected without saying goodbye. Typical.

Great. News he didn't want to hear. At least with James and Derek coming to dinner tonight, he could brief them and his brothers all at the same time.

He parked the golf cart in its designated spot at the end of the barn and jogged toward the house. Five minutes to six. Enough time to wash up and get to the dinner table on time. Mom didn't pitch many fits but coming late to her table would earn a stern lecture. She didn't tolerate rudeness, and tardiness was nothing if not poor manners and a poorer reflection of a person's upbringing. Wonder what she'd think about his time overseas. Some days beef jerky was all he had.

As Jonas stepped onto the back patio, an engine roared from the front of the house. Moments later, James's Yukon sped down the drive, kicking up gravel in its wake. They didn't get many emergencies in this sleepy little country town. What had sent James running off? Too bad. He'd miss out on Mom's roast beef.

Mallory opened the door before he could. Visibly upset, she stood in front of him, wringing her hands.

"I saw our fearless sheriff tear out of here like his pants were on fire. What's up, Mal?"

"Not his pants. There's a fire in town."

Chapter Six

Shea stared through the kitchen window and sipped her coffee. The snow had started to fall as she drove home from the diner and now a pristine white dusting lay on the ground, bright in the early twilight. An inch, perhaps two, but not enough to worry about. Unexpected all the same. Mid October was too early for the first snowfall. Way earlier than last year. The weatherman missed this call.

The yard sloped away here in the back, dropping fifteen feet over a hundred yards. A steep enough grade to make a toboggan run exciting, but not unsafe.

Memories from her childhood brought a smile. She'd learned to snowplow on Grandpa's wooden skis until the old leather bindings disintegrated. Her oldest step-brother, Eli passed his fiberglass skis down to her when he outgrew them. They were too long for her, and yet she'd made them work.

One of her favorite memories included the dented old aluminum wash basin her father hammered into a sled for them. She and her brothers had spent hours on the weekend, after chores, sliding down the slope in the south pasture. They'd laughed so hard when Daddy took her mama on a run and then tipped over halfway down the hill. Good times. For a while.

She gave the cup a quick rinse and set it in the sink. Alone in this big house, she seldom had enough dishes to run the dishwasher unless a catering gig popped up. With a wistful look out the window again, she turned toward the stairs. What a great place this would be to raise kids.

Upstairs, she gathered her clothes and headed to the connecting bathroom for a long, hot shower. Bless Dee Dee for refusing to open the diner on Sundays. No getting up before dawn tomorrow. No rushing to get dressed in the dark. And no twelve-hour day of sore feet and aching jaws from the constant smiles. She got one day off a week. Tonight, she would deep-condition her hair, shave her legs, and take care of all the housework neglected during the week. Tomorrow, she'd go to church in the morning and then do nothing the rest of the day.

As the steam filled the bathroom, she caught a whiff of a faint, unidentifiable odor. It disappeared with a second and third sniff.

After her shower, as she ran a comb through her still-damp hair, the smell returned, stronger this time. She opened the bathroom door to the smell of something burning.

Heart rate accelerating, she donned her clothes in record time. Before she finished, smoke started to curl under the bedroom door. Not a good sign.

A quick tap of her finger on the knob told her what she already knew. Hot enough to blister her skin. The fire was close. Too close.

Hurrying back to the bathroom, she grabbed the towels she'd used, soaked them in the sink, and raced back to stuff them around the bottom of the door. Wet towels would block the smoke and buy her a little time.

For what? She dared not open the door. Had no ladder to escape out the window. Which left her trapped here in her second-floor bedroom.

Panic threatened to steal her breath before the smoke could do the job. The towels dried as she watched, wisps of smoke sneaking through them, but when the white paint on the door blistered, she raced to the window and threw it open. One good shove sent the screen clattering against the side of the house as it fell.

Shea leaned out and looked down, left, right. A two-story drop to the concrete patio still littered with summer furniture. No drain pipe to shinny down. No handholds to cling to. Only the huge King Nut Hickory tree with its willowy branches standing several feet away.

Sirens rose in the distance. Too far. They'd never get here in time.

She fought off paralyzing fear. A thin brown line had appeared in the middle of the door. She watched in horror as it blackened and spread fast toward the edges.

Sweat beaded on her forehead. She had minutes, maybe seconds. The moment the fire breached her refuge, the fresh supply of oxygen from the open window would act like an accelerant. She'd be caught up in the ensuing inferno.

A new, loud, crackling sound raised the hairs on her arms. Sizzling, popping noises outside the door. Her time was up.

She shoved one leg out the window, her bottom perched on the sill. No time to think of another plan. Swinging her other leg out, Shea leaped through the air, reaching for the tree limb. The door behind her blasted inward at the same time, adding to her propulsion. Through an amazing act of grace, her hands caught and held on to the limb.

Rough bark shredded her hands. Her weight tugged the limb down and left her swaying in mid-air. She dangled there like a roast on a spit, unable to climb up, too afraid to let go.

Behind her, the fire had spread. Flames of fiercest orange, deep red, amber, and a livid purplish-blue engulfed the roof.

Whump!

Something inside the house exploded. With a loud whoosh, the glass in the windows shattered and pelted her.

The sirens drew closer, competing with the roar of the fire. Screams split the air—her screams. They'd never reach her in time.

Flames roared through the open bedroom window. Greedy tongues reached for her. Hot. So hot.

Creak!

The limb she held in a death grip jerked. Her grip slipped. The limb swayed as she lurched for a better handhold.

Crack! The limb bobbed downward ... and broke.

The volunteer fire brigade had extinguished the flames, but the acrid smell of melted paint and scorched wood made breathing unpleasant. Blackened beams, smoldering ash, and a smoke-filled sky marred an otherwise beautiful day.

James came over and put an arm around her shoulders. "Hey, you okay?"

Shea wrinkled her nose and pondered her situation. The fast-burning fire had destroyed everything—Uncle Press's beautiful home, the furnishings, his fabulous kitchen, all the equipment. And her few belongings. She had the clothes she wore, her car, and her life. That's all.

Nothing like a little life-threatening danger to put things in perspective. Other than an assortment of bruises, a sore back where the chaise lounge had broken her fall, and a knot on her head, she'd escaped unscathed. "I'm alive."

Could be worse, she tried to console herself. Had she not mailed another payment to the school yesterday, the cash collected from tips over the past two weeks would have gone up in smoke as well.

James gave her a little squeeze.

Her trembles turned violent, her entire body shaking. Deep, gut-wrenching sobs broke free.

"Hey, hey, hey, it's okay. You're safe now." James led her over to his truck and helped her sit on the open tailgate. Motioning to one of his deputies, he scrounged up a bottle of water for her. "I need to ask you some questions. Are you up to it?"

She wiped the useless tears from her face and looked away from the soggy remains of her uncle's home. "I'll try."

"Did the fire alarm go off?" James asked.

Trying to remember made her headache worse. "I ... don't think so. I don't remember it."

"Okay. Let's start from the beginning. Tell me what happened, everything you can remember."

A deep breath helped steady her voice. She recounted

the events of the morning up to the point where she woke bruised and battered from her fall ... and overheard one of the firefighters mention arson.

Her respiration escalated. "Did someone set the fire?"

James didn't answer. He concentrated on writing in a small notebook instead. "Any chance you left a burner on in the kitchen? A fire going? Maybe a candle or a cigarette?"

A tiny pocket of anger bubbled up. "No, no, and no. And I don't smoke."

He looked up with a momentary twinkle in his eyes. "Okay. Do you have any idea who would set the fire? Any run-ins at the diner? Suspicious strangers? Any men make you uneasy?"

She tried to massage away the ache in her temples. All these questions.

Wes Grainger was the one stranger to the diner lately, though she thought of him more as a regular now. He seemed open and honest. Likable, too. As for run-ins, other than Jonas she couldn't think of a single soul she might have offended. No need to mention that little confrontation. "Uh-uh. No strangers or creeps. No hard feelings."

"What about your uncle. You stay in touch with him?"

"Yes. I keep him posted on what's happening around here, but he's not the chatty type."

"Did he mention anyone upset with him?"

"Uncle Preston had already decided to leave when I

showed up in Hastings Bluff. He gave me the nickel tour, the keys, and told me to have fun. Nothing else."

"What about Starlight Catering?" James kept jotting down notes as they spoke.

"Uncle Press spent his entire career as a chef, the last fifteen years before he came here he worked at a fancy restaurant in Chicago. He opened Starlight after he retired, more as a hobby, I think, than to make money. Lord knows there's not much need for catering around these parts, or at least I haven't discovered it."

"Does he have any debt?"

"None I know of. I send him the utility bills and few tax-related documents. I've never seen any late notices so I have to assume he pays them on time."

"What about you? Anyone around here or back home you owe money?"

She couldn't attribute the heat in her cheeks to the house fire. "I owe twelve-thousand dollars to the school I attended, but we set up a payment schedule. Bottom line, they get paid before I eat. No, I'm not in debt to anyone else, here or back home."

"I'll need your uncle's contact information. He'll want a police report for the insurance claim."

"Okay. So, what's the next step? An arson investigator?"

He looked up from his notepad. "Why do you think someone set the fire?"

Shea stood from the tailgate and held his stare. "I'm stunned, upset, and traumatized, but I'm not stupid, Sheriff. I heard the firefighters. They said a fire couldn't move so fast without an accelerant. And I see Derek and Kyle over there, stringing crime scene tape around the property. I'll ask again, what is going on?"

James looked away, removed his hat, scrubbed at his scalp, and settled the Stetson on top of his head again. "Unofficially, the boys found a charred gasoline can inside. It appears the fire started in the living room right under your bedroom, engulfed the stairs, and spread from there. Honest truth, Shea, I don't know what to think. I put a call in to the Idaho Falls Fire Inspector's office. They're sending someone over tomorrow to sift through the ashes. We'll know more once he makes his report. Meanwhile, do you have someplace to stay? Somewhere safe?"

The fire happened so fast, her leap from the window, the smoldering ruins. Fear had consumed her at first, but not once had she considered that someone wanted to harm her.

Now, a new, different kind of fear crept in.

"She's staying in the apartment over the diner." Dee Dee Guthrie appeared at Shea's side and pulled her into a hug. "My no-good son stays there when he needs money. It's yours now, sweetie. As long as you need it. No charge."

Shea's tears welled up again. Her friend's warm, loving manner brought back memories of her mother before she walked out without saying goodbye.

All her life, everyone she'd ever cared about either left her or betrayed her—Mama, Daddy, her brothers. Porter and Lily. Jonas. No doubt Dee Dee would abandon her one day, too, but right now her friend and boss offered much-needed support.

Much as she hated the idea of taking charity, Shea's choices were simple: accept the offer of free rent and hope to repay her at some point, or sleep in her car like a homeless person. She had forty-six dollars and change in her wallet, and whatever tips she could earn. Not even enough for a week's stay in the cheapest room at the Primrose Motel.

"Thank you," she managed to say through the sniffles. "I promise I'll pay you back as soon as I can."

"Not happening, sweet cheeks. You staying there won't cost me a dime, so suck it up. Good thing you have the day off tomorrow because I'm pretty sure the apartment needs disinfecting."

Shea took the tissue Dee Dee offered.

Someone touched her arm. "Shea?"

Slowly, she turned to find Jonas staring down at her, worry creasing his brow. All she could think was *he'd shaved his beard.*

When he pulled her to him, she went without hesitation.

"Everything will work out. I promise," he whispered.

With her cheek against his chest and wrapped in those wonderful, big arms, she wanted to believe him.

"I'll take you to Dee Dee's. James can get someone to drive your car to the diner."

CCC

Jonas ran a cloth along the length of the reins, wiping the day's debris away. Five days had passed since the fire on Sunday, not one of which he'd gotten through without a trip to town to check on Shea. The thought of how close he'd come to losing her forever left him gutted.

Why would anyone want to hurt Shea?

Most people saw the sweet, fragile-looking girl and wanted to coddle her, not realizing it was Shea who took care of everyone else. She made homemade soup for the sick, tutored kids at the elementary school, arranged for someone to deliver the diner's leftovers to the soup kitchen in Challis every week, and drove down to Pocatello once a month on Sundays to take cookies and visit with the nursing home residents there.

Finished cleaning the tack, Jonas yelled as he grabbed his hat. "I'm heading into town now. Call if you need me."

"You've gone into town every day this week to see that little girl," Rascal called back. "Starting to get serious."

"Don't know what you're talking about." He should walk away quick, because Rascal wouldn't let up.

"Ha," Rascal snorted. "What bumfuzzles me is for all

your wicked ways, Jonas Cameron, you don't know squat about women. Clint, the new guy we hired, knows more than you and he ain't old enough to drink yet. Do us all a favor, son. Get over yourself and ask her for a date before someone snatches her from under your nose."

Jonas cocked an eyebrow at the meddlesome old man. Everyone thought Lorraine, the dispatcher at the sheriff's office, held the crown of town busybody, but boy were they wrong.

"Keep it up and Polly Prescott will learn you're sweet on her. Now I think on it, you two would make a fine pair of gossips." He grabbed his hat from the peg on the wall and slapped it on his head.

"You watch your mouth, young'un. I am not sweet on that battle-ax!" Rascal's face turned red. Any minute now, smoke would pour out of his ears.

"Wanna try convincing her after I get done?" Jonas chuckled.

"I never thought you of all the boys would grow up meaner than your dad. All right. I'll leave it for now but know this, Shea ain't one of your floozies. Hurt her and half the town will bring the tar. The other half will bring the feathers, and I'll point the way." Rascal shook his fist at Jonas before stalking off.

Laughter bubbled up at the old man's reaction. Shea brought out a protective vibe in everyone. Little did they know she had outer plating like an armadillo. She kept everyone at arm's length, especially the guys.

After Rascal's words sank in, though, indignation emerged. How dare he say such a thing? Jonas thought about going back to tell the old man he would never hurt Shea, but he sped away in his truck instead. And what floozies? The past belonged in the past. He'd suffered through a self-inflicted drought for better than a year now.

The fifteen-minute drive to town took Jonas ten, some of which he spent going over last night's conversation with his brothers about Fowler's warning. Other than alerting the hands to watch for strangers or anything unusual, how did he search for someone who looked like every other man in the state?

For the rest of the trip, Shea filled his thoughts. By now, the breakfast rush would have ended, so maybe he could get some time with her. As luck would have it, though, vehicles lined the street in front of the diner.

Jonas sighed. Ever since the fire, the place stayed full from the moment Dee Dee opened the doors until she kicked everyone out at four. He understood. He didn't like it, but he understood. The town folk loved Shea and every one of them and his brother wanted to see she was okay for themselves. They needed to tell her how sorry they felt about her misfortune.

Shea, of course, laughed and swore to them she'd survived, not that her assurances stopped them from wanting to help. On Monday, Edward Spencer brought his four sons over and replaced the rickety stairs to her apartment. The next day, Jay Red Feather, who ran the local hardware store, delivered a new door with multiple locks and had Edward come back to install it.

The Ladies Guild, headed by none other than the Gossip Queen herself, Polly Prescott, arranged to send Shea a casserole a day until she begged them to stop. How they thought someone her size could eat all they provided remained a mystery.

Not to be outdone, Mavis Dalrymple and Rosa Bea Thompson organized a group of ladies to scrub Shea's new apartment from floor to ceiling, a task which would have taken Shea all week.

Even his sisters, Mallory and Cassidy, got in on the act. They opened their closets, gifting Shea with more clothes, shoes, and coats than she'd had before the fire.

The capper, though, came from Toby, the lead mechanic at Wrangler's Auto and Repair. He'd replaced the bald tires on her car with good used ones *and* gave the old hunk of junk a much-needed tune-up. All he asked in return was some of those crepe things Shea made.

Jonas had wanted to buy her all new tires—heck, he wanted to get her a brand-new car, but she wouldn't accept it, not even for a year's worth of soggy pancakes. One day he'd earn the right to buy her everything her heart desired. Soon, he hoped.

He wound up parking down the street in front of his

brother's office. Grumbling as he walked the two blocks to the diner, he didn't notice the leggy brunette approach until she snagged his arm. His friend, Archer, would roast him for losing track of his surroundings.

"Jonas Cameron, as I live and breathe," the gorgeous brunette purred. "When did you get back?"

He stumbled to a halt. The sultry voice made his skin crawl. "Sadie Gayle Miller, how you doing, girl?"

Before he could pull back, she reached up and pinched his cheek.

Mortified, he stood there like she'd poked him with a stun gun. He didn't know what to do. If he broke away ... well, no one threw a tantrum like Sadie Gayle. He needed a scene with her out in front of God and everybody like he needed a pair of Gucci loafers.

She locked her arm with his and walked with him. Sadie Gayle stood five-feet-ten. Tall for a woman. Add the ridiculous boots she wore with heels high enough to break an ankle she could almost look him in the eye. "So, explain. I know you got home weeks ago. Why haven't I seen you at Sidewinders? I miss having you take me home."

Funny thing about the local honky-tonk. Sidewinders had served as his hideaway after he came home from overseas the first time. A place to unwind, drink, and banish his demons for a little while. Brad Garber, his best friend in high school and long after, always kept an eye on him. When he had too many, it was Brad who made sure he got home safe and sound. For the past year, Jonas had returned the favor. Whenever Brad and his longtime girlfriend, Sadie Gayle, went off on one of their crazy break-up/make-up sprees, which happened more often than it should, Jonas stepped in and rescued Sadie Gayle from her own drinking binges. Somewhere along the way, though, he'd grown tired of the mind games and playing third-wheel.

Admitting as much to her would only tick her off, so Jonas opted for a different version of the truth. "Guess I grew up."

Sadie Gayle turned her head to glare at him as they walked.

Uh, not a great answer either. Her nostrils flaring signaled a storm about to break. He took the coward's way out and told her, "Gotta go, sweetheart. Say hi to Brad for me."

You had to give her credit. Sadie Gayle didn't give up easily. When Jonas attempted to pull free, she dug her long, painted nails into his bicep hard enough to ensure he'd find crescent-shaped bruises on his arm tomorrow.

Her next move took him by complete surprise. Quick as a rattlesnake could strike, she let go of his arm and reached up to grab his ears with both hands.

"Sheesh, woman," he yelled and tried to pull her hands away. And he'd thought the claw marks on his arm hurt. "Let go.

"Hush, Jonas." Using his ears for leverage, she tugged his face down to hers and planted a wild, wet kiss on his mouth.

Unwilling to lose his earlobes, or worse hurt her feelings, Jonas stood still, his hands at his sides, and waited. She had to come up for air sooner or later.

Sadie Gayle ended the molestation after a few seconds with a not so soft pat on his cheek before she walked away.

Jonas's eyes darted all around. Could she have picked a more public place? Did anyone see?

He scrubbed a sleeve over his mouth to get rid of her red lipstick. He had no idea how Brad would react when he heard. And Sadie Gayle would make sure he did.

Right now, Jonas had more important things on his mind. Like seeing Shea.

Chapter Seven

Shea slid the plate piled high with pancakes onto the delivery window. Before she could call out the order, Dee Dee snatched it away.

Saturdays always brought in more business than the weekdays, but today seemed extra busy. The locals had swarmed the diner since the fire two weekends ago, in part to offer condolences, but also to see for themselves she was okay and get the latest gossip about who'd done what to help.

Compassionate but also competitive, they vied with one another to see who could give the most, be it food donations, clothes, household items, toiletries, tires .... She even had new stairs to the apartment. All practical needs but things she couldn't afford.

She hated taking charity, knew they'd opened their hearts, but the pitying looks and well-intentioned comments grated on her nerves.

Using a sleeve to wipe her face, Shea picked up the next order in line—three Rodeo Roundups.

"Cecil's here," Dee Dee yelled through the order window. "Hand everything over and get out here. I got too many full tables and not enough hands."

Thank goodness. They'd needed the second cook these last few days. She was desperate for a break from the stove. Plus, cooks didn't score tips, and the Lord knew she needed the money.

"*Ca va, cher?*" Cecil Delacroix strode into the kitchen. "What's cookin'?"

The first time Cecil called her cher, pronouncing it *sha*, she thought it was his accented way of saying her name. When she told him as much, he'd set her straight. "Non, girl. *Shay* be your name. *Sha* mean sweetheart or some time it mean darling."

"*Ca va*, Cecil," Shea returned his Bayou greeting using the French pronunciation of his name the way he liked. She had no idea how a Cajun born and raised in southern Louisiana had ended up here in rural Idaho, but she loved his accent. Maybe one day he'd tell her his story. "Three Rodeo Roundups and a stack of tickets."

"Leave to me, cher. Go help Dee Dee."

She changed into a clean apron and hurried to the

front.

"Grab Fred and Percy's plates, and nudge them on their way." Dee Dee instructed. "Wes will walk in any minute. We need their seats."

Shea nodded. If this were high school, Fred Robison and Percy Barnum would play the roles of class clowns. Their stories and antics kept everyone around them in stitches.

"Anything else?" She picked up their empty dishes and paused for a moment to let her meaning sink in.

Thankfully, Fred and Percy took her awkward hints because sure enough, the bell over the door jangled and Wes Grainger walked in at quarter past nine. Punctual to a fault, the man hadn't missed a day coming in, always at the same time. He'd even come on Sunday his first week in town, not realizing Dee Dee had a thing against working instead of going to church.

Shea gestured for Wes to wait.

"Mighty fine meal, Miss Shea. Thank you much." Percy tipped his hat while Fred paid their bill.

"My pleasure, gentlemen." In less than a minute, she cleared the rest of their mess, wiped down the counter, and set out a cup of coffee for Wes.

"Hey, pretty thing. What's cooking?" He flashed a huge smile.

She could depend on a compliment and a new teasing line from him every day. "Hello, shameless flirt and connoisseur of fine diners. What's cooking is whatever you're in the mood for."

Wes's eyes seemed to darken. His gaze shifted to her mouth for one long, uncomfortable moment. When he finally lifted his eyes, he hesitated before speaking. "Careful, Shea. I might take you up on your offer one day."

Heat flooded her cheeks, the curse of a fair complexion. "I ... uh ... I didn't mean ..." The ability to form a coherent sentence fled, so she clamped her lips together with a zipping motion instead. Had anyone ever died from blush combustion?

His soft, seductive chuckle worsened her embarrassment.

"I don't mean to tease but have mercy, woman. Don't go tempting the devil."

He looked to the side for a second. When he met her eyes again, the old Wes had returned, with easy laughter in his eyes and an easier smile.

Sweat-dampened hair, pants stained with grease, and smelling like bacon didn't sound like much of a temptress to her. "Uh ... your order?"

"Since you're out here, I take it Cecil has the grill today?"

She nodded.

"In that case, I'll have a plain waffle with some of that buckleberry stuff on the side."

"Huckleberry," she corrected and hid a smile. Wes had

tried one of Cecil's spicy delights—once. Waffles were safer. "Want bacon?"

"Sure. Two slices. And the warm maple syrup."

"Coming right up."

Sadness filled her at the inevitability of losing Wes as a friend. They'd talked for weeks, about the pros and cons of USDA Prime grade versus Choice, about his job, people who came into the diner, her summer camp with the kids, his frat boy days, politics, economics, and so on. Why did men have to push for more? Why couldn't they settle for simple friendship?

Time and again, Wes had revealed his intelligence, humor, and sensitivity. He was the perfect catch, and she liked him, just not the way he seemed to want.

She had to remain adamant. No relationships until she got her life back on track, and Wes didn't seem like the type to wait around for a couple of years.

According to the plan she'd mapped out based on her current income and nonexistent standard of living, it would take twenty-seven months to pay off the school loan for her unfinished degree. Add another twelve months to earn enough to pay for the final courses she needed and living expenses while she took the courses and she was looking at three and a half years of work to raise it all.

Yeah, she didn't need any distractions, and no man should have to wait so long.

Turning away to slip Wes's order to Cecil, she saw

Jonas outside the diner ... with a tall, curvy woman folded around him like a warm tortilla.

Shea stared, unable to look away when the woman pulled his head down for a kiss. Except *kiss* meant pressing lips together. This looked more like she wanted to devour him.

No!

Hurt, sharp and jagged, ripped through her. How could she un-see something so devastating?

More than a little bitter, Shea thrust Wes's order at Cecil through the window.

"*Cher? Ca va?*"

She waved him off without saying anything, grabbed the bin of dirty dishes, and carried it to the washroom before anyone else noticed her reaction. It's what always happened. She'd let someone in, start to care for them, and they'd break her heart. Birds don't swim, fish don't fly, and Jonas Cameron would never change his alley cat ways.

A few sniffles and one small tear escaped before she got herself under control. She didn't care and refused to go down such a reckless path.

Some fish do fly. And a few birds can swim. All men can't be players.

But she'd seen the woman kiss him.

And also saw Jonas stand there like a board, hands at his side.

When she thought back over the scene, it did seem

one-sided ... though he hadn't tried too hard to fight her off.

He's always been a complete gentleman.

Guilt wormed its way in. She should judge him from her own firsthand knowledge, not gossip. Actually, she had no right to judge him at all.

"You okay, honey?" Cecil poked his head around the corner

Shea forced a smile in place. "Yeah, I'm fine. Maybe a little tired."

Out front, the bell chimed again.

"Back to work," she told the still questioning cook.

Cecil nodded like he didn't believe her but returned to the kitchen.

Voices carried through the hall. She'd expected Jonas but heard Kyle instead. Her eyes rolled up in her head. Deputy Kyle Abbott. Another in a long line of arrogant males proliferating in this town, and one who thought of himself as every woman's dream. Why did guys like him find the friend zone such a challenge?

Returning from the kitchen, she greeted him. "Morning, Kyle. There's a seat at the counter. The usual?"

"You know me so well, sweet cheeks. What you don't know is that I'll take anything you're willing to give."

Wes's head snapped around. He gave Kyle a sharp look as the deputy settled onto the stool next to him.

"Be a few minutes on the coffee." She ignored Kyle's flirting, dumped the old grounds, rinsed the basket, and added a new filter and fresh grounds. The door chimed again as she pressed the start button. Would it never stop?

Still expecting Jonas, Shea schooled her features into a neutral expression. She would give him the benefit of her doubt. For now. Until she couldn't.

Clint Loomis, the hand who'd helped with the campout walked in instead. He doffed his hat and looked around, seeming unsure about what to do with all the seats taken.

"Here ya go, young feller." Gene Flowers, a frequent customer at the diner, stood up from his place at the counter. "You can have my seat."

Of course, it was on Wes's right side.

Dee Dee brushed by Shea, on her way to the back. "Need you to handle things out here for a few. I've got to call Polly and up our egg order. All this extra business has messed up my inventory."

Clint looked everywhere but at Shea as he settled onto the vacated stool. Like before at the campfire, a dark flush spread up his neck and turned his ears bright red, and yet not a drop of color reached his face.

"Hi, Clint." Shea removed the dirty dishes in front of him, wiped the counter, and handed him a menu. "What brings you to the diner?"

She hadn't seen him since the last outing with the kids. Triple C hands didn't come into the diner much. They had their own cookhouse.

He looked at her but unlike before, this time he held her gaze. "Vern and I had to pick up supplies. You remember Vern? He helped with the campouts, too. Anyway, he had some personal errands to run, so I thought I'd stop in for coffee. Maybe get a chance to see you."

The way he stared, intense and unblinking, made her squirm.

Wes snapped his head around and stared at Clint this time. To make matters worse, Kyle did the same, leaning forward on the counter to look around Wes. Both men wore heavy frowns.

Shea wanted to crawl in a hole. "Coffee's hot and plentiful. Time not so much." She nodded at the packed dining room and offered him an apologetic shrug.

Refilling the napkin dispensers, neatening up the stacks of clean dishes kept Shea busy enough to avoid conversation. She bustled about, setting out a coffee cup and creamer for Clint, additional napkins for Wes, ketchup and hot sauce for Kyle, all the while with a silent plea for Dee Dee's speedy return.

How awkward. The only three guys who'd ever shown any interest in her sat side-by-side at the counter. Some women thrived on masculine attention. Shea didn't, though she had to admit it stroked her ego.

She stole a few glances at them while they ate.

Wes had above average looks and was smart, polite, and quiet at times. But the thought of kissing him didn't launch the proverbial butterflies in her tummy. Her nose wrinkled.

Kyle was the antithesis of Wes. He had movie star looks, gave off alpha vibes, sex appeal, and charm. Too much so. He seemed harmless enough at first impression—for a domesticated cat with a feral side. But an observant person couldn't help but catch a glimpse of a predator toying with its prey.

Shea had no intention of becoming his catnip.

Clint fell somewhere between the two. Okay-looking, average height, medium build, a little shy, always polite. And young. Shea suspected she had a couple of years on him. Unlike Kyle and Wes, Clint didn't have much to say. In other words, wallpaper. Easy to forget.

An unladylike snort escaped as she grabbed another order from the window. These three men circled her like pumas stalking a rabbit, and here she stood making a calm assessment of their manly traits. Foolishness.

The door opened again and this time Jonas strolled in.

Okay, make that four big cats on the hunt.

"Mornin' everyone." He removed his hat and hung the fancy black Stetson on one of the pegs by the door.

"Jonas," she acknowledged him in a neutral voice. What in the name of mercy was keeping Dee Dee?

One of his eyebrows lifted at her cool tone. He turned to the other three men. "Kyle, Clint. Don't believe I've met you," he said to Wes. "I'm Jonas Cameron."

Wes swiveled on his stool and stuck his hand out. "Wes Grainger."

"Ahh, Lost River Development." Jonas pumped his hand a couple of times and released it. "Idaho Falls right? I heard you were surveying in the area for potential properties."

Wes nodded. "You heard right. I'd forgotten how word gets around small towns. You one of the Triple C Camerons?"

"Yep."

Another counter spot opened up—this one next to Kyle. Jonas nodded at Wes and took his seat.

The coffee finished brewing. Shea filled Clint's cup, refilled Wes's, and poured new cups for Kyle and Jonas. "Okay, Clint, you're up. What will you have?"

"Just coffee, thanks."

Shea nodded and moved past Wes. "Kyle?"

His smirky grin earned him a stern glare.

"From the menu," she prompted.

Jonas frowned, his eyes tracking from Kyle to her and back again.

As expected both Kyle and Jonas ordered the Rodeo Roundup. They never deviated. Once she had all their orders, Shea hand delivered them to Cecil in the kitchen and pounded on Dee Dee's office door on the way out. "Need some help out here."

What she needed was space from the fearsome

foursome out front. Shea fanned herself. Nothing in her life had prepared her for such a moment.

Cecil called out their orders in no time—a waffle with bacon for Wes, a Rodeo Roundup for Kyle—she didn't understand how one person could eat so much food in one sitting—and another for Jonas.

"Sorry, hon." Dee Dee hurried out, retying her apron. "You know how Polly likes to talk. Good grief, where'd they come from?" She stared at Shea's four tormenters lined up at the counter.

"Can you take them off my hands?"

"Sure. Who's the young'un?"

"Clint Loomis. He wants coffee. Nothing to eat."

"Who?"

"The new ranch hand at the Triple C. I told you about him. He helped with the kids' campout this past summer."

With all the orders served and coffees refreshed, chatter in the diner faded. Only the clink of forks on plates and an occasional moan filled the room. Satisfied diners. Music to a chef's ears.

Leaving Dee Dee in charge, Shea hurried to the kitchen for a much-needed break.

Six steps were all she managed before the bell over the door rang again. With a groan, she looked over her shoulder to see who had come in.

A chill wind blew in with the newcomer, but the cold didn't send the shiver down her spine. A face from her past did, the last man on earth she ever wanted to see again.

CCC

The bell over the door rang as Jonas watched Shea retreat. When she stopped mid-stride with all the color draining from her face, he turned to find the cause of her distress.

A man stood in the entry, a stranger who held the door wide open while he looked around.

"You raised in a barn or something? Shut the door, boy," Jeb Wharton, the retired deputy who still worked part-time, growled. Several others gave the stranger dirty looks. Local folk didn't warm up to strangers right off.

Jonas looked for Shea again, but she'd disappeared into the kitchen. Why had she run off like the ghost wolves were after her?

The man in his late twenties stood several inches under six feet. He had a slender build and dressed like he'd come from a dude ranch—dark blue, sharp-creased jeans, a pristine shearling jacket, black Resistol hat with a fancy hawk feather in the band, and Lucchese embroidered boots without a single scuff on them. No wonder the locals took an instant dislike.

The newcomer scowled, but he closed the door and then started toward the back in Shea's direction.

Dee Dee intercepted him. "Whoa, hold on there, Cowboy Ken. How can I help you?"

"I need to see Shea. And the name is not Ken." He pointed toward the back and tried to brush past.

Dee Dee blocked his way, arms folded across her chest. "Well, Mr. Whoever You Are, my kitchen is for employees only and last I looked you weren't on my payroll."

Jonas studied the newcomer and determined he posed no real threat, but no one should have to put up with such antics. He started to rise from his seat at the counter at the same moment as Kyle, Wes, and Clint.

"I got this," Kyle said. He walked over to where the confrontation escalated. As the town's deputy with a star on his chest, maybe he could convince this wannabe cowboy to back off. Or toss him out on his rear end. Legally.

"My name is Porter Townsend," the man said jabbing a thumb toward his chest. A rooster preparing to waken the dawn couldn't puff up his chest any bigger than this guy. "I'm here to see my fiancée. I demand you let me see her."

Fiancée? The single word punched Jonas in the gut. Must have affected Wes and Clint the same way, because as one they slumped down on their stools.

Not possible. Shea wouldn't bind herself to this little twerp, would she? And why did he have the same last name as her?

"I don't care who you are or what your name is, slick," Dee Dee retorted. "I've known Shea for more than two

years. Funny, she never mentioned you and she sure ain't wearing a diamond."

"I need to speak to her." Townsend's voice rose in pitch, growing louder with each word.

"Excuse me. I'm Deputy Kyle Abbott. Why don't we step outside and discuss your problem?"

"I don't have a problem, and I'm not discussing my personal business with some small-town Deputy Dawg. I have every right to see my fiancée, and I'm not leaving until I do." Townsend turned to yell toward the back. "Shea, get out here. We need to talk. There's still time to make this work. Shea? Do you hear me? I'm not leaving until we fix this."

Kyle towered over the self-proclaimed fiancé. "Sir, you can come outside with me now, or I can haul you out of here kicking and screaming and let you stew overnight in jail. Your call. You have ten seconds to decide."

"You can't arrest me. I haven't broken the law. I'm a customer like the rest of these yokels."

Every one of those yokels jeered. Some even offered to help Kyle take out the trash.

"Five seconds," Kyle warned.

"Lay a hand on me and I'll sue this hick town. I know my rights," Townsend blustered, but he edged toward the door.

"Your perceived rights do not supersede those of the owner, or the orders from an officer of the law. You disturbed the peace with your screaming and insults and made a nuisance of yourself. It's obvious to everyone here Shea doesn't want to see you. Now, the owner has asked you to leave. Do you want to add resisting arrest to your rap sheet?"

Clint jumped up and rushed ahead of them to open the door.

Townsend took a moment to glare at everyone in the room before turning to Kyle again. "You'll hear from my lawyer about this."

Kyle pulled a business card from his shirt pocket and handed it to Townsend. "Let me make it easy for you. Here's my contact information."

Townsend snatched the card from Kyle's hand, stormed out, and headed for a hot little sports car parked across the street.

Chapter Eight

Jonas hung around in the diner for almost two hours after Shea ran off, hoping she would come back. After six cups of coffee, he was wired to the max, but he had a plan. He walked back to his truck in front of his brother's office, took a quick peek around to see who might be watching, and darted behind the building to the road that paralleled Main Street. From there, he double-timed it back to the diner, or more precisely, to Shea's apartment.

After watching Kyle, the new guy, and Clint all sniffing after Shea this morning, Rascal's words haunted him. *Get over yourself and ask her for a date before someone snatches her out from under your nose.*

Yeah, not gonna happen.

He took the stairs to the upper apartment two at a time

and rapped his knuckles against the door. "Shea," he called. "It's Jonas. Can I talk to you for a moment? I have a question."

A floorboard creaked inside. A soft footstep followed. And then ... silence.

"Shea? I know you're in there. It's important. I won't take long."

Still no response. She really didn't want to see him.

Shoulders slumped, he started down the stairs again when the sound of a sliding deadbolt halted him.

The door creaked open with the chain lock still engaged. A cold front greeted him. "What do you want Jonas?" Shea asked through the narrow opening.

He retraced his steps until only inches and the flimsy wooden door separated them.

Long fair lashes a few shades darker than her glorious blonde hair cast half-moon shadows against her too-pale cheeks. Her eyes had lost their sparkle. He'd expected tears, maybe even a bit of fear or anger, but never the sad weariness that surrounded her.

"Hey. I need to ask you something. I promise it won't take long. Can I come in?"

When the door closed in his face his hopes plummeted, but the unmistakable sound of the chain disengaging revived them a second later.

Shea opened the door, stepped aside, and motioned him in.

Hat in hand, Jonas wiped his feet on the welcome mat and stepped inside. Claustrophobic came to mind. Cozy was his second thought. *Apartment* seemed a generous description given the size of the tiny space. She'd made it her own, though, with fresh paint, bright curtains, vases of wildflowers scattered throughout, a few colorful throw pillows, and two large charcoal sketches hung on the wall. He studied the pictures for a few seconds and determined the work had been done by a kid, maybe one from the campouts. "I like what you've done with the place. It's nice."

She snorted and crossed her arms over her chest. "You said this wouldn't take long."

Okay, not encouraging. Most women liked a little sweet-talk, a little lead-up to a proposition, but one thing he'd learned about her—Shea wasn't like most women, at least not today. Jonas took a deep breath, blew it out, and got to the point. "I like you. I want to take you to church tomorrow, maybe out for lunch afterward."

Well, that was about the clumsiest pickup line he'd ever used. Archer, his drinking pal and hookup wingman, would howl if he heard this drivel.

Shea's mouth opened, not to speak but in surprise. A moment more and her lips curled at the corners. Yeah, definitely a smile. She gave a soft laugh then contradicted it with a shake of her head. "Wow. Of all the questions I expected, inviting me to church wasn't one of them. Are you asking me out, Jonas? Because you know how I feel about dating."

"If calling this a date will get you to say yes, then yeah, I'm asking you out. If a date is off the table, then call it a meeting so a guy can apologize for running off and leaving his friend in the lurch without any warning. A friend who wants back in your good graces. We can call it a business meeting, an interview, a chat, a tete-a-tete, a tryst ... no, not a tryst. Friends. Talking. Nothing else. Unless ... Okay, I'm gonna shut up now."

Jonas groaned in silence. What an idiot. No recovering from this. How did she do it? How did she turn his brain to mush and his words to nonsense?

He dared to meet her gaze ... and marveled at the way the corners of her mouth spasmed despite trying to press her lips into a tight line.

"You'd do church? With me?" she asked.

His head bobbed up and down like a pogo stick on steroids.

Shea turned away and crossed six short steps to her kitchen. "I'm making tea, want some?"

Offering him a drink was good, right? "Uh, no thanks. I had six cups of coffee at the diner."

"Six cups?" She looked over her shoulder, eyebrows arched.

"Uh, yeah. I kind of hung around for a couple of hours waiting for you to come back."

"Oh." Shea reappeared with a steaming mug and a real smile on her face. She sat on the one chair in what he took for the living room space. "You can have a seat, you know."

Jonas perched on the low loveseat, prepared to jump if it started creaking. An elephant at a tea party would be more uncomfortable than he was in this oh so feminine space. He laid his hat on the seat beside him and draped an ankle over one knee. Man, his feet looked huge in here.

"So, this ... date thing." Shea prompted.

"Er, yeah."

"You do understand what you taking me—taking any girl—to church will provoke, right? The gossips will have a field day. You're willing to brave the dragons for me?"

He almost got whiplash nodding so hard. "Absolutely."

"Okay. Church. I don't know about lunch after, though. We don't want to give Lorraine, Polly, Mavis, and Rosa Bea heart attacks."

Ahhh. The spark had returned. He saw laughter in her eyes. Time to bait the hook. "Well, I thought we'd do a picnic. Out at the ranch. Maybe take a ride down by the river. I figured you might like a chance to ride Cinnamon again."

When Shea squealed and spilled her tea, he knew he had her.

"I would love to ride Cinnamon! She reminds me so

much of Kit-Kat, a horse I once had."

He grabbed a tissue from the box beside him and handed it to her so she could dab at the tea stain on her jeans. "Great. I'll pick you up in the morning at ten-forty. Wear layers. The weather calls for sunny and warmer in the afternoon, if you want to call low forties warm. So, we good?"

She set her cup on the coffee table and walked with him to the door. "Yeah. We're good. Thank you."

He took her hand and cradled it in his much larger ones. She seemed so small and feminine next to his him, but very much a lovely, desirable woman.

Shea went outside on the landing a full five minutes before Jonas said he would pick her up. The moment he pulled up, she skipped down the stairs to meet him.

He opened her door and helped her into his truck, dimples flashing with a smile. "A lady on time. Be still my heart."

"What's this on time stuff. I was early."

"True." He whistled a merry tune as he walked around to the driver's side and climbed in, the notes sharp and clear. Something about a man who could whistle brought a grin to her face.

Shea frowned when instead of turning right at the end of the street to go to the church, Jonas turned left. "This

isn't the way."

"I thought about what you said yesterday. About the dragons." He grinned the slow, sly smile of a little boy cooking up trouble. "I figured if we get there late, after they shut the doors, we can slip in all quiet like and snag a seat in the back pew."

"Won't it upset your mom if you don't sit with the family?" The Camerons all attended the same church, though some more sporadic than others, plus they all still sat together in the same pew near the front.

"She'll get over it. Anyway, before the preacher winds down, we'll slip back out and hightail it out of there. This way we can avoid all the stares, finger pointing, whispers, and worse, interrogations. Most of the people there won't even know we came until after we're gone."

She laughed at the picture he painted and visualized everything going as he described. "They'll still talk, you know."

"Yeah, but not while we're there." His grin widened. "Besides, with Halloween the night before, their focus will be on the kids who pulled pranks and got into trouble, not us."

Jonas's plan went without a hitch—until they realized teens filled the rear pews. He and Shea wound up sitting several rows closer in and caused quite a stir. Still, they slipped out as planned, right before the pastor gave the benediction.

Shea whisper-groaned when the door closed behind them. "You know the diner will be filled to capacity tomorrow, don't you? Everyone will want the scoop on us."

They laughed all the way to his truck, and most of the way back to the Triple C. At the far end of the barn, where the Camerons all parked their vehicles, Jonas helped her down, grabbed her backpack, and tugged her toward the kitchen door on the backside of the house.

"You know your way around," he told her when they stepped into the mudroom. "You can use Lucy's old room at the front of the house to change. Mallory left an old pair of boots, some jeans, and a heavier jacket for you. And Shea? You need to hurry. Knowing Mom, she'll burn rubber to catch us before we head out."

Shea made quick work of changing, but the jeans hung loose on her hips. Even though she wore the same size as his sisters, they had a few more curves than she did. Living at poverty level made for a mean diet and a lean frame. Still, it worked to her advantage. Loose clothes were more comfortable, especially for horseback riding.

She found Jonas in the kitchen pouring hot chocolate into a large thermos.

"How can I help?" she asked.

'Boots okay?" His gaze traveled from her head to her

feet.

Shea pointed a toe for him. "Yep."

"Put on your coat and button up. There's a scarf and riding gloves in a cubby by the door. I'm about done here— Mom's famous chicken salad for sandwiches, fruit chunks, cheese and crackers, walnut chocolate chip cookies, one thermos of chocolate and another of hot tea. Ready?"

Jonas had worn jeans to church, so all he had to do was shrug into his jacket, grab his gloves, and toss the saddlebag filled with food over one shoulder. He took Shea's hand and together they jogged back to the barn and the horses.

Rascal met them there. He had Cinnamon and Diablo, Jonas's horse, already saddled and ready to go. "Your dad called. Best get a move on before your mom arrives."

Shea mounted and guided Cinnamon toward the open barn door, feeling a little like a naughty child for evading Cate. Jonas settled the saddlebag on his horse and mounted, but before he could nudge Diablo forward, Rascal draped a rifle in a sling over the saddle horn. "Just in case."

Jonas nodded, nudged his horse into a trot, and took the lead. He opened the first gate without dismounting and waited for her and Cinnamon to go through before leaning down to re-latch it. "Ready?"

Shea looked over her shoulder and saw Cody Cameron's big truck roll into view. She grinned and put her heels into Cinnamon's sides. "Let's ride."

Diablo leaped forward. At seventeen hands to Cinnamon's fifteen, it didn't take the big stallion long to surge ahead.

Jonas slowed their pace before long. They rode side by side through the pastures where the Triple C herds grazed. The other horses ignored them for the most part and moved aside if they came too close. They wintered here, Jonas told her. Close to the ranch where the hands could keep watch over them. In the months of November through February when snow covered the ground and foraging became difficult, it was easy for the hands to stage hay bales around the closer pastures. Easier to watch out for the horses, too, since cold weather brought out hungry predators. Here you were either hunter or prey—eat or be eaten. A beautiful, but harsh land.

Come spring, once the snow receded and the grass greened up, they'd move the horses to the higher elevations again.

Shea threw her head back and breathed in the crisp, clean air. Gosh, she missed this—the riding, the wide-open range away from people, and the demands of ranch life.

"I've often wondered, but never got around to asking, how is it you ride so well." Jonas slowed Diablo's gait even more. "You said you had a horse once."

She'd hadn't told anyone here in Hastings Bluff about the bad stuff in her past. Hadn't even thought about it in a long time. James knew some of it because he'd ferreted out

the information, but no one knew the whole story. Did she dare share it now?

"I grew up on a ranch, too. We raised beef cattle."

"Tell me about your family. I'll bet you were the princess."

The lighthearted moment faded. "Yeah, I was ... until I wasn't."

To Jonas's credit, he didn't push. They rode in comfortable silence for several more minutes before she spoke again.

"My mother was twenty-six when she met my father. He was forty-nine, with three teenaged sons by his first wife who died the year before. I came along two years after they married, but I think things between them had already turned sour by then. He worked all the time, so I don't have many early memories of him."

"What's your earliest childhood memory?" Jonas asked.

She smiled. "Picking apples with my mom. She used to bake pies and cobblers and make applesauce. Apple muffins were a breakfast staple."

"That why you're always making all those apple desserts?"

"Yeah. Probably."

"Did you go to school in town?"

"No. We lived almost fifty miles from the nearest town with a school. The foreman's wife taught my step-brothers and the other kids on the ranch, but she died by the time I reached school age. The others were all grown up by then. That left only me, the foreman's youngest daughter, and my cousin, Porter. Daddy said it wasted too much time for someone to take us to school in town and then go back for us in the afternoon. Girls don't contribute much to a ranch's livelihood, so he got us a traveling tutor instead. Porter studied with us most mornings. The rest of the time he worked alongside my brothers."

"Well, that stinks."

"Yeah, well, I didn't know any better back then. The tutors weren't very reliable and sometimes we knew more than they did."

"Didn't your mother have a say?"

Shea took a long time to answer that question. So many years had passed, but she still hadn't gotten over Mama leaving. "Not really. I think it's part of why she left when I was twelve."

Jonas took a turn at silence. After a few minutes, he said, "I'm sorry."

Not as sorry as her. Twelve years hadn't softened the hurt one bit. She shrugged. "After she left, Gina, the other girl, and I learned about online homeschooling. My father liked the idea. It cost less than tutoring, so we set up our own curriculum and taught ourselves. Daddy signed whatever forms and reports I put in front of him. Gina was eighteen when we got our high school diplomas. I'd just turned sixteen."

"What about your brothers?"

"Step-brothers. I didn't see much of them. I was six when the youngest one left for college. Our relationship wasn't anything like you have with Garrett, Wade, Mallory, and Cassidy."

"After your mother left, did your father ...?"

"Find another wife?" She laughed. "No. We muddled along. My mother had introduced me to baking, but it was Gina's mother who taught me how to plan meals, to cook, and manage a house. It sure beat steak and beans every night. By fifteen I not only ran the house, I also worked the chuckwagon on the cattle drives. Daddy didn't like it much when I told him I wanted to go to culinary school."

"Now things begin to make sense," Jonas grinned at her. "I always wondered how you managed the cooking on the campouts so easily. Culinary school, huh? Why does a school-trained chef work at a diner at the tail end of the known world?"

Shea laughed and brushed a strand of hair off her face. A slight breeze had picked up, making her regret not tying her hair up in a ponytail. "You know what? Enough about me. It's your turn to talk."

"Deal, but we're almost to the river. See the outcropping of rocks ahead? We'll spread a blanket there facing west. The rocks will provide a windbreak, and the afternoon sun should warm us. Want to race?"

She nudged her horse into a gallop and left Jonas behind. Diablo didn't take kindly to the head start and soon overtook her and Cinnamon again. Laughing and breathing heavily, they pulled up fifteen feet from the river.

Translucent and clear, the water flowed by in deceptive tranquility. Smooth rocks lined the riverbed along this stretch, but she knew further south the current kicked up to Class II rapids when the spring runoff raised the water level.

The outcropping Jonas spoke of featured a semi-circle of stones rising some ten feet high to create a natural amphitheater. They dismounted and looped the reins around the saddle horns. Part of the Triple C training program taught the horses to stay close without the need to hobble them or tie off the reins.

After finishing most of the food Jonas had brought, they sat in silence and watched an osprey dive into the river for fish.

Shea turned to Jonas once the bird finished feeding. "Thank you for bringing me out here. You couldn't have planned a more perfect date."

"So, this is a date?" His dimples peeked out again as he tried not to smirk.

"Yes, I think so. Will you kiss me now?" Her heart picked up speed. This was new territory for her, but she never did anything by half-measures. Why dip your toe in the water when you could jump in with both feet?

His eyes stared at her mouth. His hand, rough and calloused but also gentle, cupped her cheek. He traced her lips with his thumb. "I plan on kissing you a lot, but not today."

She drew back with a frown. "Why?"

"Rascal warned me to take care with you. Others did, too. You're different, Shea. Special. I don't want to mess this up."

Her heartbeat calmed a little. "All right. When?"

"Soon. I don't think I can wait for very long. Come on, let's pack up. I want to get the horses back before the sun sets and the temperature really starts to drop."

Chapter Nine

The return journey took longer, in part because Jonas wasn't ready to give up this private time with Shea but also because he slowed the pace while he told her a few tales from his boyhood days. He stayed well clear of what had gone down after he graduated from high school, though. She didn't need to hear those ugly truths. He didn't know if he could ever talk about some of it.

"We should see Mom soon. I have no doubt she's lying in wait for us, for you in particular," he warned Shea at the gate. "In fact, it wouldn't surprise me to see the whole family at the barn."

Twilight still had a tenuous hold on the day, but the light wouldn't last much longer. Shea's tousled blonde locks fell about her shoulders, a beacon under the darkening sky. She laughed. "I adore your mother, your whole family. I don't mind spending a little time with them, but Jonas, you know I can't stay late. The morning biscuits have to go in the oven by five-thirty else we'll have a crowd of grumps when the diner opens at six."

As predicted, Cate Cameron waited in the barn. "About time. I tried to get Cody to go look for the two of you hours ago, but he said you'd straggle in about dark."

Cate held Cinnamon's bridle while Shea dismounted. She didn't need the help, but it gave his mother a reason to stay close.

Shea protested when Mom pulled into a hug. "Cate, I smell like a horse."

"So? You think this is new to me?"

"I thought I'd find you here." Rascal popped out of the small office at the back of the barn. "You two go on up to the house with Cate. I'll take care of your horses."

Jonas retrieved the saddlebag, thanked him, and bent down when the old foreman motioned him closer. "Looks like I owe you an apology. You still don't know much about women, but it looks like you figured out how to treat a lady. You'll tell me all about it tomorrow, ya hear?"

"Shea, you're frozen," his mother scolded. "What were you thinking, Jonas? Out in the cold all afternoon. Bring her to the house and I'll fix something warm to drink."

From the look on his mother's face, he'd be in the

doghouse until doomsday if he tried to spirit Shea away again.

"Yes, ma'am." He chuckled, peeled off his gloves and one of hers so he could hold her hand on the short walk to the house.

As he feared, the whole family had gathered in the family room—Dad, Garrett and TJ, Wade and Lucy, Mallory and James, and Cassie.

When he raised an eyebrow at his youngest sister, Cass answered with a twinkle in her eyes. "James put Derek on both day and night shift. Punishment for leaving law enforcement and going into the ranching business."

A wedding loomed in the future for each of his sisters. Mallory and James still danced around the idea of an engagement, but it would happen. Cassie and Derek, on the other hand, had plowed ahead. She had a diamond on her finger and lobbied for a fast wedding, but Derek had resigned his job as deputy to train the horses for the Triple C and wanted to establish himself before taking on the responsibilities of a new wife. Cassie didn't like it, but women didn't always understand a man's way of thinking.

Everyone but Derek knew their wedding would happen sooner rather than later. Mallory and James wouldn't take long either. Which left Jonas the last unattached sibling. A status he'd intended to keep for years to come until recently.

He kept his promise and dragged Shea away after

twenty minutes. A comfortable and contented silence filled their drive back to her apartment.

When he parked and opened his door, she touched his arm. "You don't have to get out, Jonas. I can get to my own door without help."

He took her hand and kissed her fingers. "My mama raised me right. I'll get your door, walk you up the stairs, and check your place before I leave you."

"Protective much?"

"You have no idea." Her smile warmed his heart and lit up his world.

Inside the apartment, he told her to wait by the door while he looked around. Small as the place was, it didn't take long. The whole unit would fit inside one of those tiny houses he'd seen on TV. "All clear."

He didn't want to leave but couldn't think of a logical reason to stay. She needed to be up early. So did he.

"Would you ... like some tea?" she asked with hesitancy.

His hands moved of their own accord to frame her face. A man could get lost in those eyes. So expressive. She couldn't hide her emotions if she tried. And she did try.

He leaned closer, thinking about the promise he'd made to her, their first kiss ...

A buzzing sound broke the moment. The vibration of his cell phone tickled his hip.

He sighed, closed his eyes, and touched his forehead

to hers. Guess now wasn't a good time after all.

"Could be important," Shea whispered in a throaty voice.

Pulling the phone from his back pocket, Jonas checked the caller ID ... and stiffened. No way. They wouldn't pull him into their games again.

"Jonas?"

He silenced the phone, knowing the caller would buzz again and again until he answered. Sure enough, a few seconds later the vibration came again. "I'm sorry. I need to take this." He opened her door and accepted the call as he stepped out on the landing.

Shea watched Jonas from the open door, not yet ready to let him go. Giddy, nervous energy filled her, the same excited anticipation she remembered from the time her brother, Ben, took her to the circus. The sensation surged through her now, only with a much different adult edge. Jonas did this. He made her dream again.

She tried not to listen to his phone conversation, but the illusion shattered when the caller's voice carried, not clear enough to make out words but loud enough to recognize a feminine laugh.

Whatever the woman said had an obvious effect on Jonas. He clamped a hand to his forehead and grimaced, paced the two-and-one-half steps back and forth across the narrow landing only to turn around and do it again.

Their conversation didn't last long. He pocketed the phone and turned to Shea with an expression of regret. "I need to go."

"To her?"

He'd already started down the stairs. Her question stopped him. Looking over his shoulder, he said, "What?"

Too late now. She might as well finish. "It's a simple question, Jonas. I saw you outside the diner kissing a woman. Now another woman calls and you go running. Is there something you need to tell me?"

His jaw clenched. Midnight-blue eyes turned cold and hard, making it difficult to recognize the man who'd charmed her all day. "Were you ever going to tell me about Porter Townsend? Your fiancé?"

The words robbed her of breath. She took a step back. Something her daddy used to say crawled into her mind. *Careful what you ask for, you might get more than you want.*

"Goodnight, Jonas."

She closed the door on him and listened to his footsteps descend the stairs. Moments later, an engine roared. Tires crunched in the snow.

Her heart shattered.

Mindless television didn't interest Shea and the five minutes it took to clean the already spotless kitchenette offered no distraction. Relief at having escaped the clutches of a serial womanizer should have consoled her. After all, it was better to know the devil than not, and she sure didn't need another Porter disaster.

Easy to say, but much more difficult to accept when her soul rivaled a desert.

She shouldn't have called Jonas out. His personal life didn't concern her. Except it did. Now. He'd taken her to church, ensured the whole town saw them together. And the picnic, the personal questions. The promise. And his mother. Was he serious? Or playing a game?

Dee Dee always said you had to fight for what you wanted. Could she do it? Did she want Jonas Cameron that much?

Shea glanced at her phone. Fifteen minutes since he left.

The telephone call played in a loop through Shea's head. The woman's loud voice. Raucous music in the background. Jonas's obvious displeasure. His regret. Guitar chords. Drums. A country song.

A bar. The woman had called from a bar.

Filled with determination, Shea found her car keys and raced down the stairs. Sidewinders was the only bar for twenty miles, a disreputable honkytonk on the northernmost outskirts of town. She'd find him there. Find *them*.

If they didn't leave before she arrived.

CCC

Jonas slammed the door of his truck and strode toward Sidewinders. He couldn't remember ever parking this far out. Of course, Friday nights meant ladies got two-for-one drinks and when the girls came out to play the guys didn't lag far behind.

Thoughts of his ruined night with Shea, all because of the mind games Sadie Gayle and Brad played, fueled his anger. He didn't know what hurt worse, knowing Shea had seen him in a lip lock with another woman or her believing him complicit in the vulgar display. How could she think so little of him after he'd shown her nothing but his good side? She had no idea ...

He stopped in his tracks. Of course, she had no idea. He'd never given her one, never shared anything because he didn't want her to see the real Jonas Cameron for fear she'd run away screaming. All she knew were the few stories he'd fed her earlier this afternoon and the salacious gossip floating around town. Unfortunately, enough truth existed in those rumors to make a grown man blush.

No, he couldn't blame this on Shea. He'd seen the hurt in her eyes, the way she withdrew after hearing Sadie Gayle on the phone with him. The look of betrayal.

This decision was all on him. All those years ago in Nigeria, he'd made the right decision even though it resulted in a little girl's death. Tonight, he made the wrong decision in a misguided attempt to ease his guilt. He chose to save Sadie Gayle from her own foolishness ... and hurt Shea in the process. He'd sabotaged any future he might have had with her.

Maybe that's what Rascal meant about him not understanding. It was different for girls. Shea possessed a core of composure and strength despite her innate shyness and uncertainty. She reacted with every emotion exposed but would rebound stronger than before. He, on the other hand, like most men, hid his pain as though showing emotion made him less of a man.

Could he fix yet another blunder?

Resigned, but determined to do his best, he entered Sidewinders to deal with the problem at hand. Tonight, he'd see Sadie Gayle safely home and put an end to his involvement in her and Brad's stupid games.

Jonas spotted Tate Murtaugh behind the bar the moment he walked through the door. The longtime proprietor/bartender waved him over and pointed at a table near the dancefloor. "I cut her off two hours ago, but she's still high. I think she's taking something."

Jonas nodded and looked around for Brad, already knowing where to find him. Sure enough, his old high school buddy leaned over one of the tables in the back, lining up for a shot. The man couldn't shoot pool for sugar, but it didn't stop him from throwing his money away after he had a few. As Jonas watched, Brad drew his arm back and ... crack! Solids and stripes ricocheted around the table, but none dropped. Instead, the cue ball slowed to a lazy crawl, teetered on the edge of the side pocket, and disappeared. Scratch. Brad stumbled to one side amid cheers and jeers.

Jonas rubbed his fist. A punch to Brad's face would make things worse, but man, it sure would feel good.

Sadie Gayle decided to dance. She grabbed a random guy and started gyrating, but thirty seconds into it, her face turned green. She was gonna blow.

Puke on the dance floor—not cool. Not with a perfectly good toilet close by. Shoving people aside, Jonas got an arm around her waist and hauled her off to the ladies' room.

He wrestled her into one of the stalls and held her while she puked. Keeping her long hair out of the way proved a major challenge.

Several minutes passed while she emptied her guts. When the dry heaves tapered off, he grabbed a handful of toilet paper to wipe her mouth, opened the stall door ... and groaned when the door opened. Of course, someone would walk in on them.

After breaking the speed limit and several more traffic laws, Shea reached Sidewinders only to find the parking lot overflowing with trucks, cars, and motorcycles. She drove

through slowly on the lookout for Jonas's truck and spotted it as far from the front door as possible.

Now what? She could wait and confront him when he came back, maybe with the brunette in tow, or she could park here on the grass beside his truck and go inside to look for him.

A woman alone? Walk through this parking lot? In the dark? Desperate might describe her state of mind but she wasn't foolish.

The front door of Sidewinders opened spilling loud music and a group of people into the night. Luck was with her. One of the couples got into a car on the first row.

Shea drove slowly toward the front and as soon as they pulled out she darted into the vacant space.

Now she had to go inside.

Doubts whirled through her head. She'd never been to a bar, never had the opportunity, and had no idea what to expect. Would she fit in wearing her horsey-smelling jeans and flannel shirt? With dusty boots and wild hair? Only one way to find out.

Shea felt more than heard the old hardwood floors creak when she stepped inside. At least a hundred people filled the place wall-to-wall, most of the men dressed in everything from dusty work clothes to fancy pearl-snap shirts and bolo ties. Outnumbered two-to-one, the women reveled in the spotlight, most of them dressed to impress in short-short denim skirts and down-to-there tank tops.

The sound hit her first—loud voices, louder music, laughter, thumping bass, the twang of a country melody, glasses clinking, a drum roll, yelling, screaming.

Overwhelmed, Shea inched her way through the crush toward the bar.

The smells assaulted her next—spilled beer, sweat, leather, wood shavings, stale air, body odor, and an underlying scent of pine cleaner masking something nasty.

Her heart pounded. Men bellied up to the bar two and three deep. The lone bartender worked like a maniac sliding foaming glasses of beer down the counter and pouring whiskey into shot glasses. The harried waitresses moved between the tables where every seat was taken. The dance floor overflowed. Even the pool tables at the back had people waiting a turn.

Despair wrapped itself around her. Jonas was the proverbial needle in Sidewinders' haystack.

Shea edged along the wall to the end of the bar and stretched up on tiptoes, but still couldn't see over the crowd. While searching for him, she noticed several men giving her a once over. Their leering grins and yellow teeth made her skin crawl.

"You okay?" the bartender asked. He leaned forward, both hands on the counter, and stared at her.

Shea laughed, hysteria bubbling up. "Other than feeling like a guppy at a shark convention? Yeah, I'm good. Have you seen Jonas Cameron?"

Surprise flashed across his face but changed to speculation a moment later. She didn't think he would answer at first.

"Other end of the bar, take a left down the hall. He's in the ladies' room."

Her mouth dropped, but the bartender had gone back to the hustle before she could ask what he meant. The ladies' room? Too many possibilities came to mind, none of them comforting.

Curiosity won out. Shea followed the bartender's directions but came face-to-face with a man not much taller than her. He wore the requisite western uniform of faded jeans, plaid shirt, and dusty boots, but the thin mustache riding his upper lip with wisps of hair crawling over the edge of his mouth made her recoil. Ugh.

She tried to step around him.

He moved with her. "What's the matter, princess? I'm not good enough?"

The bartender came to her rescue again. He pointed a finger at the smaller man and barked, "Get lost, Stanley. She's here for somebody else."

Stanley glowered at both the barkeep and her, but he slinked away.

Two more men tried to engage her before she reached the hallway. Shea darted by them both before they could take offense. Down the hallway, she saw the sign for the restrooms.

Did she really want to do this?

Steeling her resolve, Shea opened the door to the ladies' room and stepped inside. Her eyes went wide at the scene before her.

A couple stood in the open door of one of the stalls. The woman clung to man, moaning like she waited at death's door.

The man simply stood there, gaping at her.

Chapter Ten

"Jonas?" Shea couldn't believe her eyes.

Jonas, wild-eyed and a little frantic, had exited a stall in the ladies' room with his arm around a woman. Not any woman, either. The same leggy brunette she'd seen kissing him yesterday, except now she looked a lot worse for wear.

Jonas groaned. He seemed to wilt right before her eyes, but he didn't release the woman.

"Is she okay?" Shea asked. "Because she doesn't look okay."

"Yeah. No," he answered, shaking his head "I don't know. I think she's had more than beer tonight. I've never seen her this hammered."

Meaning not the first time he'd been in this situation.

The woman pushed Jonas's hands away and with great

effort stumbled forward to hang her head over the sink. "I'm right here, you know."

Shea studied the woman with her snotty nose, smeared mascara, and hair that looked like someone had taken a mixer to it ... except for the stringy clump stuck to her cheek. Wait, was that—Ew! Vomit.

Yep. The same knockout who'd laid a big, fat kiss on Jonas yesterday looked like something the pigs would fight over tonight.

Shea's nose curled at the foul odor emanating from the two. "She got a cell phone?"

"Huh?" Jonas looked confused.

"Of course, I do," the shrew snapped, still clutching at the sink.

Shea saw the outline of a phone in the back pocket of the girl's skintight jeans and slipped it out.

"Hey, give it back!"

"Oh, I plan to." She thumbed through the settings— who didn't put a password on their phone? —selected the camera app and snapped several pictures of the bedraggled woman.

"Hey!" She tried to hide behind her hands.

Now for the fun part. Shea tucked the phone in her own pocket, put her hands on her hips, and stared first at Jonas and then the woman.

"I, uh, need to get her home," Jonas announced from where he hovered in the background.

Shea pointed at him. "You guard the door. Don't let anyone in until I tell you. And you," she said poking the girl. "Lean over the sink. You've got puke in your hair, on your face, and down the front of your shirt."

"You can't tell me what to do." the woman snapped,

"Look in the mirror, honey. I promise you, it's not a pretty sight."

"My name is Sadie Gayle, not honey." Despite the snippy attitude, she turned obediently to the mirror wobbling in the highest heels Shea had ever seen.

Horror-struck, all Sadie Gayle could do was stare at herself and wail.

'Yeah, take a good look and listen. I'm the one who's going to clean you up so you don't become the laughing stock of the county when you walk out of here. Unless that's what you want? No, I didn't think so. Now head in the sink."

Jonas let out a low whistle.

Shea had worked magic but she couldn't pull off a miracle. With her makeup washed off, long hair damp from being cleaned under running water, and clothes wiped somewhat clean, Sadie Gayle stood tall and mostly steady.

He opened the door of the ladies' room and held it for the two women.

Shea locked arms with Sadie Gayle and started down

the hall. "Lead the way, Jonas. Break a path for us. I've got her."

"Coming through. Step aside, please." Reduced to acting as a one-man battering ram, he cleared a swath through the crowd. Several glances over his shoulder at Sadie Gayle gave him incentive. She'd gone from ash pale to a sickly green, taking on the hue that proclaimed her ready to blow again.

He paused outside to let his charge catch a breath of fresh air, but her recovery came slow. When Sadie Gayle could once again move forward without threat of regurgitation, Jonas slipped an arm around her waist and helped her walk to his truck, using his key remote to unlock the doors.

Shea hurried ahead of them and opened the passenger door.

"Thanks for your help. I can take it from here," he said to Shea after buckling Sadie Gayle in.

"You're welcome. I'll follow you to her house," Shea answered.

"You've done enough, Shea. You don't have to babysit her tonight."

"And you do? Don't argue with me, Jonas. I've got things to say to both of you."

He held up his hands in surrender, palms forward, and walked around to the driver side. Driving with deliberate slowness, he proceeded through the lot to where Shea had

parked near the front of the bar, keeping her in his sight the whole way.

Sadie Gayle's violent purging seemed to have gotten rid of whatever drugs she'd taken. Her wits seemed clear and her speech understandable, even though she looked like one of the walking dead.

"I'm sorry, Jonas," she mumbled.

"You're always sorry once the hangover hits." He kept his speed well below the limit and divided his time between watching the road ahead, glancing at Sadie Gayle to make sure she didn't puke in his truck, and making sure he didn't lose Shea who followed them.

"No, this time I mean it. My life has grown too crazy. I have to get off the roller coaster before I kill myself. Or kill Brad."

Could she do it? Kill Brad? He'd wanted to himself when Shea walked into the bathroom tonight. "I hope you mean it this time because I'm done."

He pulled into the driveway of Sadie Gayle's snug brick home and looked around at the freshly mown grass, tidy flower beds, and newly painted exterior. Why? Sadie Gayle had looks and style. She made enough money for a nice home and took pride in its appearance. Why did she put up with Brad? Why not find someone who would cherish and value her?

Shea parked her car on the street and met them at the front door. "I'm Shea, by the way. Thought you should know who washed your face and fixed your hair. You wouldn't happen to have some coffee in your house, would you?"

Instead of the snark Jonas had come to expect from Sadie Gayle, she smiled and said, "I'm Sadie Gayle Miller. Thank you for helping me, and yes, I have coffee."

Inside, Jonas stepped aside and let Shea take charge. She had something to prove, and he wouldn't stand in her way. He only hoped he came out standing once the storm blew over.

Shea sent Sadie Gayle to the shower and Jonas to the guest bath to wash the stench off best he could. She made the coffee and had it waiting when Jonas joined her in the kitchen.

He claimed a mug. "I, uh, want to thank you for your help tonight."

"You thanked me a dozen times already, Jonas. Let it go."

Not a warm start, but at least she'd spoken to him. He savored the aroma and took a sip. "Mmmm, good coffee."

"Really?" Shea gave him the look; the same one his sisters turned on him whenever he did something stupid in their estimation. "Good coffee is all you have to say?"

Okay, time to shut up.

They sat in uncomfortable silence until Sadie Gayle joined them, fresh from the shower with shampooed hair and clean clothes and looking like she wanted to be

anywhere but here with them.

Shea poured a cup of coffee for her.

Sadie Gayle took a cautious sip before saying, "You still have my cell phone."

Shea retrieved the phone from her back pocket and tapped it a few times before sliding it across the counter. "Check out your new screensaver. Think of it as a reminder."

Jonas leaned over to see. Wow. Harsh. Ugly didn't begin to describe the woman in the picture.

Sadie Gayle stared at the photo, looked over at Shea, and started crying. Before long, she dropped her head to the counter and shook with violent sobs.

Unmoved, Shea finished her coffee, rinsed the cup, and waited.

Jonas's skin crawled. Nothing made him more uncomfortable than a crying woman. He fidgeted for a few seconds before standing. "Uh, maybe I should go—"

The quick flash of anger in Shea's eyes told him if he did, he'd find out firsthand how a steak felt when it met a hot grill.

"Yeah, maybe not." He took his seat again, earning Shea's nod of approval.

The Sadie Gayle crying jag went on for what seemed like forever, but once she wound down to sniffles, she blubbered another apology. "I'm so sorry."

"I'm sure you are," Shea said, handing her a box of

tissues. "Listen up. I won't say this twice. You're done playing these sick mind games with Jonas. Do not ever call him again. Do not speak to him beyond hello or goodbye, and under no circumstances do you ever touch him. Not a pat on the back, not even a handshake. Got it?"

A spark of the old Sadie Gayle flared. "He's my friend. I can—"

"Before you say something you'll regret, check your camera roll and your text messages. You'll see where I sent a bunch of those disgusting pictures to my phone. Push me and I will post every one of those ugly-as-sin photos of you covered in vomit on social media. I will make sure your boss, every friend you ever had, and your family sees them. Brad, too. Do you get what I'm saying?

Sadie Gayle nodded, her eyes wide.

"And the next time you decide to get falling-down drunk at Sidewinders, know this. I explained things to Tate Murtaugh. He will call the sheriff's office and have your carcass hauled off to jail. No more free passes. No more Jonas to the rescue. Nod if you understand."

Sadie Gayle thumbed through her phone, her eyes growing even wider. The little bit of color she'd regained drained away, but she nodded.

"Hey, hey, hey, hold on a minute," Jonas interrupted. While grateful for the hard-line Shea had drawn, it seemed at odds with the woman he'd come to know. She'd grown up playing peacemaker in an all-male environment, with very few female influences. As an adult, she'd taken on a nurturer's role. Sadie Gayle would resent the heck out of this ultimatum, but guilt would eat Shea alive.

He had to divert Sadie Gayle's resentment to him. He snapped his fingers in front of his old friend's face.

She jerked around to stare at him.

"Shea's right. Hear me this time, because I won't come for you anymore. I'm done with the games."

"He broke up with me, Jonas." Tears flooded her eyes and spilled down her cheeks. More manipulation.

"He always breaks up with you, Sadie Gayle. Not the other way around. Think about it. You want to get married. He doesn't. You make a scene. He gets mad. You throw a fit. He walks away. You threaten him. He calls your bluff. The two of you break up. He laughs. You get drunk and try to guilt him. It doesn't work. What you don't get is … Brad doesn't care. He doesn't love you, girl, not the way you love him."

Sadie Gayle stared at him, her expression shocked.

"Where's your self-respect? You put yourself at risk every time you go off on one of these drunken binges." He was on a roll now. All his pent-up frustration, guilt, and anger came boiling out. "Tonight, you added some kind of drug to the mix. Why? Because the alcohol didn't get the response from Brad you wanted. Don't you see? You're not hurting him, you're hurting you."

The shock and disbelief in her expression fell away,

replaced by dawning realization, embarrassment, and a boatload of hurt.

"You know what? I've been as blind as you, but no more," Jonas went on. "Brad looked out for me during a bad time in my life. I wanted to return the favor, be there for him. My error was thinking he'd thank me for coming to your rescue. But you know what? He never did. Not once."

Shea stared at him, laser-focused while he spoke. If she didn't have questions about his past before, she would now.

A whimper escaped Sadie Gayle's lips. More tears fell, real ones this time. An outpouring of grief and betrayal.

Time to rebuild the broken woman before him. "Sadie Gayle, sweetheart, you went to college. You earned a degree in finance. You even got your CPA. The world lies at your feet and yet you left your home in Montana and settled for a bank teller position here in Nowhere, Idaho. For him. You're too smart for this. Too beautiful. Brad's a loser. He can't hold a job and he's never going to change, so cut your losses while you can. Chalk up your time with him as lessons learned and retake control of your life."

Through her sniffles, Sadie Gayle asked, "You think I should leave? Without a job?"

"Google," Shea said. "Online searches. There are tons of jobs out there. See for yourself what's available. Pick a

few and apply. You might find your dream job."

Jonas struggled not to smile.

Sadie Gayle swallowed hard, took another look at her phone, and said, "You're right. Goodbye Jonas. It's been nice knowing you. Thank you, Shea."

Jonas left his cup on the counter and hurried after Shea, not bothering with a goodbye.

Outside, the sky held the promise of more snow. She wanted to get home to the apartment before the storm broke. And before she gave in to the emotional overload of the past week.

"Shea, wait up," Jonas called. He placed a hand on top of her car to prevent her from opening the door. "You okay?"

"Yeah, I'm good." Her throat tightened, giving her a sultry tone. She knew the signs. Much more and her voice would break ... and then she would break.

"What about us? Are we good?"

She closed her eyes tight enough to see bright, geometric patterns behind her lids. Could he overlook her insecurity and jealousy, her mistrust?

Against all odds, something magical had flared between them. Logic dictated it shouldn't have happened, but this attraction, this *oneness* felt too amazing to be called a shouldn't have. Second chances didn't come around very often. This time she would grab hold with both hands and hold on for dear life. "Yeah, Jonas. We're good. We're better than good. Whatever this is ... it's so new, for both of us." She drew in a shaky breath. "I need slow. We need time to learn about each other."

He pulled her to him and pressed her cheek against his chest. "How did you get so wise?"

Shea chuckled and pulled away, turning her back on him so she could wipe her eyes without him seeing. Tears made everything personal. They revealed vulnerability, something she wasn't ready to share. One day she would.

"Get in, it's cold. I'll follow you home." Jonas opened her door and waited for her to fasten the seatbelt.

Of course, he would follow her home. He had protector ingrained in his genes. And she wouldn't change him for anything.

Jonas's cell phone buzzed as he pulled in beside Shea behind the diner. A quick glance at the screen and he let the call go to voicemail. Whatever Fowler had to say didn't need airing in front of Shea, not until he had a chance to tell her some of his secrets himself.

Taking her hand, he led the way up the stairs. Some things came second nature. He'd been trained to deal with the unexpected though he didn't anticipate any surprises this time. Still, given the apartment's isolated entrance

behind the diner and what had gone down at her uncle's house, her safety came first. Always would.

He made a mental note to talk with her about her little excursion tonight. After the fire inspector returned a verdict of arson, both he and James had warned her not to go out after dark alone. Even in the early morning hours, they told her to wait for Dee Dee's car to pull in before she went down to the diner. But Sidewinders .... He shuddered. Not a place for any self-respecting woman, much less an innocent like Shea. He'd seen the hungry looks half the men there had given her.

Tension coiled in his gut at thoughts of what could have happened tonight. And not only from the rowdies. James still didn't have any leads on who'd doused her uncle's house with gasoline and set it on fire. They didn't know if Shea was the intended target, but they didn't know she wasn't either.

When they reached the landing outside the apartment, Shea handed over her keys without a prompt. Good girl. A fast learner.

The door opened with a soft squeak. She'd left a lamp on, dispelling some of the shadows. "Wait here," he instructed ... and ignored the eye roll she gave him. Okay, they'd have to work on that.

"All clear," he said a few moments later. The apartment offered few places for an intruder to hide.

Shea still stood by the door, but her posture had gone

rigid. She stared off into space. No, at the sofa.

"Shea? What's it? What's wrong?"

She opened her mouth but no words came forth.

He followed her gaze ... not the sofa, the television. A piece of paper taped to the screen. Jonas reached it in two strides, snatched it off, and cursed under his breath. A black and white picture of two people printed on copy paper. The distance made clear features difficult, but he knew them, recognized the horses, the rock outcropping, and the river beyond. He'd know the curve of Shea's sweet body anywhere.

Someone had come onto Triple C property, followed them, taken a photo of him and Shea on their picnic. And then invaded her home, her safe space.

Rage swept through Jonas, a wildfire that threatened his control. He wanted to pound his fist into the wall, kick the television over, anything to sate the fury burning through his veins.

"Guess I'm going to need better locks," Shea said in a tiny voice.

The anger winked out. He could rage later, but right now Shea needed to know he had her back and would be her rock. Tomorrow, he'd get his brother, Wade, to come out and make recommendations to upgrade her security.

"It's okay, Shea. I'll stay here with you tonight." He led her to the sofa and pulled her against his side. "You're safe with me. I'll always keep you safe."

His ranch offered better protection. There, she'd be surrounded by him and his family plus two dozen hands. No one would get to her there.

A glimmer of a plan began to take shape. Along with it came a number of questions, foremost of which—why Shea?

Chapter Eleven

Intense relief flooded Shea when Jonas said he wouldn't leave. It had taken her awhile to admit her insecurity after leaving the only home she'd ever known in Montana and moving to Hastings Bluff. Now she could add apprehensive and vulnerable to her list of weaknesses.

Having someone set fire to a house with you in it had that effect.

Snuggled against Jonas's chest, here in the relative safety of Dee Dee's spare apartment, she felt safe again for the first time in a long while.

"Talk to me, Shea. You shiver like you jumped naked into an icy pond when you should be purring like the cat who got the cream."

She gifted him with a sharp elbow to the ribs,

scrambled away from him, and wrapped the afghan from the sofa around her shoulders.

"Ooof." He doubled over in mock pain and rubbed his side. At least his glacier expression from earlier had thawed. He'd been furious when they'd first arrived, angry that an intruder had entered her home. Shea suspected he'd inadvertently revealed a side few people ever saw.

"I'd like to peek inside your mind for a minute to see the fairytale you're living in," she told him.

Snap. The glacier returned, darker this time, and cold enough to freeze her blood. "No, you wouldn't."

The simple statement sounded more like a threat than a denial.

Jonas had always seemed a little dangerous to her. Now, after having witnessed his rage firsthand she had no doubts about his lethality.

Not toward her. Jonas would never hurt her. At least not in a physical sense. Her heart was another story.

She looked at him and wondered how his personality could change in such drastic fashion in the span of seconds. A chameleon had nothing on this man. He could hide in plain sight. Creep about without anyone hearing him. And prevaricate with the best.

What are you hiding, Jonas Cameron? What don't you want me to see?

The unsaid words hung between them like fairy dust, sending yet another shiver down her spine. "All right. How about some coffee? I can make a pot in a couple of minutes. Won't take long at all. I mean, if we're going to stay up all night, caffeine will help, right? A lot of people use it to wake up and stay awake. It's what we need, right? Caffeine. To keep us awake. Of course, if you prefer—"

"Whoa, whoa, whoa. Slow down there, speedy. You're rambling. Why?"

She gaped at him. Another metamorphosis, from iceberg back to Prince Charming with the flip of a switch. How did he do it?

"What's the real problem, Shea?"

Like she would tell him how much his close proximity affected her. "You won't fit on my bed," she blurted out. Of all the things she could have said ... She needed a hole to crawl into. Right now.

Of course, he grinned. "Oh, I think I'll fit."

"Don't," she said, holding up a hand to punctuate her demand. One side of the afghan dropped, and she had to scramble to right it. "Not what I meant, and you know it. This apartment has one bed, a twin size. I thought to let you have it, but your legs are so long I'm afraid your feet will hang off. The loveseat is even smaller than the bed, so the logical solution is we both stay up and keep watch. With coffee."

"And do we stay up all night again tomorrow night? And the night after?"

He didn't even try to hide his laughter. How rude.

Sometimes her cheeks acted like a thermometer. Like now. She could feel the heat rising. "There's more."

Okay, she had his attention again. He calmed down enough to say, "Go on."

"It's ... your truck."

She'd fallen in love with Hastings Bluff and its residents, but the small community held tight to their provincial moral beliefs. While most of the town folk accepted her, they still saw her as an outsider and that would make it easy to brand her a Jezebel.

"My truck."

"Yeah, your truck."

His laughter stopped, the grin turned into a frown. Had she hit a vulnerable spot?

"What's wrong with my truck? I washed it yesterday, vacuumed it, too."

"Your truck is very pretty. I like the chrome. But not parked outside my door all night."

It took him a moment to realize what she was saying. He collapsed then, fell to his knees laughing so hard tears rolled down his face.

"Stop it." She stamped her foot.

"Sorry. I haven't laughed like a crazy man in ... well, ever. And my truck is not pretty. it's rugged, rad, bad—"

She dismissed him with a wave. "Whatever. You need to move it. Maybe you could park it down by your brother's office?"

He sighed, climbed to his feet, and grabbed his hat and coat. "Lock the door behind me and don't open it until you hear my voice. It will take me ten minutes tops. Better put the coffee on, too. We'll need it if we're going to swap bedtime stories."

Shea heard Jonas's heavy tread coming up the outside stairs. True to his word, nine minutes had elapsed since he left, long enough for her to start the coffee and heat a pot of water with the oats, corn grits, and quinoa to boiling. She waited for him to call out as instructed and used the time to scoop a portion of the porridge mixture into a bowl. To it, she added a pat of butter, some diced apple, chopped walnuts, a spoonful of brown sugar, a few raisins, and a dollop of milk.

A series of solid thumps made the door jump. "Shea, it's me. Jonas. Open up. It's freezing out here."

She hurried to unbolt the door and stepped aside while he raked his boots over the welcome mat.

"Storm's here. Got about a foot on the ground already." He leaned over to remove his boots. After setting them next to the door, he shed the heavy jacket and lifted his nose high. "I smell heaven."

Shea smiled and made her way back to the kitchen. "My favorite snack. You hungry?"

"Starved. What did you make? I'm not picky." He

flashed his naughty little boy grin and wandered over to see for himself.

"Comfort food. Something that will stick to your ribs and warm your insides. Here, try a taste." She scooped up a small amount with a spoon and held it out.

He wrinkled his nose and backed away. "Oatmeal?"

"Porridge. My own special recipe." Miffed, she stuck the spoon in her mouth, took her bowl and coffee cup into the other room, and left him to fend for himself.

The sounds of his foraging carried across the room— a cabinet door clanged, refrigerator door opened, a drawer, rattle of silverware, the fridge again. She ignored it all. If he wanted help, he could ask. Finally, he came out carrying a saucer with two humongous sandwiches.

He started laughing before he sat down.

Shea glared at him. "What?"

"You. You remind me of Little Miss Muffet, sitting there with your feet tucked up under your tuffet, eating your porridge. Cute. You need one of those frilly Bo-Peep bonnets now."

"You're mixing your nursery rhymes. Bo-Peep tended sheep. Miss Muffet ate curds and whey. Goldilocks ate the porridge."

"Yeah, well you look a little like a Goldilocks. What do you know about curds and whey? Where do they come from?"

"They both come from cottage cheese. Whey is the

watery part left over after the curds form." Shea held her bowl out. "Does this look like cottage cheese? By the way, I don't have a tuffet, thank you very much."

When he didn't respond, she looked at him suspiciously. "You do know what a tuffet is, right?"

His smile took on a mischievous glint, as his eyes roamed. "I always thought it meant her backside."

Teasing wretch. She needed to step outside and cool her flaming face. "No. It's a footstool. Look around. No footstools here."

"But the scene fits the moment now that your little friend has come to sit down beside you."

She pointed her spoon at him, ready to scold some more, but followed his gaze instead ... and squealed. Bugs, rodents, even bats she could handle, but not spiders.

An eight-legged creepy-crawly thing skittered toward the sofa.

"Get it out of here!" she squealed again and climbed onto the back of the loveseat.

Instead of laughing at her antics or coming to her rescue, Jonas stared with something akin to fascination in his expression. "Don't tell me you're afraid of a little spider?"

"I mean it, Jonas, get it out of here!"

He started toward the creature while shaking his head.

"Don't squish it, not in here. Throw it outside."

The spider froze as though awaiting its fate.

Jonas looked from Shea to the spider, and back to her again. "You think it's kinder to let it freeze to death outside?" He tsked.

"Absolutely."

Sighing, he set his saucer down and went to the tiny kitchenette, returning a moment later with a glass. With the spider captured he tossed it out the door. "Shay-Shay, I will always fight your monsters for you."

His words opened the door on an old memory she'd thought locked away for good. A sunny afternoon. Sheets on the clothesline, smelling like sunshine and fresh air. Her mother's smiling face. All of it snapped into focus like a clouded glass wiped clean. "What did you say?"

"I said I will always fight—"

"No, what did you call me?"

"Shay-Shay."

Her eyes closed as she tried to block the bittersweet recollection. "My mother used to call me Shay-Shay."

"Then I will, too. Will you tell me about her?"

She slid down to the sofa cushions, muscles gone limp. Shay-Shay. A happier, better time.

The past poured out of her like poison from a lanced wound. Her mother's laugh. Picking peas with her in the garden. The first time they tried to catch a fish in the pond. They'd used bread chunks not wanting to hurt the worms only to have the bread dissolve when it hit the water. Her first cake. How proud her mother had been even if it was

lopsided. Smiles. Bedtime stories. Chores made into games. Laughter. And tears on her birthday when Mama left without a goodbye. How she'd cried herself to sleep for too many nights to count.

CCC

Jonas stared at the sleeping woman lying against his side. Somewhere around one in the morning despite her best intentions, Shea gave up the fight to stay awake. She didn't stir when he carried her to bed, tucked her in, and closed the door.

She'd given him her trust tonight and shared the treasure of her past, her most beloved and most painful memories. A gift he didn't deserve ... because he couldn't reciprocate. Shea gave light to his darkness. Good to his evil. One glimpse into his past and she'd run as far and as fast as she could. He should leave her, walk away ... but he couldn't, not knowing someone meant her harm.

With no immediate answers in sight and since he had no intention of torturing himself by trying to sleep on a midget-sized sofa, he checked the voicemail Fowler had left earlier.

Two words, "Call me."

Terse, but typical Fowler. *Never leave information on any device not secured by the Bureau's technology.* Jonas had lost track of the number of times he'd heard the man say it.

He dialed Fowler's number, knowing he would answer despite the lateness of the hour.

Three rings later a series of squawks, chirps, and buzzes kicked in to signify a scrambled connection. Jonas jerked the phone away from his ear. They needed to adjust the volume on the blasted encryption software.

"Nice of you to return my call, Cameron," Fowler answered. "Hope I didn't inconvenience you."

Fowler's distinctive, raspy voice sounded like a two-pack-a-day habit, but the man didn't smoke. Didn't drink or cuss either because of his kids.

The thought of Fowler with kids boggled the mind. Six of them, last Jonas heard, all adopted. "Tell me you have a lead on our missing terrorist."

"Some chatter. When our quarry's contact didn't respond he reached out to the now deceased Sebastian Toure."

"And?"

"The Mayakan don't know him from Ali Baba's turban. They suggested if he wanted to join them, he should bring ten thousand American dollars in cash to Nigeria."

"Doesn't tell me much."

"We don't have much. Our profilers think he's a white male, belligerent, and with a perceived injustice from some level of authority."

"So, an ordinary Joe you think is dangerous."

"Given the propaganda ISIS puts out and what we've

learned from other cells taken down here in the States, yeah, I think he's dangerous. Add in the culture we've cultivated for the younger generation, all the violence in video games, telephone, radio, music, and movies, plus the negative slant the news media put out, and we've done the work for them. Sometimes it's hard to remember why I keep fighting."

"No, you don't forget. You get hugged by six little reminders every time you go home. Seven, counting your wife."

"Yeah." The sound of deep sigh carried over the line. "Anyway, our analysts traced the computer IP address he used to contact Nigeria to somewhere within a one-hundred-fifty-mile radius of Jackson Hole, Wyoming. This guy is close. Don't let your guard down for a second. There won't be a neon sign on his forehead. He'll look like a well-dressed stranger, an old friend, one of your ranch hands, or even your sister's ex-boyfriend. If you get one of your famous itchy feelings, call me. I can put a team on the ground in under three hours."

After the call ended, Jonas spent the remainder of the night thinking about what Fowler said—a stranger, an old friend, a ranch hand, an ex-boyfriend. Maybe the ranch didn't offer the level of safety he thought it did.

CCC

Shea dreamed of warm lips on her cheek, a deep voice

whispering sweet nothings in her ear, calloused hands on her arms, shaking her ...

Wait. Shaking her?

Her eyelids popped open.

Jonas sat on the side of her bed looking down at her. "Wakey-wakey."

She groaned and tried to turn over, but he wouldn't let her. "Your alarm will go off any minute. I have to leave now before we give the old dragons more gossip, but I'll stop by the diner later this morning. Come slide the deadbolt behind me, okay?"

Still in a sleep stupor, she nodded.

He moved in silence through her apartment, only the soft click of the door and one creaky stair step telling her he'd left.

Little by little, the fog cleared. She stumbled through the apartment to lock the front door and then spent a long time under the hot shower.

Dressed and waiting, Shea kept the security chain in place and opened the door a crack to watch for Dee Dee's car. The two of them used the area behind the diner, along with a couple of delivery trucks during the week. No one else. After Jonas's comments about the isolation though, she no longer saw their private parking area as a benefit.

A car turned in, ten minutes later than usual. Headlights illuminated the darkness. The familiar Honda Pilot pulled into the space near the rear entrance.

Shea went down the stairs, taking care to step in the snow tracks Jonas left, while wondering why she bothered to lock up. Her mysterious visitor had no trouble getting in.

Inside the diner, Dee Dee turned up the heat and went into her office to stow her outerwear, after which she began readying the dining room for their customers.

Shea could see her breath in the air, but she took off the dark red coat Cassie Cameron had given her anyway and dropped it on the counter by the door. The heater would kick in soon, but the biscuits couldn't wait. And she didn't want to get flour on her pretty coat.

After the first batch of biscuits went into the oven she started throwing the ingredients together for blueberry muffins. She would put her stuff away later once the bakery items were underway. Customers couldn't see the messy kitchen but they would sure notice the lack of muffins.

Dee Dee's displeased yell startled her. A moment later the older woman stomped into the kitchen holding an overstuffed garbage bag.

"That good for nothing ... Cecil forgot to take the trash out and now the place reeks." She wrenched the back door open still muttering under her breath.

"Wait. It's freezing out there. You need a coat." The trash dumpster sat in a niche at the far end of the alley.

"I don't have time—"

"Here, take mine." She picked up her coat and held it out.

Holding the trash bag in one hand, Dee Dee slipped one arm into the coat's sleeve, switched hands, and shrugged the coat on. She even waited while Shea draped the scarf around her neck. "Thanks. Leave the door open so the place can air out."

"Careful out there. It's slippery," Shea called after her and watched until the darkness swallowed her friend.

High winds during the night had formed deep snow drifts against the buildings but all seemed calm now.

Shea turned back to her work. She'd toyed with a new recipe for a skillet scramble with all the fixings and wanted to try it out. Healthier than a Rodeo Roundup and every bit as filling.

A muffled shout pulled her attention to the door. "Dee Dee?"

Silence.

At the door, Shea looked in the direction her friend had gone. It shouldn't take this long to walk to the dumpster and back.

The faintest promise of day lay on the horizon. Black fading to indigo, but enough to see a figure in the distance. She squinted. Not a figure. Two.

Dee Dee screamed.

Fear for her friend's safety surged through Shea. Frantic, she reached for the cell phone in her pocket. Should she call the sheriff? Jonas? No time. She looked around the kitchen for a weapon—a butcher knife, her

rolling pin. She spotted the small cast iron skillet and grabbed it.

With no heed for her own safety, Shea raced out the door and toward her friend. "Let me be in time, Lord."

One good thing about snow, it muffled her footsteps. Although how they didn't hear her slipping, sliding, and gasping shocked her. She sounded like a horse blowing after a long, hard run.

Closer now, she could make them out. A man stood behind her friend. He had his arm around her neck, choking her. As Shea watched, Dee Dee clawed at the man's arm, but her efforts grew weaker until her legs gave way and she dropped to her knees.

The attacker went down with her. He never looked back, never heard Shea approach.

Filled with fear and fury, Shea raised the skillet and swung down at the attacker. The blow caught him on his shoulder.

He screamed and rolled away. Holding his arm, he tried to rise but slipped and fell to his knees.

Her second swing caught him on his hip, earning another wail. Skillet raised, she aimed for his head.

Before she could deliver the hit, though, he scrambled to his hands and knees and scurried out of reach.

She went after him but slipped.

He made it to his feet and fled down the alley still clutching his arm. He turned once, stared for a moment, and vanished.

"Is he gone?" Dee Dee croaked.

"Oh, my gosh, did he hurt you? Yes, he's gone." Heart pounding out of control, Shea dropped to her knees beside the other woman.

"Call James." Dee Dee sat in the snow and hugged herself, rocking while Shea got her phone.

James answered on the second ring. "Shea?"

"We need you," she sobbed through chattering teeth.

Chapter Twelve

"What's going on?"

Simple questions should have easy answers except Shea couldn't seem to form the right words. Her whole body shook, whether from the cold or an overload of fear, she couldn't tell. "I don't know," she wailed.

"Shea, calm down. Where you are?"

"Behind the diner. A man attacked Dee Dee." Her teeth could have been castanets they chattered so hard.

"Stay with me. I'm sending help."

She heard a door slam, an engine start, tires squealing, and snippets of James talking to someone else. "... attacker. Go. You're closest."

Dee Dee scooted through the snow until she could put her arms around Shea. "You're freezing."

The embrace offered comfort but little warmth. She should try to get them both back inside.

"Shea." James's voice snapped her back. "Archer's across the street at the station. He's on the way."

"Who?"

"John Archer, my new deputy."

Returning to the diner where it was warm seemed like the best idea but also the hardest to do. How would she get Dee Dee inside when she couldn't move her own body?

She heard someone running and looked both ways down the alley. The snow muffled sound making it impossible to determine from which direction the footsteps came.

There! A man emerged at the far end near the dumpster. Not running now, but cautious. He made a one-eighty sweep of the area as he moved steadily toward them. Was it James's deputy? Or the man who'd attacked Dee Dee?

O sweet mercy, what if the attacker had returned to finish the job? Shea pushed Dee Dee down, covered her, and prayed like never before.

"Shea? It's John Archer."

Shea drew a deep, shuddering breath. The terrible cold burned her lungs. Her tears froze on her cheeks. "I thought he'd come back," she sobbed.

"Stay here. Don't move."

"No, wait. Where—?"

"I need to make sure he's gone. Stay put. The sheriff is on his way."

James arrived while Archer searched the alley. "Shea, you okay?"

"Ye-es-s-s." She couldn't remember ever being this cold.

"Dee Dee?"

"I'm good, but Shea's freezing."

"Sheez, you're a block of ice, girl. Let's get you inside." James put his arm around her and whistled for Archer.

The deputy returned and helped a wobbling Dee Dee back to the diner's rear door.

When Shea stumbled, James lifted her with ease and carried her back inside.

The oven timer was dinging when they entered the kitchen.

"My biscuits," Shea exclaimed and struggled in James's arms.

He settled her in a chair Archer confiscated from Dee Dee's office. "You need to sit before you fall over. John, get the biscuits."

"On it." Archer found the oven mitts, donned them, and removed the pans from the oven like a pro.

"Now, both of you sit here in front of the oven and tell me what happened." James chafed Shea's arms and hands. "Dee Dee, you go first."

"Cecil forgot to take the trash out Saturday night," she said, scooting closer to the open oven. "I found it first thing this morning because of the stink. Can't have that with my customers coming in, so I ran it out to the dumpster. I had just started back when this guy came up behind me and wrapped his arm around my neck. He choked me and tried to drag me down the alley. I couldn't get a breath and almost passed out. That's when Shea whacked him with the skillet."

"My skillet!" Shea yelled. "It will rust if we leave it out in the snow."

"Shhh, we'll get your skillet. Go on, Dee Dee. Any idea who it might've been?"

"I've lived and worked in this town for more than twenty years. Other than a few heated arguments with Polly Prescott, there's not a soul here I'd suspect of doing something like this, and I'm pretty sure it wasn't Polly. I could take her. Besides, it was a man."

"How'd you know? Did you see his face?"

"No, I didn't see his face. He was behind me, but I know the difference between a man's biceps and a woman's, not to mention he had a deep voice."

"Sheriff," Archer interrupted. "I'll go scout around."

James nodded and pulled a little notepad from his shirt pocket. "How tall? What kind of build?"

"Taller than me," she said, shaking her head. "Not anywhere as tall as you, though. Maybe five-eight or five-

ten and plenty strong. If Shea hadn't come along when she did ...."

"What did he say?"

"'Stop fighting me,' and 'I don't want to hurt you.'"

James ducked his head while he jotted several things in his notebook. When he looked up again, those gray-green eyes held no humor. "Okay, Shea, your turn."

"Dee Dee didn't have her coat on so I made her wear mine."

"Go on."

"She told me to leave the door open so the air would clear the stench, and then she hurried off toward the dumpster. I went back to my baking and slipped the biscuits in the oven. That's when I heard something outside. I called Dee Dee's name. When she didn't answer, I stepped outside and called again. I saw her, or rather I saw two people struggling in the alley."

James kept writing.

"I freaked. I knew one of them was Dee Dee, that she was in trouble, but I didn't know what to do. I thought to call you, but she needed help now. You would take too long to get here. I looked around for something to use as a weapon, grabbed the skillet, and ran. He never heard me coming, so I clobbered him on the shoulder."

Shea had the impression very little caught James by surprise, but he looked a little stunned now.

"Go on."

"He yelled and grabbed his arm, which let Dee Dee get away from him. I whacked him again, on the hip that time."

"Did you injure him or draw blood? Did he limp?"

"Blood? I don't think so but he held his arm as he limped off. I was going for his head next."

James's mouth had drawn down in an obvious attempt to forestall a grin. "Hmmm."

"I've never hit anyone before." Her insides started to churn. She recalled how her brothers used to roughhouse. Bloody knuckles, bruises, scrapes, and once a broken arm. She'd thrown up while trying to clean their wounds that time.

"You okay, hon?" Dee Dee asked.

Shea nodded yes. She would not throw up in front of the sheriff.

James looked thoughtful. "Shea said you didn't stop for a coat. Is this hers then?" He fingered the red sleeve.

"Yeah. I'd already hung mine up in the back. Shea insisted," Dee Dee said.

"So, you had on Shea's coat?" He turned to Shea. "This your scarf, too?"

Shea nodded, fearful of where this line of questioning would take them. "You think he mistook her for me?"

"What?" Dee Dee cried.

"Oh, my word, that guy thought you were me."

Her friend's eyes were filled with shock.

"We don't know that for sure. Now, did either of you

get a look at his face? Can you describe him?"

"No. He wore a ski mask," Shea answered.

"What about his clothes?"

"Jeans, boots, a quilted jacket in some kind of camo pattern."

"Gloves?"

"He wore gloves," Dee Dee said. "I tried to bite him but got a mouthful of leather instead."

Shea tried to visualize the scene. "They were thick work gloves. Leather, with fringed cuffs."

"Anything else?"

A frown drew her eyebrows together as she tried to recall, but all the nods and head shakes had given her a pounding headache. "He stopped at the far end of the alley after he ran off. Not by the dumpster, the other end. He seemed familiar." Shea shook her head and groaned. "I'm sorry. That's it."

Archer returned from his scouting.

"Find anything?" James asked him.

"Four sets of tracks. One leads from the back door of the diner to the dumpster. The tread looks consistent with Ms. Dee Dee's footwear. They start back this way but turn into a free for all where I found the ladies. A second set, a man's footprints from the width of the boot, first appeared near the dumpster. Looks like he stood there a while."

James wrote in his notebook again. "And the other two?"

"A second set of smaller tracks, consistent with Shea's shoes, lead down from her apartment to the back door here. They follow after Ms. Dee Dee's tracks to the point of confrontation."

James looked up when he finished writing and quirked his eyebrows at Archer. "And?"

Shea shrunk into her seat. She knew who owned those last footprints. She'd tried to step in them herself when she came downstairs but found the stride much too wide for her. From the look on Archer's face, he knew, too.

"The, uh, fourth set of prints?" Archer said.

"Yes, the fourth set." James folded his arms across his chest and waited.

"They, uh, originate from the apartment. The smaller tracks overlay some of them. They lead down the alley to the side street, and from there, south on Main. They, uh, continue to, uh ... for a couple of blocks."

Yep. He knew. The snow had already started to fall when she made Jonas move his truck, and Archer followed his tracks all the way to his brother's office building.

"What about the tread?" James prompted.

"Uh, yeah, tread."

"So, this fourth set of prints had tread?"

Archer blushed. "Yeah. Boots. Similar to mine."

James's eyebrows lifted.

Shea groaned. Of all the men in these parts, only James, Kyle, Jonas, and now Archer hadn't succumbed to

the smooth-soled cowboy boots most men around these parts wore. They preferred military-style boots with heavy-tread, the same type they'd worn in service. A simple process of elimination would identify the owner.

"Oh." Dee Dee's complexion turned rosy as she made the connection. "Oh, my."

Knowing her own face mimicked the red pepper she'd laid out for the new breakfast scramble recipe, Shea thought about crawling into the cold storage room and locking herself in for the next three days.

Shea squirmed on her chair. Even after James had dismissed Archer and Dee Dee, she still couldn't look at him. Now she understood the true meaning of mortification.

"Shea, you'll get no judgment from me but I need to understand the sequence of events. Talk to me."

"I—we planned to talk to you today." Face on fire, she fumbled the photo from her back pocket and handed it to James.

A sweet picture, flattering even. Her stalker had captured the two of them, bundled up in jackets, all alone, out in the middle of nowhere. He'd caught that magical moment Jonas slipped his hand behind her head and pulled her toward him until their foreheads touched. Nothing more.

"Nice picture. Who took it?"

Leave it to James to find the major point. She shrugged. "I found it taped to my television when I got home last night ... er, this morning."

"Maybe you should start from the beginning."

Enough. She had nothing to be ashamed or embarrassed about. Shea looked up, owning her actions. "Jonas asked me on a date. We went to church together."

"I heard about that."

"Then you also heard we went riding down by the river. On Triple C property. We had a picnic, but someone followed us. They watched and took pictures."

"This was yesterday afternoon?"

She nodded and then proceeded to tell him all the gory details, from Sadie Gayle's phone call to Jonas, how she followed him to Sidewinders, of finding Sadie Gayle with Jonas in the ladies' room and then taking her home, and how Jonas's safety check of her apartment led to the picture taped to the television.

"Someone broke into your apartment."

"Yeah, but Jonas didn't see any signs of forced entry."

"Why didn't you call me last night?"

She ducked her head again. Jonas had intended to help her tell this story. "It was late."

His eyebrows lifted. "How late?"

"Very."

James tucked the picture in his jacket pocket. "Well,

knowing Dee Dee this won't stop her from opening as usual. Take a break when things slow down. Come over to my office. I'll call Jonas in, too."

"Okay."

"What do you mean, Clint fell off his horse?" Jonas stomped away from Rascal, slammed his saddle on the wooden rail, and went back to groom Diablo. He'd hired Clint and Vern back at the start of the summer, before all the stuff with his sister went down. Vern was a shoo-in as a hand, having grown up on a small cattle farm. Clint showed promise, but he had little to no experience on a working ranch. A likable kid, though, and he got along well with the other hands. Better yet, the horses liked him.

"Stuff happens. Like when Diablo stepped on your foot last year, and when the gate malfunctioned and broke the tail light on your truck. Sometimes you hit your finger with a hammer." Rascal held up his swollen thumb with the blackened nail. "Or one of the horses body-slams you into the wall."

"The gate didn't malfunction. Somebody tampered with it. Anyway, I didn't give Mallory permission to drive my truck. I also didn't give Clint permission to fall off his horse. He's better than that, or so I thought. Who got slammed into the wall?"

"Vern, he's a little lame, but fine. In fact, he's helping

me pick up Clint's slack. We got this. Deal with it." Rascal stormed off.

Jonas sighed. Of all times to be shorthanded. James wanted him to come by his office this morning at ten. A summons, not a request.

On the drive into town, he checked his messages. Still no response from Shea. He'd texted her over an hour ago, telling her to expect him soon. The diner probably kept her busier than usual given their church appearance. Still, he'd expected some kind of response.

Trucks filled most of the parking spaces in front of the diner again. He found a spot at the end of the row and pulled in. Maybe things would have slowed up by the time James got through with him.

"Hey, Lorraine," he greeted the town's long-time dispatcher. "James in?"

"Hi, Jonas. He's expecting you. Go on back."

He heard voices as he started down the short hallway. James's deep bass finished speaking and a new, higher pitched voice piped up, one he knew all too well. Why was Shea here?

"Hey, man, you're right on time." James left his chair behind the desk and came over to shake his hand before closing the door.

Jonas lifted one eyebrow.

"Privacy." James grinned. "Some ears tend to hear more than they ought."

True. Lorraine had a corner on most of the news in town given her role in the midst of the action. "What's going on?" Jonas asked.

"I wanted to ask you the same thing." James slid a piece of paper across the desk—the photo Shea had found taped to her television.

Jonas glanced at the picture. They'd agreed to tell James about the intruder together. Why had she felt the need to jump the gun?

"It slipped out, Jonas," she whispered, her eyes pleading.

"How?" He hated the way his voice tightened up. She would notice, of course. Had already noticed from the way her shoulders stiffened.

"Hold on, you two. Let's start at the beginning," James said.

Tight-lipped, Jonas gave him one quick nod.

"Somebody attacked Dee Dee this morning in the alley behind the diner."

"What?" Jonas launched himself from the chair, every muscle tense and ready for action. "Is she all right?"

"She's fine," James answered. "Archer got there within minutes of Shea's call. He had the area secured by the time I arrived."

Concern for Dee Dee and fear for Shea left Jonas feeling weak-kneed. He dropped into his chair again.

"After we got the ladies inside, Archer did a thorough

recon of the area while I got their stories," James went on. "He found four sets of tracks. Three belonged to Dee Dee, Shea, and the attacker. I bulldozed Shea into identifying the last set. She explained about following you to Sidewinders and going to Sadie Gayle's, how you saw her home and found the picture on her TV."

"I couldn't leave her there alone and scared." Jonas scrubbed a hand through his short hair. He glanced over at Shea.

She looked up at him, eyes of brown sugar and cinnamon filled with apology. The strange connection between them locked into place. "I couldn't leave her unprotected with this madman still on the loose and it was too late to take her anywhere else."

"I explained why you left first," she whispered. Her cheeks had a rosier than normal hue. "Why I made you move your truck."

"Ahem."

The sound of James clearing his throat snapped Jonas back to attention. "A fire, a stalker, an intruder making unclear threats, and now an attack on her friend. Tell me you have a suspect or at least some leads."

"No suspects. Dee Dee had on Shea's coat, so we have to assume he wanted Shea. The question is why?"

Both he and James turned inquisitive looks on her.

Chapter Thirteen

Okay, now she was mad. "I told you, I don't know who's doing this or why."

Shea glared at the two men. After she'd spilled her guts to James and Jonas, telling them more than she'd told anyone else in her entire life, they'd ignored her, discussing her like she wasn't even there.

"All right," James said. "Let's assume for the moment you have a stalker. What do we know about stalkers?"

"They're scary. The thought that someone would spy on me, take pictures, and come into my home while I'm not there frightens me." She shuddered.

"Most stalkers suffer from Borderline Personality Disorder, or they have full-blown psychological issues," Jonas replied. "Many times, though not always, victims know their stalkers."

"You think it's someone I know?" The incredulous look on her face had to tell him what she thought of that idea.

"Well, look at the basic stalker categories. They include rejected partners who want to reclaim the relationship. Then there's the resentful ones who imagine a wrong done to them, or the predatory jerk who enjoys hurting his victims. There are those who imagine themselves in love and believe they can convince their victim to love them in return, and let's not forget the morbid fascination some crazies have. Those creeps don't need a reason for what they do. There are tons of other combinations, but these are the most common. I think several might fit in Shea's case."

Shea stared, seeing yet another side of Jonas as he recited the information in clinical, impersonal detail. How did he know this stuff?

"He's got a point, Shea," James added.

"You've analyzed my life and solved my problem, all in fifteen minutes? I can't believe this." She crossed her legs, foot swinging. Yes, Jonas was arrogant, conceited, controlling—both men were—but she'd had no idea to what extent.

What other option did she have than to hear them out. Storming out of James's office might soothe her ruffled feathers, but it wouldn't find her stalker. She needed

James's help, Jonas's, too. With a long sigh, she nodded for him to proceed.

"Kyle told me about this Townsend fellow who claims you're his fiancée." James jotted something down on his ever-present notepad.

"He's not my fiancé," she all but shouted through clenched teeth. "He never was."

James held up both hands as though fending her off. "Not saying it's true, only repeating his claim. I think we have to consider him as a rejected suitor stalker. What do you think? Could he have set fire to your uncle's house?"

For someone who didn't know her cousin, she could see how James would come to such a conclusion. "You'll find Porter's picture in the dictionary next to the word narcissist. He's arrogant, conceited, and short-tempered, but set a fire? No. He wouldn't know how. Nor would he follow me on horseback, because the man can barely ride, and while he knows his way around a camera, I'm positive breaking and entering lies beyond his capability."

"How about the new guy, Grainger?" Jonas prompted. "He's been very attentive since he hit town. Spends a lot of time at the diner."

Shea frowned. Who would have told him such a thing? Wes did flirt, and she'd wondered if he might ask her out. With the thought came realization—Wes hadn't come into the diner this morning. The first time in two months. "Wes Grainger is a gentleman."

Jonas snorted and tried to cover it up with a cough.

She glared at him before continuing. "He's outgoing and funny and spends as much time talking to Dee Dee as he does with me. While I can see how you might lump him into one of those absurd categories, he has zero interest in me beyond friendship. He's not a stalker. Is this all you've got?"

"We're trying to point out possibilities," James said. "Stalkers don't come with a sign around their neck. They're everyday people you'd never suspect. Take Kyle, for instance. He's fascinated by you, always talking about your cooking, how you go out of your way to help others, how you're sweet and funny and smart. I could make a case for him as a stalker, even though I've known him for years. And don't read anything into what I just said. I know he's not your stalker."

Jonas grumbled under his breath, "I'm going to kill him anyway."

Shea pressed her lips together. "You make my point for me, sheriff."

James, always stoic and unbothered, looked like he might come undone. "I'm not finished. Most of the men in town find you attractive, woman. Every single guy under forty who's not already taken would give their left arm for a shot with you. Admit it, business at the diner has boomed since you came to town, and it's men who comprise the majority of your customers. Right?"

"They like my cooking."

Jonas raised an eyebrow.

How many times had she tried to copy that move only to wind up making ridiculous faces? Impossible. He had to have a special eyebrow muscle to arch it so high.

James went on when she didn't say anything more.

"Any one of those guys at the diner, this Porter guy, Kyle, Jonas, Grainger, Loomis, Fred Robison, heck, even Rascal, we can't rule any of them out."

"You're saying I'm a suspect?" Jonas leaned forward in his chair, tension roiling off of him.

"No. But I'm beginning to wonder if you might not have a connection to Shea's problems."

They both looked at her.

"What are you not saying?" she asked.

James and Jonas looked at each other again. Had she not watched them closely, the tiny headshake Jonas made would have gone unnoticed.

Secrets. All her life, people had kept things from her. Her parents, her step-brothers, her best friend, even the man she'd thought to marry one day. Now, she could add the sheriff. And the man who'd crawled inside her heart. "You said I could trust you. I can't if you keep me in the dark. Tell me what's going on."

"I can't." Jonas clamped his lips together.

"Can't? Or won't?"

"Is there a difference?" he snapped.

Her sharp, indrawn breath sounded loud in the silence.

"Hey, now," James said with a forced laugh. "Don't go getting your underfrillies all knotted up, Shea. Jo means you don't have clearance to hear some of this stuff."

"My underfrillies?" Shea bounded to her feet, put her fists on top of James's desk, and leaned forward. "Seriously?"

"Oh, man," Jonas hung his head.

James blanched. "Sorry. It's something Rascal says all the time. It slipped out."

"Shades of sexual harassment here, sheriff," Shea snapped. She glared at them both. "I want answers. What do you mean about me not having clearance? You mean like all the top-secret stuff you hear about in the movies? What are you, spies? Secret agents? Undercover operatives?"

Their squirming and inability to look her in the eye spoke volumes.

"Oh my gosh." She clapped a hand over her mouth. "You are."

"No, we're not," Jonas answered.

"You are so busted." She laughed, but not in a humorous manner. "Tell me everything."

"Shea," James's voice took on a pleading element.

"No." Jonas's voice held no such weakness. "We can't."

"Fine," she snapped. "I'm done here."

CCC

Jonas started after Shea but hesitated after two steps. For the first time in his life, he had no idea what to do.

"Give her time," James said still seated at his desk. "This is a lot for anyone to take in. She'll come around."

"I hope you're right." He'd worked so hard to gain her trust, and now he'd blown it over something he had no control over. "Shea can't stay in the apartment. It's not safe. I thought I might convince her to stay at the ranch, but there's not even a remote chance now."

"Looks like a long night for you, my man. Out in the cold, keeping watch, or ..." James grinned. "You could call your mother."

"Why would I call my mother?"

"Because when you run into trouble, you call for backup. In this case, Cate Cameron. The heavy artillery. She's invincible."

Jonas felt a grin take form. "Garrett always said you were a sly one. Guess my brother knows you pretty well."

The more he thought about the idea, the more he liked it. Dad had once described Mom as a tornado, hurricane, and blizzard all rolled in one because when she set her mind on something, *watch out world*. Shea's mule-headedness couldn't hold out against a fully-engaged Cate Cameron, not once she learned of the danger Shea faced.

"See you later, man." Jonas all but danced from the

room.

"Hold on a sec. I need you here for a meeting tomorrow, one o'clock. It's time to pool intel and come up with a plan. Can you let your brothers know?"

"Sure. Who's in?"

"The usual suspects—me, Derek, Kyle, you, your brothers. Archer, too. Thanks for sending him my way."

Jonas nodded. "He's a good man. The best. I'll tell Garrett and Wade. Gotta go now. I have to call Mom."

On the drive home, Jonas dialed his mother and told her about Shea's predicament. "She's so independent. There's no way she'll come if I ask."

"Oh, that poor girl. You leave it to me, Jonas. No one will touch her here on the ranch. And if she insists on continuing at the diner, we have plenty of drivers who can take her to work in the mornings and pick her up in the afternoon."

"I plan on driving her."

"I'm proud of you, son. And never more than at this moment. Mark my word, I'll have Shea tucked up in Lucy's old bedroom tonight. Now, let me go so I can get it ready."

"Thanks, Mom. I love you."

"I know you do, son. I love you, too, but you still owe me."

He laughed, his spirits soaring. "Yes, ma'am. Whatever you want."

"Careful what you promise. You already know what I want."

Somehow, the thought of giving her more grandbabies didn't make him shudder this time.

The diner had every seat filled when Shea marched through the front door at five past eleven.

"Thank goodness," Dee Dee exclaimed. "I don't know where I need you more, out here or in the kitchen helping that insane Cajun."

Shea nodded and headed for the kitchen. "I'll get Cecil caught up and run the food orders for you. By the way, did Wes ever show up?"

Concern touched her friend's face as she picked up a tray filled with food hot off the grill. "No, he didn't. Not like him, is it? Maybe he got called back to Idaho Falls for work or something."

"Yeah, maybe." His absence bothered Shea, too.

The post-lunch slowdown didn't hit until almost three. Two people remained, but they had their coats in hand and would soon leave.

Shea grabbed a cup of coffee and took her usual seat at the counter.

Dee Dee joined her after the couple checked out.

"Can't complain about business of late. I'm thinking about bringing Maggie Willoughby on full time."

"Great idea, though you might want to consider hiring another part-timer, as well. I hear Jerrica Holmes has some interest in working here."

The bell over the door rang, prompting a groan from both of them.

"Finish your coffee. I've got this." Shea whirled around on the stool and almost fell on her face.

Porter Townsend stood there, one arm in a sling, his jacket draped over his shoulders. He closed the door and looked around.

"What are you doing here?" Shea demanded, her temper spiking.

"We need to talk and this looks like a good time. Unless you have another deputy waiting to beat me up."

"Kyle didn't touch you, Porter."

He moved his injured arm. "According to the lawsuit I filed against the sheriff's office and Deputy Kyle Abbott in particular, he did."

"Good luck," Dee Dee called from behind the counter. "There's about two dozen witnesses here, me included."

"Hostile witnesses, all predisposed toward the deputy makes your testimony a conflict of interest. I like my odds." He smirked.

"One more time, why are you here, Porter?"

"As I said, we need to talk."

"You want me to call the sheriff?" Dee Dee held up the phone.

James thought Porter could be her stalker. She still didn't think so, but perhaps talking to him might give some insight. Whether she liked it or not, she knew him. He wasn't going away until they talked. "I'll give him ten minutes."

Porter took a seat in one of the booths by the window. "I'd like some coffee."

"Nope." Dee Dee marched over to the entrance, flipped the 'open' sign to 'closed,' and locked the door. "We're no longer serving. Your ten minutes start now."

Shea slid into the other side of the booth and tried not to smile at the sour expression on Porter's face. "Why, Porter?"

"I miss you. Don't you miss me, Shea? A little bit? We were friends once, more than friends."

"What about Gina?" Darn, she didn't mean to mention her.

Porter hung his head, the picture of regret.

Shea searched her heart but found it devoid of feelings for this man she'd considered marrying. Would have had she not caught them in the act.

"I made a mistake. I ended it with Gina the day you walked out."

He expected her to believe him? "Two years without a peep. Why now?"

"Did you know your brother, Eli added to his brood? He and Trina had twins right before Christmas."

She frowned at the change of topics. "Trina couldn't handle the first two, how in the world will they manage with four?"

"Eli hired a housekeeper and a nanny after you left."

Shea loved those kids with all her heart, but not their mother. Eli had moved his family into the old farmhouse with her after their father died, and Trina expected Shea to act as cook, housekeeper, and surrogate mother while she spent time with her country club friends.

"What about Noah and Ben?" she asked.

"Noah and Lisa have two kids now, a boy and a girl. To hear him tell it, they're done. Ben and Katy Barnaby tied the knot last October. You and me, Shea. We're the last."

"There is no 'we,' Porter. We're cousins. That's icky."

He didn't bat an eyelash at her rebuke. "You should come home, you know. Everyone misses you. They'd welcome you with open arms. No one cares what Wallace said."

Maybe no one cared, but she did. She'd given up her dream for Wallace Townsend. Left school with one semester remaining to take care of him in his dying days. Wallace. Not Father, not Daddy. Never again.

"You know, the brothers have done well for themselves," Porter went on. "Now that Eli has free rein to

run the place the way he wants, the net worth of the ranch has almost doubled. The share designated for you is still on the table, but not for long. Your twenty-fifth birthday is coming up. Think about it. You could finish school, get a place in the city, find a real job. We still have time."

Ahh, now she understood. He knew about Wallace's codicil. The one tiny little amendment to her part of the inheritance. "He boxed me into a corner, Porter. Wallace had my life mapped out with you as my only option. I'm not even sure marriage between cousins is legal. Anyway, I know better now, and I've discovered I don't like you very much. I sure don't want to marry you."

"I'm adopted, Shea. It's quite legal. Besides, we don't have to make it a real marriage. We can sign the papers and go our separate ways. In a couple of years, if you want out, we can file for divorce."

"No."

All the earnestness slid from his face, replaced by grief. "Please, Shea. I need the money. For Mama. The doctors diagnosed her with Stage 4 breast cancer last summer. The bills ...." His voice broke.

Ella Townsend, Porter's mother, represented one of the only bright spots in Shea's life after her mother left. Miss Ella deserved whatever help she could give her, except too many holes riddled Porter's sob story.

"Not buying it, Porter. I saw the will. Wallace might not have loved me, but he cared for your mother. He left her the house, along with a very generous stipend to live out her days, medical included. Have you gone through all her money?"

His face turned hard. "Twenty percent, Shea. Marry me and inherit. We can sell it back to your brothers and walk away with a million-five for each of us. Not bad for a scribble on a paper."

"No. I want nothing from Wallace. Please leave, Porter. And don't come back. I won't change my mind."

His face turned an alarming shade of purple. Violence hung in the air. For a moment, she feared Porter might strike her.

He strode to the door instead but had to pause and fumble with the lock. With a last hate-filled glance, he made his parting shot. "You'll be sorry, Shea."

Dee Dee rushed over and locked the door after he left. She turned to Shea with a worried look but held her tongue.

A long, drawn-out shiver coursed down Shea's spine. Maybe he could be her stalker.

Chapter Fourteen

Shea tied off the trash bag and looked over at the big clock on the wall. This had to go down as one of the longest days in history "Want to walk me to the dumpster?" She asked Dee Dee who had finished tallying the day's receipts.

"Safety in numbers, you mean? No, thanks. Leave it for Cecil. I'm parking in front of the diner and using the front door from now on."

"But—" Shea didn't finish the thought. With the single access to her apartment at the rear of the building, it meant she'd be alone when she went down in the mornings. The alternative was to wait until Dee Dee turned on the lights and opened the back door for her. Another possibility crossed her mind. She could always ask Jonas about getting a gun.

Scratch that. After meeting with him and James this morning, she wouldn't ask him for a thing.

Her gaze strayed to the big wooden block on the counter and the selection of kitchen knives it held. Could she use one of those on another person? Her stomach turned at the thought, but yeah, a butcher knife would work. A really big one. She would take it home with her tonight. One never knew full capabilities until faced with a decision. And if parking in the front made Dee Dee feel safer, she couldn't deny her.

A pounding on the diner's front door that afternoon startled her. Couldn't people read? Even though it wasn't the normal closing time, they couldn't miss the closed sign.

Voices drifted down the hallway.

Shea blew a strand of hair out of her face in frustration. She wanted to go back to the apartment, run a hot bath, and forget her troubles for a while. Now she couldn't, not with more customers.

"She's in the kitchen. Go on back. Shea, honey, Cate Cameron is here to see you," Dee Dee yelled.

Oh, brother. She didn't want to see Jonas, much less his mother. Good manners won out, though. Always. "Hello, Mrs. Cameron. What can I do for you?"

"Shea, dear, I told you to call me Cate. I've worried so since Jonas told me about all the nasty things going on in your life. He's worried sick about you staying all alone in an isolated apartment and says it's not safe."

"He's over-reacting. I'm fine."

"I'm not sure I agree with you which is why I came over today. I want you to come out to the ranch and stay with us until they catch this cretin. We have lots of room since our two oldest sons moved into their own places."

The offer shouldn't have surprised Shea, but it did. "Uh, that's very sweet of you, but—"

"I confess my motives aren't entirely altruistic. I've tried to duplicate some of those canapes you made for Wade and Lucy's wedding reception, but I had to toss every batch in the garbage. I hoped you might give me a few tips."

"I'm happy to help you, but—"

"Cassie and Mallory got so excited when I told them about you coming to stay. It's all they've talked of all day. They have so many girl-outings planned for you, but I promise to not let them monopolize all your time. I mean, between work, church, and all the baking you do for the senior citizens in town." Cate laughed. "You're a busy woman."

Unable to get a word in edgewise, and not knowing what to say if she could, Shea kept silent until Cate ran out of gas. Of course, this move had Jonas written all over it. What was he thinking? She couldn't go live with him. Even with his parents there, the gossips would have a field day. "I don't know. Not sure it's a good idea. I mean ... such a surprise."

Cate beamed. "I know, dear. I love surprises. Now, if you're finished here, let's go upstairs and pack your stuff. I brought Cody along to carry everything. Do you think we can get it all in one trip? I can always call one of the boys to bring another truck."

Cody Cameron came up behind Cate and put his big, gnarled hands on her shoulders. "You saying I can't handle this little lady's stuff?"

His sons had a remarkable resemblance to their father, even though Cody's hair had more silver than black in it these days. Jonas had the same penetrating, blue eyes. He would look this way in another thirty years. Not bad. Not bad at all.

"I'll bring my truck around." Cody slipped away.

Wait. This had gotten out of hand. "Listen, Cate. I appreciate your thoughtfulness, but—"

"Nonsense." Cate hooked her arm through Shea's. "It's what neighbors do. Now, let's get your coat and get started."

Unlike the rest of her family, Cate stood no more than a few inches over five feet, but she had the personality of a steamroller.

Shea refused to let them roll over her.

"No. I'm sorry. I don't want to be rude, but I can't go to your ranch. I have a job. I'm here before daybreak, and I'm pretty sure my car can't handle going back and forth through the snow. Besides, what would people say? Thank you, but no."

"Don't you worry about opening the diner." Dee Dee said from the corner. "I got hold of both Maggie and Jerrica while you talked with the idiot from your past. The girls start tomorrow morning, and since it's Cecil's day to open, you can come in for the lunch crowd. Or take the day off. You've earned it."

She hadn't forgotten about Shea's predicament after all. The wily woman had known Cate planned to come here, knew of this whole setup. And supported it. Anger flared, but it didn't hang around for long. She owed Dee Dee too much to stay angry with her. "No, I—"

"Excuse me," Cody came in through the back door. "You don't need to worry about your car making the run from the ranch into town."

Shea turned in a huff. "Why?"

"Somebody took a knife to all four of your tires."

Jonas whistled along to a snappy tune on the radio as he drove home. Finally, the world seemed aligned in his favor. True, Shea didn't like him much right now, but she'd get over it. His dad always said men forget but don't forgive, while women forgive but don't forget. He could live with her anger, but her safety would always take priority. The Triple C stood like a fortress with tons of people there to watch over her.

The whistling gave way to a grin that grew wider with the realization he had happiness within his grasp for the first time in a very long while.

His cell phone rang as he turned onto their private drive. He thumbed the remote on the truck's sun visor to open the gate and hit the Bluetooth button on the steering wheel. "Hello."

"Jonas? It's your mother."

The grin grew wider still. "You have good news for me?"

"Yes and no."

Some of his joy dimmed. "Please tell me I'll see Shea at the ranch tonight."

"Yes, but under duress. And something else, Jonas. There's been another incident."

A terrible fear gripped him. His fists tightened on the steering wheel until the darned thing creaked in protest. "Explain."

"When your father pulled his truck into the alley behind the diner to get Shea's things, he discovered someone had slashed her tires."

"What?" he yelled.

"Lower your voice, son. Cody said someone used a knife on all four of them."

A red mist settled over his vision. He pulled to the side of the road and slammed the gearshift into park. When he found the one who did this—

"Jonas, are you still there?"

He closed his eyes and unclenched his jaw enough to answer. "Yeah, Mom. Is Shea okay?"

"Shea's more than fine. She's ready to rip someone's head off. Oh, one more thing. You'll need to stay with one of your brothers tonight, maybe for several nights. Shea's request. Oh, here they come with the last of her stuff. I have to go. You can pick her up at quarter of nine in the morning and take her to the diner. Goodbye, Jonas."

"Wait—what?"

Too late, His mother had already hung up. Well, his plan sure hadn't worked out the way he'd intended.

CCC

Not much frightened Jonas, but William Michael Cameron, his four-month-old nephew terrified him. Weighing in at a whopping seventeen pounds, the little guy ruled his world with drooling smiles or ear-splitting screams, all dependent on the time of day and the condition of his diaper.

At the moment, all seemed right in Will's world. He lay on his belly on a blanket in the middle of the family room, arms and legs flailing, and blowing spit bubbles.

Jonas lay on his belly, nose-to-nose with the prince, flapping his arms, and making the same funny noises.

"Now, that's a sight you don't see every day." His brother, Garrett came down the stairs, his hair still damp from his shower. "Two masters of the universe going head to head, winner take all."

"My money is on Will. I already know how this story ends." TJ, his sister-in-law and the mother of little Will, watched from where she worked in the kitchen.

Will protested with a loud squawk.

"And that's the dinner bell," TJ said. "Bring him here before he launches into full battle cry."

Jonas got to his knees and reached for the baby but a dire, rumbling sound had him backing away. "Uh, TJ?"

"Come on, Jo. He's a squirmy little thing, but if you hold him close, you'll be fine."

"No, uh, it's not—." Jonas wondered if it would hurt TJ's feeling if he skipped dinner.

Garrett had doubled over with laughter, one finger pointing Jonas's way.

TJ looked from her husband to Jonas. "What?" It took a moment for her to understand and join Garrett in laughing.

Another rumble filled the air, longer and louder this time. Little Will's face turned an alarming shade of red.

Jonas gagged and backpedaled as fast as he could, trying hard to hold his breath. "Man, that's rank."

TJ regained control first. Wiping her eyes, she turned to Garrett and blew him an air kiss. "Why don't you show your baby brother how a real man diapers his son while I finish supper, hmm?"

The look on Garrett's face left Jonas laughing. A mistake. Laughter required breathing, which resulted in a full inhale of Will's odoriferous contribution to the world. This time Garrett joined him in a second round of gagging. Eyes streaming, Jonas stumbled to the front door, opened it, and stuck his head out. Sweet, sweet air. How could something so cute and sweet smell so bad?

Wade dropped by after dinner. TJ excused herself to take the sleepy baby upstairs, while the three men settled in the family room. Never one to beat around the bush, Wade started right in. "I need to bring you up to date on some things. Kevin Fowler called asking for help."

An uneasy feeling settled in Jonas's gut. The only kind of help Fowler wanted from Wade and his wife, Lucy, involved technology. When Lucy first came to Hastings Bluff, Fowler had used her unorthodox computer skills to help the BII capture an international terrorist. In return, he'd thrown his considerable resources at taking down the stalker who had followed Lucy from Atlanta. In the end, everything worked out and they called it even, but everyone knew Fowler wouldn't hesitate to use them again if the need arose.

"What does he want this time?" Jonas asked.

"A little hocus-pocus. Seems your missing terrorist recruit made two more phone calls to Nigeria. The last one reached an interested party, the same one Toure had promised a set of American twins. Sound familiar?"

Jonas's mouth went dry. The information hit him like a sucker punch. This joker was supposed to be hunting him, not his sisters. How many more people would end up a victim because of him?

"Still with us, Jo?" Garrett asked.

Jonas nodded and let the cold, clinical aspect of his personality assume control. "Yeah. What did you find?"

"Lucy worked some of her magic and got the one-hundred-fifty-mile search radius down to twenty-five. Bet you can guess the red zone's new midpoint."

"Hastings Bluff," Garrett leaned back and crossed an ankle over his knee. He never showed emotion. Ever. He did now.

Of course, he did. His family lived in the red zone.

"Bingo. He's here, Jo," Wade went on. "Right under our noses."

Another punch to his midsection. He'd faced graver threats than this many time before, but not when it involved his family. And now the jerk had crawled into his own backyard.

"There's more," Wade said.

"Spit it out."

"Fowler asked Lucy if she could pinpoint the computer's IP address, but he also wanted her to grab the associated files, similar to what she did in Atlanta while working for the bureau."

"I take it she did?" Jonas asked.

"Yeah. She had some doubts about the distances involved, but she got it to work. Fowler has his analysts pouring over the data as we speak."

"And?" Jonas knew Wade had more to say, could see it in his eyes, none of it good.

"We saw the latest transmission. It had an attachment—the photo of you and Shea, the same one you found taped to her TV."

Chapter Fifteen

"Whoa, Tiki," Jonas spoke softly. He reached out in a slow, steady movement, not wanting to spook the agitated horse, but she jerked her head to one side and backed up as far as the stall would allow. "What are her symptoms and their progression?"

Tiki Fire came from a long line of pedigreed winners bred for speed. Her owners touted the thoroughbred mare as the next *Winning Colors*, the last filly to win the Kentucky Derby back in 1988. With her dark, reddish-brown coat and jet-black mane and tail, the cameras loved her. She ran like the Santa Ana winds, fast and furious. Unfortunately, speed doesn't always come with a competitive spirit. After two full years on the circuit, Tiki Fire finished dead last in all but two of her races.

"She ate from the nosebag yesterday morning," Rascal answered. "The special Ration Balance feed, vitamins, and minerals as usual. We turned her and the others out into the small pasture around nine. Derek noticed she didn't forage in her normal way. She hung around near the gate instead, restless, circling, and pawing at the ground."

Jonas eased the gate open enough to slip inside and latched it behind him. Since winter weather posed nutritional challenges for gestating mares, at first snowfall he had his people move the mares inside at night. Weather permitting, they let them out to graze each morning in a small pasture adjacent to the breeding barn, one planted with their nutritional needs in mind. But sometimes noxious weeds found their way into the long grasses. "Sounds a little like colic. Did you check the pasture?"

"I did a quick look but dusk had fallen. I'll do a thorough search in the morning."

Tiki's first owner, embarrassed by her failures on the track, decided to cut his losses. But few racers wind up in grassy pastures to live out their days. Horse racing's dirty secret. Everyone in the industry knew horses that outlive their value get shipped to auctions where kill pen buyers pick them up at meat market prices. Everyone in the industry knew unwanted horses were sold to slaughterhouses and often processed for human consumption overseas. And everyone in the industry turned a blind eye and pretended it didn't happen.

Jonas nodded. "Let me know what you find."

Two years ago, at a horse show he and Garrett had gone to in Coeur d'Alene, they heard of Tiki Fire's fate from a friend. Outraged, they'd tracked down the particulars, showed up at the auction, and drove away with the four-year-old filly. A five-hundred-fifty-dollar steal, an incredible deal given her bloodlines.

At last, the mare settled enough to let Jonas touch her. Using a soft-bristled brush and moderate pressure, he ran it the length of her back, widening his circuit with each stroke.

Tiki had a sweet temperament, well-mannered, and was a quick learner. With her heritage and calm temperament, he'd had no qualms about breeding her. And so far, her first gestation had gone by the textbook. Until now.

The pregnant mare trembled like the horse he'd first seen in the auction pen. Her skin flinched and rippled under his hands. She shifted constantly and turned her head to watch him, every now and again letting out a soft groan. All sure signs of agitation and discomfort.

"When did she last eat?"

"Yesterday morning. Same time as always. She balked at the nosebag last night, and again this morning. Didn't touch the hay flake in her stall either."

Using constant movements, Jonas ran his hand along the mare's flank. As he suspected, her belly tightened, rumbled, and loosened. Digestive spasms, not labor-related. "Her water bucket's empty."

"I filled it myself last night. Found it empty this morning and filled it again. She drained it right away. Don't want to give her anymore right now."

She showed signs of having ingested something disagreeable. Were she not pregnant, he'd watch her for a few days and see if she got better. But not this late in her term. A pregnant mare could miss a few meals, but nutrition became more and more important as the birthing date drew closer. The foal inside her would put on most of its weight in the next sixty or so days. Any weight the mother lost in these last few weeks would be difficult to regain.

No, he wouldn't take a chance with Tiki. Not after having already lost a mare and foal earlier in the year. "Give Tom Blackburn a call. See if he can make room in his schedule to get out here today."

"You do recall he's the only vet for twenty-five miles and has a four-week waitlist, right?"

"Yeah, well tell him it's an emergency He owes me a couple of favors. Tell him so if you have to."

Rascal nodded, filled Tiki's water bucket part way, and pulled out his cell phone to make the call.

Jonas pulled his own cell phone out. He'd been checking the time every five or so minutes since arriving before sunup. Mom said to get there by nine-forty-five.

He headed over for the big sink in the wash area, debating whether to go early. Knowing Mom, she'd want to impress Shea on her first morning at the house, which meant maybe he'd have time to snag some breakfast. He could almost taste the aromas emanating from the kitchen.

The truck's interior warmed up on the drive from the big barn to the ranch house, making it nice and toasty for Shea. He pulled up in the front circle drive, threw the gearshift into park, and started toward the house when the door opened.

Shea came out, bundled up in her red coat and a stocking cap.

"Well, good morning." He tipped his hat.

She ignored him, hurried down the steps, and made a beeline for the passenger side. No greeting, no smile, not even a wave.

Jonas busted his chops to get to the door before she did. He opened it with a, "Hey, what's the hurry? I got here early in hopes of grabbing a cup of coffee."

She glared up at him but held her tongue. Without waiting for his help, she stepped onto the running board, caught the grab handle, and pulled herself up.

With a soft whistle of admiration, Jonas closed her door, retreated around the front of the cab, and climbed in behind the wheel. He'd added a lift kit to his F-150, raising the chassis to accommodate his height. A side benefit he'd discovered was women found getting in difficult without help. Not Shea, though.

No problem. He liked independent women and could get an excellent cup of joe at the diner.

"So," he said as they started down the drive. "Sleep well last night?"

"Yes."

Silence.

"The weatherman's forecasting a winter storm. Says it could rival the big one back in 1949."

"Mmm."

Silence.

"The brunt of the storm will hit Magic Valley to the south, but I expect we'll feel it, too. You might want to mention it to Dee Dee. Make sure she's well stocked with food at her place. Gas for her generator, too."

"Mmm."

Silence.

"Is this how it's going to go, Shea? You freezing me out?" Jonas slowed and came to a stop at the end of the drive. He twisted in his seat to look at her.

Shea stared back at him, though confronted seemed more appropriate. Something about the way she didn't take guff from him or anybody else pleased him no end.

"I make small talk all day long every day, Jonas. Forgive me if I don't find it appealing when I'm not working. If you have something to say, say it."

"Are you still mad because you couldn't pry out all my

deep, dark secrets?"

"You mean do I still have my underfrillies in a knot?" Her nostrils flared. Flames flickered in her brown eyes. "You can keep your deep, dark secrets. I want nothing to do with them.

He rubbed a hand over his mouth and chin. "Shea, you know—"

"I've been surrounded by people with secrets my whole life. No more. If you can't trust me, how can I trust you?"

He had no idea what to say. Instinct told him she'd know if he lied. "Uh—"

"Did I hit a sore spot? Let's go, Jonas. I'm already way later than I like."

"Shea, I made a commitment when I joined the Army. I swore an oath. Yes, I have secrets, information I've promised on my life not to divulge. This isn't about you or me. I'll tell you whatever I can."

A speculative look entered her eyes. "Fine. Tell me what you did while in the Army. Where did you serve? Did your absence this past summer have anything to do with Mallory's disappearance? Because she's not the same since she came home and you aren't either. And what about your nightmares? I heard you go off to the mountains for days at a time."

His mouth fell open. After a moment, he snapped it shut again and looked away. "My sisters talk too much."

"Your sisters didn't tell me. Your mother did."

"Shea, you're asking me to reveal classified information. I wish I could." No, he didn't. Not really. You couldn't uncross lines you stepped over. The less she knew of the real Jonas Cameron, the better for her. So why couldn't he leave her alone? "Let it go. Please."

The soft jawline he'd come to love turned to stone. She folded her arms across her chest and turned to face the road. "I told you my mother left. Eight years later, I dropped out of school to care for my father in his dying days. When he died, I learned why she took off.

"After we buried Wallace Townsend, my so-called father, my stepbrothers and I met with the estate attorney. The will stipulated forty percent of everything—land, assets, stocks, and cash—went to Elijah, the oldest of the brothers. It seemed reasonable to the rest of us, given the well-known fact Eli had run the ranch for the previous few years."

Jonas put the truck in park and waited.

"Noah, Ben, and I each received twenty percent," she went on. "Except as we started to leave the office, the attorney asked me to remain. That's when I learned my whole life was a lie. It turned out Wallace had a slow-growing brain tumor. Cancer. It stole his wits, changed his personality, and plunged him into paranoia. When my mother first noticed the symptoms, she tried to get him to see a doctor. Instead, he turned paranoid and refused to

seek treatment until long after she'd gone. It was too late by then."

Shea's voice faltered. She swallowed repeatedly and took several long breaths until control returned.

He waited. She needed to get this out on her own terms, in her own time.

"My *father* added a codicil to his will, to my part of the inheritance. Mr. Rickerby, the attorney was embarrassed, so he handed the addendum to me to read. Wallace had included a handwritten note. It turns out my mother didn't abandon me after all. He kicked her out. Claimed she had an affair, and he wasn't my biological father. He said she tried to paint him insane to get his money."

Shea brushed tears from her eyes with an angry swipe.

"The amendment specified I would have to marry Porter Townsend by my twenty-fifth birthday to *qualify* for the inheritance since I didn't have Townsend blood. Once we produced a marriage certificate, both Porter and I would inherit equally, but if the marriage didn't occur, my twenty percent would go to Eli, Noah, and Ben."

He tried to imagine his own father doing something so hurtful to one of his children but couldn't. He had no frame of reference for the rejection she'd experienced and had to hold back his anger to let her finish.

"I always believed I'd marry Porter one day. We grew up together, became good friends. When I left the attorney's office that day, I drove to Porter's place and used the spare key he kept under the front step." She stared off in the distance, lost in another place and time until Jonas cleared his throat. "I found him ... with Gina."

Jonas reached for her hand.

"It hurt seeing them together, but not like I thought it should. What hurt more was finding out everyone knew everything—how Wallace had thrown my mother out for cheating, my illegitimacy, and the relationship Porter and Gina had been in for a couple of years while I didn't know any of it."

Never had he known a person more in need of comfort than Shea at this particular moment. He pulled her into his arms and let her blubber into his shirt.

After a long time, she put some distance between them. "Let me finish. Once I'm done, we'll never speak of this again. I ran home crying. Eli and his family had lived in this tiny, one-bedroom cabin on the property, but with two kids they needed a bigger place. After Wallace died they moved into the homestead with me. Trina, my sister-in-law met me at the door that day. She handed me a letter, a bill from the culinary school I'd attended. They said I owed fifteen-thousand dollars. Trina told me Wallace took out a loan in my name for my tuition, but since I left before finishing the deferment was voided. The bank wanted the full amount owed within thirty days."

"That's ... awful." He didn't know what else to say.

"Trina told me since I didn't have any income I could live with them. She needed help with the cooking, taking care of the house, and the kids."

"That's when you left."

Shea nodded. "Yes. I packed up what I could fit in my car, went by the bank and withdrew all seven-hundred-forty-five dollars I had to my name, made arrangements for a payment plan, and left. Another three years with Dee Dee and I should have the loan paid off. You want to know something else? Something really ironic? Porter is adopted. He doesn't have Townsend blood either."

Jonas's family meant the world to him. How had she survived having no one? "You never told me where you're from."

Shea choked on a laugh. "I grew up on a cattle ranch in Montana. The ironic thing is the closest town, if you can call it a town, is Cameron. Imagine my surprise when I looked up my uncle and found him here in Hastings Bluff surrounded by Camerons."

Chapter Sixteen

Two tissues and ten minutes later, Shea waved goodbye to Jonas. Her confessions had eased the tension between them but hadn't changed their stalemate. He and James were keeping secrets that concerned her.

At least a dozen heads swiveled around to stare when the bell over the door announced her arrival. The breakfast rush should have already passed by now.

"It's her," someone called out.

"About time, little girl. When you gonna chase Cecil out of the kitchen and make me my crepes again?"

"Pour out the motor oil and let's get some real coffee going, Shea. Please? I swear, you make it best."

Dee Dee raised her voice to be heard over the excited chatter. "Maybe Calvin's onto something there. We could market a new brand of 'Shea's Java' and charge double."

Her comment garnered a few groans, but most of the customers smiled and grinned. A few even nodded.

Darned if her tears didn't start to leak again. She'd come here, to a town of strangers, intent on keeping her distance, but here she stood, four hours past her usual arrival time, and they acted like she'd gone missing for a month. Caring for them in return was never in the plan. But she did.

Running the gauntlet from the door to the counter, she smiled, greeted, touched, and hugged her way through. After stopping in the back office to hang her coat and lock up her purse, she donned a freshly pressed apron, said hi to Cecil, and headed back out front to help Dee Dee with the customers ... and spotted Wes at the far end of the counter.

He offered her a two-finger salute, but his smile seemed strained.

"Make some more coffee, would you?" Dee Dee whispered. "Then go talk to Wes. He's moving like an old man this morning. See if you can find out what happened."

Shea bantered back and forth with a few of the regulars while she made a fresh pot of coffee. After fifteen minutes, a slow parade of customers left until five remained, Wes one of them.

Pouring herself a cup of the steaming fresh brew, Shea walked over to where he sat alone. "You act like you got hit by a Mack truck. What happened? We worried when you didn't come in."

A smile lit his face up like a Christmas tree. "You missed me?"

"Yeah. Seriously, though, you okay?"

Wes hung his head, shaking it side to side with a soft, self-conscious laugh. When he looked up again, amusement filled his eyes. "Not a Mack truck, a 1942 Ford pickup."

"Oh, no. Not Judd Wheeler?"

"Yep. Me and my team had set up out on Route 93 south of Challis when this old dude decided to take his half of the road on the shoulder. I jumped out of the way, but my transit didn't make it."

"You sit like you have a rod in your spine, so I'm pretty sure you didn't get away scot-free."

"A couple of bruised ribs, that's all."

"I'm sorry, Wes, and I'm glad it's not serious."

"Thanks, Shea. I was surprised when I didn't see you here this morning. Dee Dee said you've cut back on your hours."

"Yeah. With the way business has picked up over the past few months, I talked her into bringing on more wait staff. This way I can get back to my kitchen. Cecil and I plan to trade off breakfast and lunch shifts, so this week I'll come in late."

"Thanks for letting me know. Maybe I'll switch to brunch or lunch this week. Right now, I need to get going.

My little sabbatical put my crew behind schedule." He winked and a semblance of the old Wes returned.

Shea waved when he looked back over his shoulder.

"Curious." Dee Dee gathered up the last of the dirty dishes from the booths.

"What is?"

"Your friend, Porter, showing up here with a sling."

"He's a jerk, and I doubt he's injured at all."

"Mmm-huh. And I heard Kyle, a.k.a. Deputy Dawg slipped on the ice and hurt his back. Now he's walking funny."

Shea looked askance at her friend.

"I also heard Clint Loomis fell off his horse and whacked his shoulder, and now Wes has hurt his ribs."

"What are you getting at, Dee Dee?"

"Odd how all the guys flirting with you came up lame after you clobbered my attacker. I'm wondering if Jonas Cameron will start hobbling, too."

Shea frowned as she put the oddities together. "You think one of them attacked you."

Her friend shrugged and started for the kitchen. "Maybe, maybe not, but I don't believe in coincidence."

The next week brought temperatures in the low teens, which was brutal for November. At least the forecasted snow storm had stalled over the Cascades. For now, blue skies and sunshine prevailed. A perfect winter day for anyone who didn't have to work outside.

Jonas slid the barn door shut behind him, and stomped his boots on the ground, more to warm them than to shake loose the snow he'd tromped through. The foaling horses needed exercise in spite of the weather, but he didn't like leaving them outside for very long. A quick romp through the small pasture adjacent to the barn and right back inside the heated barn. Not Tiki, though. Jonas wanted to keep careful control over her environment for the next few days, which meant she couldn't free-roam to graze.

"She looks better this morning. Like she got whatever was bothering her out of her system," Rascal said from where he leaned against the side of Tiki Fire's stall.

At the far end of the barn, Clint worked at a slow, but steady pace mucking the stalls.

"Yeah, she does look good," Jonas answered. "We'll treat this as a one-off digestive upset like the vet said but keep a close watch on her anyway. Clint back up to speed?"

"Not in the saddle yet. Shoulder's still sore."

Jonas shook his head.

"He's not a slacker, Jo. Clint keeps up with his chores around the barn. Takes him a bit longer, but he stays at it till he gets it done."

Jonas stared at the younger man for a long time before he answered. "If he's not better by tomorrow, haul him in to see Doc Burdette. Vern, too, if he needs it."

"Will do." Rascal looked over Jonas's shoulder and smiled. "Well, lookee who's come for a visit. Morning, Shea."

Jonas turned and couldn't contain his own smile as Shea unwound the heavy scarf from around her neck. Her nose and cheeks glowed red as a rose. "Hey, there."

He'd offered to show her around several times, but she'd not shown any interest until now.

"Hi. I hope I'm not interrupting. Your dad brought me over. I thought I'd take you up on a tour if you have time."

"One deluxe guided tour coming right up. Step this way, ma'am." Jonas crooked his arm out. When she slipped her hand into the bend of his elbow, something warm unfurled inside his chest. He patted her hand, liking the feel of her skin. What was she doing to him? Why her? Why now?

As he introduced her to each of the pregnant mares and let her get acquainted with the two new babies and their mamas, he pondered the questions. Yes, Shea had an ethereal beauty with a killer figure, knock-out blonde hair and brown sugar eyes. She turned every man's head. But the *why her* answer involved more than mere physical appeal. His attraction to Shea and—unless he'd gone blind and dumb—her attraction to him, had become a living force between them. It stripped him of any ability to deny her. Even now watching her fascination with the newborn foals mesmerized him. He wanted to memorize every detail—from the curve of her hip as she bent over to pet the foals to the tiny corkscrew curls at the nape of her neck revealed by her high ponytail.

His nose lifted, breathing in the clean soap and sunshine smell of her skin.

"What?"

Uh-oh. She'd caught him sniffing her like a wild animal.

"Is there hay in my hair or something?" Shea touched her head in search of the elusive straw.

He stared like a lovesick puppy and decided on the spot he didn't care if she or anyone else knew it. "No, there's not a single thing wrong with you."

Her rosy cheeks had faded some being away from the cold, but now they burst into full bloom again. How did he never realize before this moment the appeal of a woman's blush?

The *why now* answer came to him despite the Shea-fog that clouded his mind. His dad called it male mating instinct. All guys experienced the here-today-gone-tomorrow lustiness of youth. It was a rite of passage. But the subconscious takes over as maturity sets in, a longing for one woman, a mate who can give him a home and family.

"I, uh ... I don't ..." Shea looked everywhere but at him. Skittish. A little bit wild-eyed. A woodland sprite.

Jonas backed away a step to give her space. He'd come

on too strong, crowded her. Shea didn't fit the same profile as most of the women he'd known. She came with a whole different set of rules and required delicate handling.

A horse in a nearby stall snorted, giving them both a reprieve.

"Ah, you need to meet Lilly. She has quite a story."

Jonas stroked the velvet-soft nose of the smallish roan mare. "Shea, come meet Lillian Laughingwater. We call her Lilly. She ran with the herd of wild horses on our land until she injured a fetlock. Dad found her a few years back. The herd had abandoned her when she couldn't keep up. Abandonment for a herd animal means a death sentence in the wild. Lone animals, injured ones in particular, make easy prey for predators. Starved, half frozen, and too weak to fight, she went docile as a lamb when Dad loaded her into one of the horse trailers and brought her here. Now, look at her. Healthy, content, and nursing her baby."

Shea placed her hand next to his and rubbed the horse's forehead. "She's a beauty. Did you ever consider sending her back to the herd?"

He shook his head. "No. Lilly's prone to hoof problems. Sooner or later she'd wind up in trouble again. None of us want to lose her. Besides, she's adapted well to domestic life. Sorry to cut this short, but we need to get going if you intend to make it to the diner by nine."

"Speaking of the diner, can I ask a favor?"

"Of course."

"Tomorrow, would it be okay if we go in a little earlier? Say, seven o'clock?"

"Dee Dee already reneging on the new schedule?"

"No, I've been working up a new recipe, but there's never time when I'm on grill duty or waiting tables."

"You could use Mom's kitchen. I'm sure she wouldn't mind."

"Oh, no, I couldn't impose. Besides, all the equipment and ingredients at the diner, and it's a messy process, perfecting a recipe."

"Okay. I'll pick you up in front of the house at seven sharp tomorrow, but I have a condition." He grinned at her. "I get to be your guinea pig. Deal?"

She laughed. "You might regret it, but you have a deal."

Chapter Seventeen

An intermittent buzzing sound broke through the barriers of sleep. Jonas fumbled for his cell phone on the nightstand thinking to turn the alarm off but the noise stopped. Puzzled, he sat up on the side of the bed and squinted at the screen with bleary eyes.

One missed call.

The phone buzzed and vibrated in his hand. Startled, he dropped it on the floor. One thought penetrated—calls in the middle of the night seldom brought good news.

He slid to his knees and ran his hands around the wooden floor but couldn't locate the still buzzing phone. A light blinked under his bed, in sync with the rings. He leaned down and spotted it halfway underneath the bed.

Dropping to his belly, he stretched an arm out, got his

fingertips on it, and tickled it back toward him.

Rascal's name flashed on the screen

"H'lo."

"You need to get over to the big barn. Tiki's in bad shape. I already called Doc Blackburn." The call disconnected.

Jonas dropped his phone on the bed, dressed in the clothes he'd worn the day before, and ran out the back door to his truck in under three minutes.

What went wrong? She'd looked good before he came home last night. He'd measured her feed himself with meticulous care.

The big breeding barn shone like a beacon in the distance. Rascal had turned on every light, inside and out. Jonas threw the gearshift into park and jumped out.

Nervous whickers greeted him when he strode inside. Most people didn't realize horses had a heightened sensitivity. They recognized when a human feared them, could discern a greenhorn holding the reins, and knew with absolute certainty when something was wrong with another horse.

Tiki Fire stood in the stall, her head down, breathing labored. A sheen of sweat covered her body, along with a thin layer of froth around her mouth. Every now and again she would turn her head and try to nip at her belly, an almost impossible feat given the distention of her late-term pregnancy.

"How did this happen?" Jonas growled.

"I've had Clint help me watch over Tiki these past two nights. He woke me fifteen minutes ago, worried. I took one look at her and called Tom Blackburn and you."

Jonas glanced over Rascal's shoulder and spotted Clint and Vern hanging nearby. "What happened?"

Vern patted the younger ranch hand on the shoulder and disappeared through the rear door.

Clint shuffled forward a few steps. "I've been here since midnight and checked on all the horses every half hour like Rascal instructed. Tiki was fine up until about three-thirty. She seemed restless, pacing back and forth in her stall, so I stayed with her. The sweats started about four, the hard breathing not long after. That's when I called him."

"You give her anything to eat or drink?"

Clint's lips flatlined. His hands clenched into fists at his side, but he didn't waver under Jonas's stare. "No, sir. I heard your orders. Nobody feeds Tiki but you, not to even top off her water."

Jonas wiped the ailing mare down with a damp rag while they waited for the vet to arrive. Doc Blackburn pulled up a half-hour later.

"I'll go help bring his stuff in," Clint muttered and hurried out the barn door.

Tom Blackburn had practiced in the area for more than forty years. He knew a thing or two because he'd treated thousands of large animals in his lifetime. If anybody could help Tiki, Tom could.

He walked through the door, waddling from side to side like the seventy-one-years he'd attained.

Clint followed, lugging the big medical bag and an even bigger toolbox.

"How long she been like this?" Doc asked.

"Clint here says she got restless around three," Rascal said. "The sweats and labored breathing followed not long after. The groans have continued ever since. Nips at her belly, too."

"What's she eaten?" The old vet opened his cracked leather bag, retrieved a stethoscope, and entered the stall to listen to the distressed mare's chest.

"Quarter ration of bran mash last night about seven," Jonas answered. "I left her a flake of hay, too, but she hasn't touched it. I measured out the mash and chose the flake myself."

Doc looked up, a puzzled frown on his face. "Nothing since?"

Jonas looked at Rascal.

"No, sir. I watched over her and the others up until midnight when Clint took over. Neither of us gave her anything.

"What about the pasture? Did she graze out there yesterday?"

"I walked her around the corral several times during

the day for exercise," Jonas said. "But no pasture. Didn't want to take any chances." He rubbed the back of his neck, not liking the mystery.

Doc Blackburn checked the mare's eyes, examined the slobber around her mouth, felt along her swollen belly, and sighed.

"What are you thinking Doc?" Jonas asked.

"She's got classic signs of colic, but what you gave her shouldn't create this kind of discomfort. With strict control over her diet as you claim, we have to look for some kind of bowel obstruction. But let's worry about that later. Right now, we need to get her and her foal out of distress. Open my toolbox and get me the medium tubing. I'll need a bucket of water to soften it, a second bucket of clean water, and a third bucket to catch the contents. Fetch my pump, too."

Jonas had assisted with the insertion of nasogastric tubes many times before, sometimes to administer medicine directly to the horse's stomach, but also to lavage any undigestible contents. He always found it surprising when the horse didn't seem to mind having a plastic tube shoved through their nose and down their throat. Maybe since horses couldn't vomit, they didn't have a gag reflex.

He found the proper size tubing, while Clint ran off to get the pump and the buckets.

Rascal remained by Tiki's neck and held the bridle while Doc stroked her nose and talked to the anxious horse.

"You're a fine girl, Tiki. We'll get you fixed up in no time. Good girl."

Doc lubed up the end of the tubing, gripped one of Tiki's big nostrils, and began sliding the tube in with slow, downward pressure.

Siphoning off the contents of her stomach yielded little results—a few twig-like pieces and some residual mash.

"Here." Doc handed the bucket to Jonas. "Hang onto it."

Two hours passed from the time Doc started his treatment until they saw improvement. The sweating stopped first. Tiki's labored breathing eased and she stopped biting at her side. Not long after, she started tossing her head, a sure sign of improvement.

"Crisis averted for now," Doc said. "Give her some water, but no food until tonight. If the symptoms start up again, load her up and bring her to my office. I'll need to run some tests to check for a blockage. Meanwhile, I need you to show me step-by-step what you did last night to feed her—the bag of feed, how you mixed it, the water source, the measuring scoop. And get me her water pail with any remaining water and her nosebag. I want to run tests on them and the stomach contents."

Rascal tugged on Jonas's sleeve and motioned him to the side. "It's almost seven. You told Shea you'd take her in early today. Want me to go?"

"Rascal," Doc said. "I need you to walk me around the

pasture and point out where Tiki likes to graze."

Jonas clapped a hand to his forehead and groaned. He'd let the time slip up on him. Worse, he'd forgotten all about Shea. She would understand, wouldn't she? "I can't leave right now. Neither can you."

He searched for his cell phone to call her, patted every pocket, but came up empty. Great. He'd dropped the phone on his bed when he got dressed this morning and never picked it back up.

"I'll take her." Clint spoke from where he leaned against the stall. "Shea knows me. I helped her with the campouts last summer."

Jonas bristled. The thought of any man taking his place with Shea made his jaw tighten. Before he could react though, Rascal patted his chest and pushed him back a step, kept him from making a fool of himself. "Thanks, Clint. You be sure and pick her up at the front of the house, seven sharp. Tell her we had an emergency and Jonas will call her later."

Clint nodded and headed off without bothering to look at Jonas.

Shea grabbed her backpack and headed to the kitchen. The morning meal during the week was a hit or miss thing in the Cameron household. With the family coming and going at different times, each one got their own breakfast, but woe to whoever took the last cup of coffee without making more.

Cate sat at the counter with a steaming cup and a newspaper. "Good morning, Shea. Did you sleep well?"

"I did, thanks." With fifteen minutes to kill she had plenty of time. And if Jonas arrived early, as usual, he would come inside.

"Looks like our reprieve from the storm ends today," Cate said pointing to an article in the newspaper. "The weatherman says we'll feel the effects later this morning. Make sure you bundle up."

Shea nodded. The storm had already dumped more than twenty inches of snow on eastern Oregon and now had the southern half of Idaho in its sights. She'd packed an overnight kit in case the roads closed and she had to stay with Dee Dee.

When the big grandfather clock in the foyer struck seven and Jonas still hadn't come in, she shrugged into her parka, wrapped her scarf around her neck, and pulled the stocking cap down over her ears. With a goodbye for Cate, Shea tugged on her gloves, grabbed the backpack, and went to wait by the front door.

Seven came and went. Not a big deal for most people, but it created a niggle of worry for Shea. No one took punctuality to heart more than Jonas. The man had a serious hang-up about being on time.

The front window afforded a picture-perfect view of

the pastures, Cate's rose garden, and the long drive to the main highway. A vehicle appeared moments later. Not Jonas's truck, but an older model car, dark in color. Maybe he had to borrow someone else's ride. She stepped outside.

When it pulled up in front of the house, some of the anxiety squeezing her chest eased a little. Until Clint opened the door and stepped out.

"I hear you need a taxi," he called from the driver's side.

"Where's Jonas?" she yelled from the porch steps.

"We had an emergency at the barn. Jonas sent me to drive you this morning. Said he'd call later."

Shea nodded but didn't want to get into a car with Clint, even for the short drive into town. For a moment, she considered asking Cate to take her.

Clint ducked back inside the car, closed his door, and waited. No gentleman's manners from him.

Disappointed and a little wary, she made her way down the front steps and got in on the passenger side. "Thanks. I appreciate the lift."

"No problem." He pulled around and headed back down the drive.

"So, what's the emergency? Which horse?"

"Tiki Fire. She took sick in the middle of the night. Mr. Sutcliff called the vet in, and all three of us have been working on her ever since."

"She's okay, though?"

He shrugged. "Maybe. I think so. Doc says she has colic, but he can't figure out why she keeps getting it. With her due to deliver in another month, they tend to worry about the foal. She looked better when I left."

"What did he do?"

Clint's eyes lit up. "Man, it was awesome. Doc shoved this long, plastic tube through Tiki's nose. I could see it move down her throat. Once he got it into her stomach, Doc sucked on the end to get a siphon going. I thought he'd get a mouthful of horse puke for sure."

"Ew. Hey, look there." Shea pointed to a truck parked on the side of the road ahead with the hood up. A man stood by the driver's door waving his arms overhead. "That's, uh, Vern, right?"

"Yeah. Looks like his truck broke down, though I don't remember him having such a fancy one." Clint slowed, flipped the right turn blinker on, and pulled up beside the stranded vehicle.

Vernon Beauchamp strolled over to the passenger side, so Shea lowered her window using the old hand crank. No electronics for Clint.

"Car trouble?" she asked.

Vern propped his folded forearms in the open window and looked in. "Yeah. Rascal sent me for some emergency stuff for Tiki. You're the mechanical genius, Clint. Can you take a quick look?"

Shea leaned away from the window, not liking the way

Vern invaded her space.

"You mind, Shea?" Clint asked. "It'll only take a minute."

"No, go ahead." Anything to get Vern's rancid breath out of her face.

Clint put his car in park, got out, and followed Vern to the front of the truck and out of Shea's sight.

She breathed in the fresh air, closed the window, and took the time to check her phone for messages. Why, she had no idea. The emails she received included ads with an occasional bill notification.

No more than a minute passed before Vern returned and opened her door.

"What—hey!"

He reached across her, popped the seatbelt free, and hauled her from the car by the arm.

"Let go! What are you doing?"

His huge hand gripped her upper arm. The harder she tried to jerk free, the tighter he held on. She'd have bruises tomorrow.

Free of the car and still struggling, Shea lost her footing and landed hard on one knee. "Let go of me," she screamed. "You're crazy!"

Vern didn't stop. He shifted his grip to her wrist and dragged her to his truck.

"Clint!" Heart racing, she twisted and kicked him, missed, and struck out with her free arm. "Clint, help me!"

Vern grunted, his sole acknowledgment of her pitiful blow. He opened the rear door of his truck and hauled her upright. "Get in," he growled through clenched teeth.

"No." Fear escalated into full-blown panic. She kicked again, catching him square in the shin this time. "Let go, you're hurting me!"

She drew back to kick him again, but never got the chance.

"I don't have time for this." Wham! Vern's huge fist caught her on the side of the face, right below her left temple.

Pain exploded in her head but quickly faded into nothingness.

Chapter Eighteen

"Come, look at this."

Jonas closed and locked the feed room door and walked over to where Doc stood outside Tiki Fire's stall. "You find something?"

"Maybe. Maybe not. Look here." He held out Tiki's nosebag turned inside out and shook it over a cloth he'd spread on a nearby bale. A few small particles of feed and twigs fell out.

"I didn't give her a nosebag last night. She got her mash in a feed bucket," Jonas told him. "Where'd you find this?"

"On the floor behind her stall."

Anger, concern, fear, and betrayal made a stomach-turning cocktail. Jonas had to make a conscious effort to unclench his teeth and fists. They always collected the feedbags once the horse finished. They turned them inside out and shook them to get rid of any leftover particles. Afterward, they hung them on a hook inside the feed room.

"Tell me again what all you put in the mash," Doc instructed.

Jonas tipped his hat back on his head. He'd already gone over the mash recipe three other times with Doc. "Three quarts dry wheat bran, two quarts coarse-chopped carrots and apples, and a gallon of warm water."

"No molasses?" Doc asked.

"Nope."

"What about her regular grain ration?"

"Nope."

"Oats?"

He shook his head.

"Look at this." Doc worked a gnarled finger through the debris from the nosebag.

Frowning, Jonas leaned down to study the fragments. "Oats and ... twigs?"

"Now look at this." Doc used a mixing paddle to stir the meager contents he'd siphoned from Tiki's stomach.

"Looks like oats and some of those same twigs." Acid churned in Jonas's gut.

Doc nodded. "You fed her at six last night, right?"

Jonas nodded.

"Of the ingredients you listed, carrots are the hardest

to digest." Doc stirred the mess again. "I don't see any carrots."

Jonas turned in a full circle and kicked the bale of hay.

Startled, Tiki jerked back from the gate of her stall and snorted.

"Whoa, girl, whoa. He's not mad at you," Rascal ran a hand down the horse's neck and flank to soothe her. "He's mad someone tried to hurt you."

Pulling his self-control around him like a blanket, Jonas turned to Doc. "You got any idea what those twigs are? If they have any lasting harm?"

"I'll send them off for analysis, but it'll take a week to get the results. Meanwhile, keep an eye on her like I said. And keep a tight control on who has access to the feed room. Call me if you need me, day or night." Doc tipped his hat and grabbed his bag.

Jonas collected the rest of the medical gear and carried it out to the truck for the old vet. "Thanks, Doc. I appreciate you coming out in the middle of the night."

"Don't worry, I'll send you a bill."

They shook hands before the vet drove away.

Back inside the barn, Jonas went straight to the feed room door. It had a simple latch lock to keep the door closed. He sent hands into town all the time to buy feed and they'd stack it here. Anyone determined to get into the room, lock or no lock, could do it.

"I'll call Wade," he said to Rascal. "We need to rethink

access to the feed room and some of the other supplies. I also need you to make a list of everyone who came to the barn yesterday."

Rascal nodded. "It's a sad day when one bad apple causes you to distrust all your men."

At five till nine, Jonas settled in a chair across from Wade's desk. "Need your help, big brother."

"Welcome to Cameron Security Services. Happy to help you out but don't go expecting any family discounts." Wade leaned back in his chair, hands behind his head. "What's up, little brother?"

Jonas explained the events of the morning, and the conclusions he'd drawn. "This is the second instance where someone fed Tiki Fire an unknown irritant with the intention of causing her harm. I have to restrict access to the feed room, but I don't know how."

Wade leaned forward with a soft whistle. "Seems to me if someone wanted to harm the horse, they'd have done it the first time. Sounds more like they're playing with you. Have you considered the guy Fowler's worried about?"

The idea of someone who worked for him, someone who knew his comings and goings every day ... The thought terrified Jonas. If they could get to his horses, they could get to his family. And he'd brought Shea into the middle of it. "I'm going to need a complete background check on every single ranch hand we've hired in the last year. Heck, make it the last two years."

"Okay, but it'll take time, and I'm thinking time's a luxury right now. Whoever's doing this has to know he's tipped his hand. Let me call Garrett."

Jonas nodded, hating the out of control feeling. *He* was the covert operative, the one who hid in the shadows and brush. *He* did the stalking. Acting as prey put him at a distinct disadvantage. Hopefully, he could turn the tables.

"Let's head over to the diner. Garrett and James will meet us there. Seeing your pretty little girl will cheer you up."

Yes, it would. Despite the new risk, he still liked his odds of keeping her safe at the ranch better than in that ridiculous apartment.

The two brothers shrugged into heavy jackets, crammed their big white Stetsons on their heads, and tugged on winter gloves. As they walked down the sidewalk to the Calico Diner, they saw James come out from the sheriff's office across the street. He met them at the diner door as his brother, Garrett, pulled up.

"Perfect timing," the oldest Cameron brother called out. "Now, what's this about someone trying to poison one of the mares?"

"Let's go inside where it's warm and I'll fill you in." Jonas opened the door and held it while the other three stomped their boots on the mat in the entry vestibule and hung their coats and hats on a wall peg inside the door.

Dee Dee looked over at them and waved, but a puzzled look crossed her face. "You can have the booth in the back corner. I'll bring coffee."

Garret and James took one side, while Jonas crowded in next to Wade. "Shove over, would you. I'm hanging off the edge here."

Wade grumbled but managed to give Jonas a few more inches. "She needs to invest in larger booths. These aren't designed for men our size."

Jonas, the smaller of the four stood six-feet-three and weighed in at a solid two-twenty-two. He conceded Wade had a point.

Dee Dee approached, carrying a tray with four mugs and a pot of coffee. "Here you go. It's piping hot and fresh off the brewer." She set the mugs down on the table, filled each one, and slid them across to each man. Turning to Jonas, she said, "Shea not coming in today?"

All the blood in his body turned into ice water. For the first time in his life, Jonas thought he might faint. "She's not here?" he managed to croak.

When she shook her head no, he whipped out his cell phone and dialed. "Mom, is Shea there?"

"No, dear. She left at seven. Clint came to pick her up. Why? What's wrong?"

"Nothing." He hung up on his mother without saying goodbye and dialed Rascal.

"You and Wade got all our problems solved?" the old foreman answered.

"Clint there?"

"I don't know. He didn't check in with me after taking Shea to work. Hold on, let me ask the other guys."

The phone clattered when Rascal set it down. The few minutes of waiting seemed like a lifetime ... one where every moment spent with Shea flashed through his mind. A new kind of fear reared its ugly head, taunting him for his inability to protect her on his own land, from the evil that had targeted him.

"Nope," Rascal said. "No one's seen him. Why?"

"He picked Shea up from the house at seven, but she never made it to the diner. I gotta go." He ended the call and stared at his two brothers and James. "I ... I ... don't know what to do."

James's cell phone rang. "Evers. Yeah, hold on. I'm going to put you on speaker."

The knot in Jonas's stomach tightened.

"It's Archer," James said to the others and tapped a button on his phone. "Go ahead, John."

"Fred Robison called the office. He told Lorraine about a car parked half on, half off the road with the front passenger door open and the engine running. I found signs of a struggle nearby. Clint Loomis lay over the side of the hill with his head bashed in. Doc Burdette came when I called, but now he's asking for an air evac."

The knot in Jonas's chest expanded to boulder-size, making it difficult to breathe. "Shea?"

"Any sign of Shea Townsend? She was with Loomis."

"No, but there's a single footprint near the passenger side of Loomis's car smaller than the others. And a trail like something being drug through the snow. I didn't find anything of hers in Loomis's car."

"Can Clint talk?" James asked.

"No. He's unconscious. From the dent in his skull, I don't know if he'll ever talk. One more thing." He hesitated for a couple of seconds. "I found blood where I think the struggle ended. Not much, but some."

Jonas looked at his watch. Nine-twenty-seven. Two and a half hours had passed since Clint had picked Shea up at seven. She could be anywhere. The pressure inside him increased to bursting point.

"Give me your coordinates. I'll be there in five." James left the booth, grabbed his hat and coat from the peg by the door, and left the diner running.

When Jonas got up to follow, Wade caught his arm. "Hold on, Jo. I got an idea."

Jonas stared at his computer-genius brother for the longest time before he nodded. "Okay. What is it?"

"Come back to my office with me. If you've got Shea's cell phone number, I can track it. If she's still got it, we can find her quicker than James."

Garrett agreed. "It's more than he has right now."

Jonas gave one sharp nod and headed for the door. "Let's do it."

Dee Dee stopped him on the way out "What's going on, Jonas? Where's Shea?"

"We don't know," Garrett told her. "But we're gonna find her."

Dee Dee covered her mouth with a hand, a horrified expression in her eyes.

Outside, the three brothers headed toward Wade's office as fast as the slippery sidewalk allowed.

Garrett had his phone out. "Rascal, it's Garrett. I need a head count of all the hands. Let me know who's missing. Call me back as soon as you can."

He turned to Jonas. "Given the events surrounding Tiki Fire, this seems more premeditated than opportunistic. Tell me the name of every person you saw in the barn yesterday. Today, too."

Entering through the glass front doors of his office, Wade led them to a small conference room.

Jonas fell into one of the chairs. "Yesterday—me, Rascal, Clint, Robby, Dusty, Bertram, Vern, and Herb. And Shea. I gave her a tour of the barn. That's when she asked me about going in early today."

"Think," Wade prompted. "Who was around when Shea asked to go in early?"

Fingers to his head, Jonas closed his eyes and tried to remember. "No one."

"What about this morning?" Garrett asked.

This memory came easier. "Me, Rascal, Clint, and Doc. Rascal kept watch over the horses up until midnight when Clint took over. He called Rascal around four. Wait. Vern was there. He left shortly after I arrived.

Garrett's phone rang. "Talk to me, Rascal." He listened, nodded, and offered a few uh-huhs before he hung up. "Rascal accounted for all the men except Clint and Vern."

"Well," Wade said. "I think we can rule out Clint."

"I need to let James know." Garrett got up and walked out of the room, the phone pressed to his ear.

Wade handed Jonas a small notepad. "Write down Shea's phone number and let's go into my office." He led the way past two more doors, sat behind his desk, and fired up his equipment.

Jonas knew his way around computers, but Wade played in a different class. He and his wife, Lucy, had extraordinary abilities when it came to the cyber world.

Jonas handed the pad back across to his brother, the action making him realize how helpless he was. Not a comfortable or familiar feeling. He squirmed while Wade typed, clicked, and talked to himself in a quiet monotone.

Garrett came in and sat next to Jonas. "James has Vern's license plate number and a description of his vehicle. He'll put out an APB for him. We need a picture of Shea."

Jonas thumbed through his phone and selected one of the many pictures he had of Shea, some she'd posed for, others she didn't know about. He chose a front view and messaged it to James.

"I think I might have something." Wade spoke but never took his eyes off the monitor. "Her phone is still active. GPS shows them heading north toward Montana, but I don't know how long I can keep the signal with this storm brewing."

"We need to let James know," Garrett said.

Montana. A two and one-half hour head start. Anything could happen before he got to her. Jonas got up to pace the room which seemed to have grown smaller.

His phone pinged with a text message. What he saw almost made his heart stop. The message came from Shea's phone. It showed a picture of her sprawled in the backseat of a truck. Her hands were tied behind her back, her eyes closed. An ugly bruise covered one side of her face and she had a bloody gash over one eyebrow.

Jonas fell into his chair.

"Jo? You're white as the snow outside, man. What gives?" Garrett snatched the cell phone from Jonas and looked at the message. "That's gonna get somebody killed."

The message chime pinged again.

"What now?" Jonas managed to ask.

Garrett stared at the message for the longest time. He

swallowed hard before he met Jonas's eyes. "He sent a message. 'Find me, find your woman. Come alone, and I might let her live.'"

Chapter Nineteen

A jouncing motion dragged Shea up from oblivion. An unpleasant, earthy smell brought her fully awake. She wrinkled her nose ... and hissed through clenched teeth, almost passing out again at the agony burning the left side of her face.

Seconds, perhaps minutes passed before the pain and nausea subsided enough to fill her lungs again. The dirty rug smell remained.

A floorboard. She lay on the floor in the backseat of a vehicle. From the swaying and bouncing, the road had more potholes than pavement. Where in the world?

Not yet willing to sit up and risk the fiery ache again, she lay still and took stock of her injuries. Her cheek pulsed with a dull, throbbing ache. Her legs worked, but not her arms. Concentrating, she realized her hands were tied behind her back.

The diner. Jonas had promised to pick her up at seven instead of nine because she wanted to test a new recipe. Clint Loomis had come for her instead.

A rush of memories swamped her in dizzying succession, the encounter with Vern foremost. How he'd dragged her out of Clint's car and hit her. No, he'd punched her. With his fist. In the face. Oh, dear Lord, he'd kidnapped her.

The vehicle slowed, made a hard right, and kept going. A crunching sound resonated through the floorboard. She knew this sound. Tires on snow. And from the gravity pull, they were climbing.

Pressure built in her ears. She swallowed to clear them. Higher elevation meant mountains. Why would he go there with a storm on the way?

Bracing for more pain, Shea worked her elbow into a position where she could leverage herself and push up. The throbbing in her cheek increased, but not unbearably. Taking it as a good sign, she eased to a semi-sitting position, but couldn't hold back a groan.

"You awake?" The driver turned his head and looked down at her.

Yep. Vernon Beauchamp. She'd thought him such a nice guy when he helped with the kids' campouts.

"I wondered if you were dead," he added.

The lackadaisical comment sent a terrible chill through her. It sounded like he didn't care if she lived or not.

"Stop," she cried out. "Sick." The upright position set her stomach in a freefall. Or the blow to her head had given her a concussion.

"Oh, heck, no!" Vern yelled. "Don't you dare puke in my truck." He slammed on the brakes and brought the vehicle to a jarring stop.

"Oooooh." Shea's head banged into the back of the front passenger seat and set off another explosion inside her head. She clenched her teeth through the pain.

In a flash, Vern yanked open the back door. "Out. Now."

As he pulled her out by her ankles, her eyes locked on the gloves he wore. Heavy leather. Fringed.

She landed on her butt in three feet of snow. A quick snip with his knife rid her of her bindings. Somehow, she managed to defy the pain in her arms and crawl a few feet away before her stomach purged itself of breakfast.

When the dry heaves abated, she collapsed to the ground, her face cushioned by the fresh powder. The cold felt wonderful against the fire in her cheek. She scooped a handful of snow into her mouth. Once it melted, she swished and spit, and repeated the process two more times.

"You through?" Vern asked from where he leaned against the side of the truck and watched.

She pushed to a sitting position, knees up, rested the

uninjured side of her face on her forearm, and studied him. "Not sure."

"We've wasted enough time here. Let's get going. I want to get to the cabin before this storm hits." He reached for her arm, but she warded him off.

"Don't. Give me a moment." She'd learned her lesson about quick movements. And Vern had already proven he didn't care whether he hurt her or not. Moving onto all fours, she got to her feet with slow, steady movements. It took several more minutes to shuffle her way to the truck.

Vern slammed her door and climbed in behind the wheel. They started forward again, slower this time. More cautious.

Shea scooted all the way to the right side, wanting as much distance as possible between them, but also to study her surroundings. For any chance of escape, she needed a basic understanding of what she faced, both inside the truck and outside.

The landscape changed as they drove. Their ascent grew steeper, the road narrower—if one could call it a road. A goat trail maybe. Heaven forbid they meet an oncoming car. Not that a sane person would test fate in this weather.

On the driver's side, the trees drooped low, their branches laden with snow. What little bit of pavement was still visible disappeared in rapid order. White covered everything and left a two-inch accumulation on the hood of the truck. The heat from the engine no longer melted it

away. Fat snowflakes fell making it difficult to see more than ten feet in any direction.

She looked out the window on her side ... and wished she hadn't. No shoulder. No guardrail. Just a sheer drop as far as she could see. A few scraggly pine trees grew from the sides of the rocky precipice.

It hurt to breathe, whether from the higher altitude or the fear coiled in her chest, she didn't know. "I can't see the edge of the road anymore. Maybe we should turn around."

Vern sat hunched over the steering wheel as though leaning forward would help him see better. His gloved hands gripped the steering wheel, the fringe swaying with every jounce.

She knew those gloves. "It was you who attacked Dee Dee. Why?"

"I thought she was you."

"So, you intended to kidnap me all along? Why?"

"You sound like a parrot. Why-why-why. It's simple. You were bait."

"Did you set the fire in my uncle's house, too? Because I almost died in there."

"Yeah, well, the fire got out of hand."

"And my tires?" she pushed. "Was that a scare tactic?"

The truck fishtailed on a tight S-turn.

"Enough. I need to concentrate."

The defroster fought a losing battle against the ice

forming around the edges of the windshield. The wipers swished back and forth, more scrape than wipe now.

"Vern, this road isn't safe. We have to go back." Could he hear the fear in her voice? The way it trembled? She could.

"Anybody ever say you talk too much? Now, shut up. I need to concentrate."

Every muscle in Shea's body tensed. Her heart fluttered like a wild thing. What kind of insanity drove a man to challenge Mother Nature in this way?

"You've almost gone over the side twice in the last two minutes. Do you even know where you're going?"

"Of course, I know," he snapped. "I got a hunting cabin up here. Been in my family for years and now it's all I have left. The government couldn't take it because they don't know about it. Your boyfriend will have a hard time finding us, but he will. That's what he does." He laughed, a nasty, evil sound.

Despair crept in. "Your beef lies with the government. Not me. And I don't have a boyfriend."

"I'm not a fool, Shea. I watched you for weeks, how you pranced around the diner trying to draw Jonas Cameron's attention. It worked, didn't it? He doesn't know which side is up when you're around."

"It's not like that."

"Don't much matter whether it is or not. He'll come after you. His pride demands it."

She shook her head and swallowed back tears. A bully like Vern thrived on such weakness. He was right. Jonas would come. "Why do you want to hurt Jonas?"

"There you go with the why-ing again."

The truck slid toward the drop-off.

"Watch out!" Shea yelled.

He righted the truck. "Jonas Cameron represents everything wrong with the country, just like the government he works for, the one that's supposed to protect people like me. He goes and sticks his nose where it doesn't belong and steals what ain't his. This time he crossed the wrong people."

Vern glanced sideways at her. "He didn't tell you what he used to do in the Army, did he? How he sneaked around and killed people for the government, the same bunch of politicians who took everything from me. I might not be able to hurt them, but I can make Cameron an example and see he gets what he deserves from the people he wronged."

Her eyes met Vern's in the rearview mirror for a fleeting moment. Pure hatred and a large dose of insanity stared back at her.

"What does all this have to do with me?"

"Like I said, you're the bait. Jonas can no more resist coming after you than a wolf can stop howling at the moon. Now shut up, behave yourself, and don't give me any trouble, and you might live long enough to see the inside of some sheik's tent."

He would ... sell her? His words evoked a horrific image that reduced her to shudders. "Jonas won't know where to find me."

Another wicked chuckle assaulted her ears. "He really didn't tell you anything, did he? Don't worry, if anybody can track you down, he can. It's what he does, finds people and ...." Vern folded his hand like a gun, pointed his index finger, and fired. "But I'll be waiting for him."

Shea flinched from the evil emanating from her captor. Much as she hated the thought, Vern's insinuations struck a chord. Was Jonas a killer?

He'd always had an air of danger about him. Given the right motivation, she had no doubt his ruthless side could respond with exacting precision as circumstances dictated. But the man she'd come to know was no murderer.

The truck slipped again. The rear wheels lost traction, slewed sideways, and caught once more. Sooner or later their luck would run out. "We have to get off this mountain. You're going to kill us."

Vern shrugged. "No place to turn around. Besides, we're almost there. Another mile, two at most. We'll go as far as the truck will take us, and then hoof it."

The thought of walking through knee-deep snow in arctic temperatures, clad in a thin parka, jeans, and sneakers raised Shea's anxiety to a new level. If she didn't tumble down the ravine, break her neck, and freeze to death first her idiot captor's plan would freeze her feet off.

Ahead, the road sloped downward. The drop-off lessened on her side. The descent seemed less steep here with trees and bushes dotting the hillside.

Shea breathed a little easier for a moment ... until she saw the big bull moose in the middle of the road ahead.

Taller than a man by a foot or more and weighing in at over a thousand pounds, the big animal sported a rack bigger than she'd ever seen. A moose this size could do serious damage.

Vern honked his horn and continued to inch forward.

"I don't think you should mess with him."

"Shut up." He continued to creep forward, hand on the horn.

Agitated, the moose lowered his head, snorted, and pawed the ground.

"Big or not, it's still an animal. Animals can't win against a GMC."

"Moose are big, mean, stupid, and very strong. They're all about ruling their territory and proving their strength to hold it. I assure you, this guy will have little trouble pushing your truck off the road. The snow will grease the way."

"We'll see." Vern pressed the gas a little harder, heading straight for the moose.

The animal didn't give an inch.

Neither did Vern.

When the inevitable clash came, the moose's bellow

turned Shea's blood to ice. Wham! The slam of his great horns scraped against the truck and rocked it sideways. The huge animal backed up and head-butted the truck again. Crack! And again.

With each hit, the truck inched closer to the edge.

Vern, sweating now, kept one hand on the wheel and the other on the gearshift. He worked the brake and the clutch with both feet and tried to right their trajectory.

Shea screamed when one of the back wheels slid off the road. The truck rocked for a moment.

CCC

Jonas snatched his phone from Garrett and turned to Wade. "Get me the GPS coordinates."

He turned to leave, but Garrett caught his arm. "Hold on, Jo. You can't go off with incomplete information."

The hardened, emotionless void enveloped him. It always came before a mission. Jonas looked his brother in the eye. "I know what I'm doing. Call me with any additional information. I can't wait any longer."

"We can help you, Jo. Let us in."

Jonas took a deep breath. "Okay. I'm going home to gear up. You can help me by getting everything together."

Wade waved to get his attention. "I'm loading the tracking app onto a spare notebook computer, but it'll take a few minutes. I'll follow you home. Don't leave until I get there."

Jonas nodded and bolted out the door.

Garrett rode his heels. "I'll follow you in my truck."

Jonas nodded again and cranked the engine with a roar. White powder sprayed as he tore off for home.

A welcoming party met them at the small barn by the house—Dad, James, Derek, Kyle, and Archer had all arrived by the time he and Garrett got there. Jonas left his truck running, stepped out, and started issuing orders.

"Dad, take my truck and top off the gas."

His father jumped in behind the wheel of the black and chrome F-150 and headed for the gas pump they used to fuel the ranch vehicles.

"Garrett, I need clothes. Fix me a cold weather pack."

His oldest brother nodded and loped to the house. A couple of changes of underwear, spare socks, and his cold-weather gear should do it. Throw in a few air-activated hand warmers and a thermal blanket, and he'd be all set.

"I'm going with you." John Archer said behind him.

Jonas turned fast, a reflexive action. "No. He said to come alone."

"I've had your back for years and I'm not stopping now. Besides, I'm already packed." He hefted a well-stuffed backpack.

A long tense moment held between the two men. Other than his family, there was no one he trusted more than Archer. If anyone could find Shea and get her out alive, it was him. "Thanks." He turned back to the others. "I need help with the munitions."

"Whatever you need," Derek said.

Jonas led them to a dark corner inside the barn, well away from the stalls. "Help me shove this stuff aside."

With Jonas, Archer, Derek, James, and Kyle working together, the heap of what looked like abandoned equipment was cleared away in minutes and exposed a large, square trapdoor.

Digging a key from his wallet, Jonas inserted it into the embedded lock, grabbed the ring handle, and pulled the hinged door open. Stairs led down, lit by a naked bulb on the ceiling. The others followed him one by one.

At the bottom, he felt for the switch on the wall and flipped it. Brilliant fluorescent light filled the place, chasing all the shadows from the corners.

"Hokey Joe," mumbled one of the men.

"Welcome to the munitions room," Jonas said. His brother, Garrett, had set the storeroom up after he joined the Bureau of International Intelligence. A year later, Wade added to it, and then Jonas. Today, both Garrett and Wade had set up new rooms in their new homes, leaving this one for Jonas alone. No one but the three of them had ever seen the inside before today. Not even their dad.

Several dozen assault rifles of varying design were displayed under glass—Heckler & Koch G36 from Germany, Russian-made AK-12, M4 Carbine from the U.S., and a TAR-21 used by the Israelis. He also had shotguns and too many handguns to count.

Shelves on one side of the room held box upon box of ammunition for the different weapons, while another wall of shelving held specialized equipment—night-vision scopes, thermal imaging, communications gear, grenades, explosives, knives.

"Man, you got a full armory here. This is awesome," Kyle spun in a circle as he tried to take everything in. "Is that a grenade launcher?"

Jonas started snatching up items and handing them off. "Arch, see anything you need, take it."

His dad appeared on the bottom stairstep, eyes wide as he looked around. "Truck is ready to go."

Upstairs again, Jonas locked the trapdoor, but when he started to cover it his dad stopped him. "We'll take care of this part son. You focus on the mission."

Garrett returned with two packs, one on each shoulder. "Unlock the hard shell on the back. We need to stow everything under cover. Derek, grab a case of water from the barn office. I took some MREs from your closet, but why do you have those things? They're awful."

Jonas returned a tight smile. Once upon a time, he'd thought the Meals Ready to Eat a delicacy, a staple of his life. Call it a doomsday mentality, or an inherent need to stay ahead of the game, but he never wanted to be caught unprepared—like today.

With the truck loaded, all the men gathered around.

"He's driving a dark blue, late model GMC truck," James reported.

"We don't pay our hands the kind of money one of those cost. I should have picked up on it." Garrett added.

"Vern didn't keep it here at the ranch," Rascal said walking up. He clapped Jonas on the shoulder. "He always used one of the ranch vehicles. Hey, Jo. I wanted you to know Tiki Fire is fine. No need to split any time worrying about her. We got this end covered."

"I called the State Police for an APB, but if he's gone to ground, they won't find him," James said. "I also put a call into Fowler. I'm guessing you have six hours, eight at the most before he and his team arrives."

Jonas glanced at his watch. "Shea's been gone between three and four hours and I still don't know where to start yet."

Wade's truck screeched to stop beside Jonas's. "I got it," he said and climbed out. "Give me a couple of minutes to show you how to use the app." At the back of his truck, Wade opened a small notebook computer. As promised, Jonas and Archer climbed into Jonas's truck two minutes later.

"Godspeed, son. Bring Shea home and make an honest woman of her, would you?" Dad gripped his hand.

"I plan to, Dad."

Once everyone said their farewell good wishes, Jonas revved the engine and pointed the truck north on Route 93.

"Montana, huh?" Archer asked.

"James says Vern grew up in the mountains near a little town called Sula. See if you can pull it up on a map and calculate the drive time."

Some minutes later, Archer had a route mapped out ."Rand McNally says it's two and a half hours from here. I have to disagree with them given today's weather. Make it three hours, unless the weather deteriorates even more."

Jonas pressed harder on the accelerator.

Archer motioned for him to slow down. "You wrap us around a tree and we'll never find her. Get yourself under control or I'll dump you on the side of the road and go by myself."

Jonas glared at his longtime friend and partner, but he eased off the gas. "Try it."

Chapter Twenty

Shea grabbed onto the back of the seat. "Vern, watch out!"

The moose had backed up several steps. One front hoof still pawed the ground while its head bobbed up and down.

"Shift over to my side," he yelled. "Now!"

She scooted as fast as she could, but the moose had already started its charge.

Metal screeched with the impact.

The truck see-sawed on the edge of the road. More metallic screeching filled the air. The driver's window shattered.

"Turn off the engine!" Shea screamed and covered her face with her arms.

The car started its slide down the slope, rear end first. It picked up speed until the bumper clipped a tree. They ricocheted off in a violent spin and hit a boulder a glancing blow. The jolt flipped the car up on its side where it teetered for an eternity before giving way to gravity.

Over and over they rolled, bounced, and slid until Shea couldn't tell up from down. Without the restraint of a seat belt, she tumbled inside the cab like wet clothes in a dryer, from one side to the other, against the windows, the floorboard, the ceiling, sideways, upside down, and right side up again. The car hit broadside against something solid. Shrieking metal and a harsh rending noise hurt her ears. The truck shuddered twice and settled.

Shock held Shea still for long seconds. Opening her eyes, she discovered the truck had landed on its right side at a sixty-degree angle. She'd ended up in a ball between the front and back seats with the door handle pressing into her spine.

The tricky position afforded her a surreal, tunnel-vision look at the path of destruction left by the truck in its downhill plunge—broken trees, gouged earth, torn bushes, saplings uprooted or sheared off. And snow. Big flakes swirled through the air, a curtain of white blanketing everything. She'd fallen into a nightmare snow globe, one shaken too hard.

A single snowflake drifted through the rear door window now devoid of glass. It landed on her nose. Cold

air curled around her, a reminder of the imminent danger of the storm closing in.

"Vern?" she whispered.

No response.

Devastation lay inside the truck as well. Windows shattered. Doors bowed. Shards of glass everywhere. Trash, pens, a jacket, his hat, a shoe—no rhyme or reason.

"Vern?" she called, louder this time.

Still no answer.

Her breaths came in shallow gasps. An anvil sat on her chest, even as her heart raced with the realization of her predicament. Light faded in and out while pinpoints of darkness flickered at the edge of her vision. Panicking wouldn't help. She had to calm down.

Several deep breaths brought her pulse under control, but crane her neck as she might, Shea couldn't see much from her awkward position. She moved her legs one at a time in slow precise movements until she managed to unfold from the cramped space. She worked her way to a semi-recumbent posture, surprised to not find any significant injuries beyond what she'd already sustained at the hands of her kidnapper. Pain aplenty. Tomorrow might find her bedridden, but for now, the shock and adrenalin flooding her body masked the minor stuff.

The truck shifted when she tried to stand, not much, but enough to freeze her movements. A large tree blocked both the front and rear passenger windows. From what she could tell, the truck had ended up near the bottom of the slope. Sounds of rushing water gurgled somewhere nearby.

Stretching and contorting, she managed a glimpse into the front of the truck cab. The windshield remained intact. The laminated glass had done its job, though the spiderweb of cracks made it impossible to see much.

Fearful of setting another slide in motion but knowing she had to get out before the storm turned the truck into her tomb, Shea eased upright, got her feet under her, and leaned between the front seats.

Nope, no Vern. With the driver's door ripped off, had he fallen out? Or bailed on purpose?

He didn't matter at this point. She had to help herself first. Had to get out of this mangled jumble of metal and then survive the coming storm.

First, a scavenger hunt. Her backpack was in the front. She leaned forward, stretched out, and caught one of the straps. She added two loose bottles of water, a crushed bag of chips, a package of beef jerky, a flashlight, and a small duffel.

Inching forward a little more provoked another groan, but the truck remained stable. In the dash jockey box, she found a lighter, a pack of chewing gum ... and a handgun.

Stuffing everything into her pack or the duffel, Shea stood on the door that had become her floor. Now came the hard part—climbing out.

She could kick out the windshield and risk tipping the

balance of the truck. What were the chances she'd survive a second roll? Into the freezing water?

Turning to the rear window, she studied it. Intact, but too small for her to easily fit through.

With a heavy sigh, she looked up at the open window above. Her last option. All the moving around had reignited the fire in her cheek and behind her eye. Other little twinges, aches, and stings made themselves known, too. She wiped wetness from eyes.

"If you put your mind to something, chances are you can make it happen, but tears won't help," she whispered. The thought arrived unsolicited. Something her father used to say. *Mind over matter.* While she couldn't conquer the physical discomfort, she could overlook the pain long enough to get out of this death trap.

Hoisting her backpack and the small duffel over one shoulder, Shea put a foot on the right front seat headrest and pushed up. Just like stepping into a stirrup only with the wrong foot. She chucked the backpack through the window opening, threw the duffel after it, and then slipped both of her arms through. Balancing on one leg, she found the driver's headrest with her other foot and pushed off. Tearing sounds told her the ragged remains of the window glass were shredding her jacket. No matter. She couldn't stop now.

Grunting and praying, lurching and pushing paid off at last. It took more effort than she anticipated to hoist herself up and out, but she did it. Freed herself from what could have become her coffin. She rounded up the pack and duffel, slid to the edge of the undercarriage, and dropped to the ground.

Her poor head throbbed more than ever, but she dared not stop, not with the temperature dropping. Exposure was her number one concern.

The snow continued to fall in the eerie silence, slower now but steady. Shea knew all too well how it muffled sounds. She glanced around in nervous suspense, half expecting a bear or a wolf to appear. Or worse, Vern.

Without her phone, she had no idea of the time, but the darkening sky concerned her. Sundown came early in the mountains anyway, but with the storm, she had a feeling it would come sooner than she wanted.

She looked around the immediate area. Vern's GMC lay on its side, dented and scraped and almost unrecognizable, and tilted at a crazy angle. No wonder she'd had a hard time getting out.

The truck bed was empty. All the carefully packed supplies he'd stowed in the back littered the mountainside—granola bars, bottles of water, bottles of cola, cans of soup, clothing—and a single cowboy boot.

Excited at the prospect of putting something other than canvas on her feet, Shea looked farther afield until she spied the boot's mate several yards uphill. Dropping her backpack and the duffel on the ground, she started

crawling. The leather boots and scattered supplies might very well make the difference in whether she survived the coming night. She needed to gather what she could and get back to the top as soon as possible.

The steep grade made reaching the second boot difficult, but she reached it and then let gravity pull her back down to the truck. The boots looked way too big for her size sevens but with luck, she might be able to squeeze her sneaker-clad feet into them.

Her short foray up the hill brought a new point home— no way she'd be able to climb all the way back up, at least not from here. The incline was too steep and without much to hold onto. She'd have to make her way along the bottom until the grade lessened.

Holding on to the side of the truck, she moved to the rear of the vehicle. From there, she had a clear look at the stream below, iced over at the edges. Lucky the truck hadn't plunged into the freezing water.

Now to gather her supplies. Vern's duffel was the first target. Inside it, she found a flannel shirt, a thermal undershirt, and a pair of woolen socks. Doffing her coat and thin cotton blouse, she slipped on the undershirt, added the flannel over it, and slipped her coat on again. The socks she stuffed back in the duffel. Brrr. So cold.

The rest of the stuff she emptied on the ground with the items from the truck, the gun in particular. Foraging through the debris on the hillside, she scored a small medical kit, two granola bars, and a whole case of water. She added several bottles to the duffel as well.

As she rounded the truck again, Shea caught her reflection in the still intact driver-side mirror. Creeping closer, she knelt and peered at her image. A bloody gash split her left eyebrow near her temple, crusted over now. More worrisome was the swelling around her left eye. Her cheek had purpled, her eye bloodshot and almost swollen closed.

Her fingers feathered across the damaged skin before moving to the side of her skull. She found a lump there the size of a lemon. From Vern's fist or from the crash? No wonder her head ached.

Nothing she could do about it at the moment. With the snow coming down and hypothermia a real danger, she had to get moving. Find shelter. Somehow, she had to get up this ravine and back on the road. Right before they went over the side he'd said, "Another mile or so." If she could reach the top and find the road, maybe she could find this mysterious cabin.

Hoisting her backpack and the duffel over one shoulder, she took another look at the steep, almost impossible grade above her, and set out to follow the river for a bit.

Distance and time lost all meaning as she stumbled over exposed roots, loose rocks, and treacherous sinkholes. The stream grew wider as she traveled. Deeper, too. But the slope remained steep.

At some point, she decided to climb again. The ascent didn't appear it would get any easier, and she didn't want to be down here after dark. Finding the road seemed her only hope for surviving this disaster. No one would look for her here and she surely wouldn't find Vern's cabin from the bottom of a ravine.

Choosing her way with care, Shea grabbed onto spindly trees, branches, rocks, roots—whatever afforded a hand or foothold. The backpack and duffel shifted and threatened to throw her off balance every time she reached for another grip. She had to readjust them several times.

A quarter of the way up the embankment, she reached for a rock and found a small animal instead. Startled, the critter skittered off. Equally startled, Shea jerked her hand away.

The duffel slipped off and tumbled back down the hill.

"Agggghhh!" she screamed in frustration. Did she continue on, or go back down to retrieve it? How much did she need the supplies it held?

The decision was made for her when the root she stood on pulled free from the ground. She grabbed onto a sapling but lost the backpack. A moment later, the sapling broke and sent her plummeting after the supplies.

Shea rolled, bounced, banged off a tree, and slid right on past the backpack feet first into the icy water. Old hurts screamed with renewed pain. New hurts joined them. In the blink of an eye, her situation had gone beyond desperate to dire.

Submerged to her hips, the boots filled with water. The freezing water stole her breath and numbed her feet.

Gasping, she struggled out of the water and into the wooded area, her body convulsing with shudders. Desperation soon gave way to lethargy. So tired. Every step forward came with two steps back. Was this how it all ended?

Chapter Twenty-One

"Stop here, before the snow gets any deeper. We need the chains."

Jonas hit the steering wheel with his open palm. He didn't want to stop, didn't want to lose the time, but Archer was right. With the snow falling and the weather forecast calling for twenty inches accumulation, they needed the chains.

The GPS showed Shea's phone well off the main road in the mountains ahead. The snow would be deeper in the higher elevations. And slippery as a pig sty.

He slowed the F-150 and pulled off the road onto a somewhat flat shoulder and put the truck in park. He opened his door the same time as his friend did and met him at the rear. Under the hard cover, they found the box of chains and took two each for the tires on their respective side. Spreading the chains so they lay straight and flat with the hook locks on the outside, Jonas spread one set over the rear tire and straightened them. He did the same with the front tire. With the chains in place he stood and called across the roof. "Ready?"

"Almost." Archer rose from his crouch a few minutes later and gave a thumb's up.

Jonas climbed back in behind the wheel, put both windows down, and yelled, "Tell me when."

"Ready when you are. Slow and easy."

Putting the truck in gear, Jonas eased off the brake enough to allow the torque converter to inch the truck forward.

Archer made hand gestures to keep him moving. "Keep coming. A little more. Stop." Throwing the gear into park again, Jonas got out and began the task of locking the chains in place and tightening the links on his two tires. Fifteen minutes after stopping, they started off again. Another fifteen minutes and Archer motioned him to slow down.

"There's a side road up ahead on the right. It's the last turn on the map for thirty miles."

"Does her signal lead there?"

"Yeah. I didn't say anything before because I wasn't sure, but the signal hasn't moved much in the last half hour. They've either stopped or are going so slow it doesn't measure. I'm guessing they aren't far now."

Jonas spotted the turnoff. Didn't get much traffic from the looks of the snow covering it. At least they still had pavement.

Ten miles in, the road narrowed and the incline began. Up the side of the mountain, isolated and icy, it didn't bode well with the storm gathering momentum. What was that fool thinking?

The snow came down in earnest now. Big flakes, and lots of them. The few glimpses of asphalt disappeared. Not long after, the feel of the road changed again when the pavement gave way to dirt. Worse, it narrowed still more until the truck had no more than two feet clearance on either side.

"Looks like we're on the right track." Archer turned the notebook toward Jonas and pointed at the map.

Jonas chewed his lip. His shoulders ached, a side effect of anxiety. He'd never had a problem compartmentalizing before, but now, with Shea in danger, everything seemed heightened. How had he let this happen?

"Man, you need to ease up on the steering wheel. You grip it much harder and it's going to crumble in your hands."

Jonas flexed his hands and loosened his white-knuckled grip. Thank goodness for Archer and his voice of reason.

"Better," Archer said. "Remember. Frosty. We stay

frosty. Shouldn't be difficult in these temperatures."

Words didn't want to form, so he nodded instead. Frosty. Loose. Focused on the goal. Nothing more.

They wound up and down, around S-curves and hairpin turns for another thirty minutes. Finally, near the bottom of one of the twists, Archer pointed to a rough patch in the road ahead. "Look there. Pull over."

"Do you not see this road? I can't pull over. There's no shoulder." He stopped in the middle instead.

Archer hopped out and side-stepped with his back against the truck to where the snow had been disturbed.

Jonas followed.

In full tracker mode, Archer went to the uphill side and pointed at the ground. "Moose tracks. Looks like it tangled with a vehicle. And look here," he strode to the other side where the embankment fell away. Several broken saplings and a good-sized tree a foot below the road had been snapped in two. Raw dirt showed through the pristine snow on both sides and all the way across the road.

Gut clenching with dread, Jonas peered over the side. "Looks like a demolition team went through here."

"More like a GMC truck. Look down toward the bottom. You can see a glimmer of chrome. We need to get down there." Archer started toward the rear of their truck.

Heart hammering, Jonas didn't move. "But the GPS shows Shea's phone further ahead. She's my priority right now. We can't afford any more delays."

Archer changed course and got in Jonas's face. "It shows Shea's cell phone, not her. Vern had her phone. He sent you the picture from it. Shea could be down there, hurt. Do you want to take the chance she's not?"

No. He couldn't take that chance. If she was with Vern, at least she was alive. Down there, she could die from her injuries or exposure by the time they figured it out. "We need rope. Lots of it. Looks like a hundred-fifty-foot drop. I'll go down first, and relay what I find. Tell you what we'll need."

He returned to the truck and switched off the engine before joining Archer at the rear again.

"Cell coverage is nonexistent up here but these should work over a short distance. Channel six." He handed one of the walkie-talkies to Jonas, did a squawk test, and dropped his into one of his cargo pants pockets.

Jonas tied one of the longer ropes to the trailer hitch, looped a length around his waist and started his descent in short bouncing jumps. One-hundred-twenty-feet down he reached the crashed GMC.

Pressing the talk button on the walkie-talkie, he said, "Looks like the slide started out butt first and banged off a couple of trees before rolling. The right side is wedged against a big Ponderosa. No one inside. I'm checking for tracks."

"Roger."

He spotted the shoe prints first. Smallish. Tennis shoes

if he wasn't mistaken. They'd slipped in the snow trying to climb up the hill and left a swath sliding down the hill again. There, where the slide ended, more tracks. Footprints. Handprints, too. And a thin, gauzy-looking blouse.

Excitement slammed into him, making his heart race again. But with it came the fear. Shea had been here, but where had she gone?

A couple of steps away, he spotted more tracks. Bigger. From the size of them and the narrow, square-shaped heel, he guessed they came from a man's cowboy boots. The prints led down toward the bubbling stream at the bottom.

But no tennis shoes?

The radio squawked in his hand. "Go ahead," Jonas answered.

"I got the binoculars out to scan the upper area. I think I found a set of footprints about twenty-five yards down."

"Man or woman?"

"Can't tell from here. I'd guess man. They lead west and up toward the road."

Jonas smiled. The boot-sized prints he found had to be Shea's. She'd recognized the folly of tromping around in the snow in flimsy canvas shoes. She must have shoved her feet into a pair of Vern's boots. That had to be it. Smart girl.

"Sounds like Vern bailed. I found footprints here, too.

Smaller ones. They lead west and down toward the water. "I'm going to follow them. Do what you can to stay with me. And keep an eye on where your prints lead. Squawk me if you find anything."

"Ditto."

As he'd surmised, the boot prints did indeed lead down to the water. One of his greatest abilities allowed him to get inside the head of his prey to gain insight into their reasoning.

Jonas couldn't think of Shea as his prey or his target, though. She was his life. A mistake here and he could lose her.

With a mighty effort, he shoved those thoughts aside and trudged on. When she couldn't get up the hill back at the crash site, she must have moved on in hopes of finding a lesser grade she could climb.

She couldn't have gotten far in this rough terrain. With her much shorter legs, exhaustion would soon take a toll.

A sense of urgency gripped him. Prolonged exposure in freezing temperatures could result in frostbite or worse. The 'worse' scenario worried him.

The snow obscured the tracks, but not enough to lose them ... until they played out.

He whirled around, eyes searching everywhere with frantic urgency. And then he spotted her. She lay on her back several feet up the hill, partially hidden by a low bush.

"Shea!" He scrambled to her side. "Shea, baby, wake

up." Oh, dear Lord in heaven help me, she was soaking wet. And her face ...

He stripped his gloves off and tugged at the oversized cowboy boots on her feet. Water spilled out when he finally got them off. He quickly stripped the thin sneakers and soggy socks off her, too.

Her feet and toes were ghostly white and icy cold. Not good. Her jeans were wet as well and had already formed an ice crust. Thankfully, she remained dry above the waist. A miracle.

He glanced up, saw the slide marks in the snow, and concluded she'd tried to climb up the embankment. Unsuccessfully. The momentum of her fall must have taken her into the water.

Pressing her small feet inside his jacket, he called Archer on the walkie-talkie. She needed out of her wet jeans in the worst way, but he had nothing to wrap her in.

"Go ahead," Archer said.

"I found her. Twelve-hundred yards west of the crash site. I need the hand warmers and the thermal blanket. And bring rope for a sling. Fast, Archer. She's conscious but unresponsive."

"On it."

He heard the roar of his truck above. The next minute, Archer called on the walkie-talkie. "I think I'm above you. Can you see me?"

"No, but I hear the truck. Close enough. Get down

here."

"Two minutes. I need to collect everything."

A short time later, Archer rappelled his way down the mountainside. Disengaging at the bottom he ran the few feet to Shea's side, carrying all the gear Jonas had requested.

"What in the world happened?"

"Don't know. My guess is she tried to climb up." He pointed to the slide area. "But fell and tumbled into the water. I got her shoes off, but didn't want to remove her jeans without something to wrap her in."

"Got the thermal blanket right here, man. Strip her down." Archer unloaded an extra coil of rope from his shoulders and pulled the hand warmers and thermal blanket from the pack on his back. "I brought a med kit, too."

Jonas looked at the gash over her eyebrow. It had crusted over and no longer bled. He decided it could wait for now.

The wet denim wanted to cling to her skin, while the frosted bits of the fabric made it inflexible. He got the pants over her hips but needed Archer's help shimmying them down her legs. He pulled Shea onto his lap and turned to his partner. "Tug the pants off her legs for me."

Archer grabbed hold of the waistband and pulled, but with little result.

Jonas glared when the other man had to work his big hands under the fabric over and over again to peel the jeans away from her skin.

"Not looking man, just doing my job. Here's the Mylar. Wrap her up while I open the Hot Hands."

A quick shake unfolded the silver blanket, but he needed Archer's help again to wrap it around her. Resourceful as ever, Archer pulled a roll of duct tape from his pack and tore off several strips. "Wrap this tape around her legs and waist to hold it in place. I'll get the rope for the sling."

Jonas made quick work of securing the blanket and shoved the hand warmers on her feet.

Archer pulled his Ka-Bar knife from its leg sheath, measured out several lengths of nylon cord, cut them, and tossed them to Jonas one by one.

The trip back up would be arduous. Using the lengths of rope Archer had prepared, Jonas weaved a piggyback litter arrangement—one under her bottom, another around her back and under her armpits, with butterfly loops for his shoulders. A carabiner at his chest secured the ropes through the spring-loaded shackle clip. He'd have Archer add an additional rope at her waist to bind her to him and stabilize any movement during the climb. Essentially, she'd be strapped on his back, legs dangling. Dead weight.

While Archer finished the sling, Jonas tried to wake Shea. "C'mon, baby. I need you to wake up." He patted the uninjured side of her face but couldn't bring himself to apply more than a gentle tap. "Shay-Shay. Wake up, honey.

Imperfect Lies

I need to see those beautiful eyes."

Her good eye fluttered open. The injured one had swollen shut. "Jonas?" she croaked.

"Yeah, baby. I got you. Listen up, I need you to understand what we're doing."

"Cold. Head hurts."

"I know. We need to get you up this hill. My truck's up there. It's warmed up and waiting for you."

"I tried ... fell. The water."

"You're safe now. We got you out of those wet clothes and shoes. Now we need to get you up the hill. Okay?"

"I don't think I can climb. Everything hurts. Why are there two of you?"

"Archer's here."

"No. Two of *you*."

"You had a knock on the head. No worries. And you don't have to climb, baby. We're going to tie you on my back. Arch will pull us up. Ready for a bumpy ride?"

She drew her head back and stared at him, her one good eye tracking back and forth between his. "I'm too heavy."

He grinned. "Nah, if I can carry Cinnamon you're a cinch."

Her lips twitched at his silliness. "You saying I weigh as much as a horse?"

"No, not that much."

"Stop," she groaned. "Please. Hurts to laugh."

"Okay, pay attention. Archer's going to pick you up and drape you over my back. You have one job—wrap your arms around me but don't choke me. And hang on."

"That's two jobs."

With her securely tied in place, Archer placed her hands on the rope attached to the carabiner on Jonas's chest. "Hold here. Lay your head against his back. Close your eyes if you want, but don't wiggle once we start moving. Got it?"

"Got it," she answered.

"Okay, I'm heading back. I'll use the truck hitch to pull you both up real slow."

"No, there's a winch in the back. Use it."

"You got a winch? Anything you don't have?"

"Yeah, a doctor."

"Soon, my brother. Soon. I'll holler when I've got the winch ready."

Several minutes passed before they heard Archer's yell.

"Here we go, baby. My truck has a nice, warm heater waiting for us."

The winch took longer but offered a smoother, steadier journey. He wanted to go slow for Shea's sake. The gash on her forehead, the swelling and heavy bruising, seeing double—her injuries worried him. You shouldn't take chances with a concussion, not that they had a choice.

Fifteen agonizing minutes later, Archer grabbed

Jonas's harness and pulled him over the edge. Less than a minute more, he had Shea untied. "Get the door, man. Let's get her out of this cold."

Jonas hurried to the truck's rear door and yanked it open, ignoring his screaming muscles. He climbed inside, reached for Shea, and pulled her onto his lap. "Shut the door."

Archer eased the door closed. After stowing their gear, he slid in behind the wheel. "Visibility has worsened. I'm not sure if we can make it down the mountain."

Jonas peered through the window at the sky. "Well, we can't stay out here. The gas will run out before this storm passes," Jonas answered.

"Cabin," Shea mumbled.

He had to strain to hear her whisper. "What?"

"Vern has a hunting cabin. Close. He said if the road got too bad, we would walk."

Archer grabbed the notebook computer. "Fowler didn't say anything about a cabin. You sure?"

"No. But it's what he said."

"The tracker shows her phone's signal is somewhere off to the right. You thinking what I'm thinking?"

Jonas nodded. "Let's find the cabin before he does."

Chapter Twenty-Two

Here on the leeward side of the mountain, the snowfall had all but stopped. The wind had also died down, leaving an eerie hush as though Mother Nature took a nap.

Inches of fresh snow covered the ground, making it difficult to discern the road's boundary.

"You okay?" Jonas asked from the backseat where he held Shea close to share his body heat.

"I don't know, man. Snow's let up, but there's not enough traction with this much accumulation on the ground. I learned to drive in Alaska when I was ten. I can drive anywhere, but this makes me nervous. One good slide and we're going over."

"Stop the truck. I'll get out and break trail for you."

When the truck eased to a stop, Jonas slid Shea off his

lap to the seat. "Rest, pretty girl. I'll be right back." He zipped his coat to the chin, snugged his musher hat down over his ears, and tugged his gloves back on before opening the door. Outside, he donned a pair of Z87 certified goggles. A necessity in these temperatures. Tempered, anti-fog, and with UV protection. No one wanted frozen eyeballs.

Snow reached his knees and forced him to slog his way to the front of the vehicle. From here the road descended into a shallow valley with no more than a foot clearance on either side for the truck. The drop-off remained on the passenger side, but it had a lesser grade here.

Survivable if they went over but losing the truck would pose a huge problem. It was their sole heat source at the moment and might very well make the difference in whether they got out once the storm passed. If he slid over the side, on the other hand, Archer could throw him a rope and pull him up. Supposing he didn't break his neck.

Shelter topped their priority list. They had to find this enigmatic cabin while the lull in the storm lasted.

Jonas moved with slow, cautious lunges through the deep snow, feeling his way to find the edge of the road. Once he identified it, he gestured for Archer to stay well left of where he walked.

The insidious cold penetrated to his bones despite his winter gear. The temperature had to have dropped into the low teens, maybe lower. Prolonged exposure in these conditions meant certain death. He couldn't help but wonder whether Vernon Beauchamp still lived but wouldn't count him out. Desperation and determination made powerful motivators.

Twenty minutes passed with a slow but diligent exploration of the road. Still no sign of the cabin. He hoped for all their sakes she hadn't hallucinated it.

Archer lowered his window and shouted. "Hey."

Jonas looked back, but Arch had put the window up again and now pointed off to the left at a clearing that extended a good thirty yards into the side of the mountain. And there it was. The small cabin. Weathered timbers provided a disguise for the building in the woods.

Jonas made his way over in search of a place where a vehicle could enter. He discovered it ten feet ahead and motioned for Archer to follow him.

"Hold up," Archer yelled through the window again. He put the truck in park and pulled on his own ski mask and cold weather goggles. "My turn. You warm up while I recon."

Nodding, Jonas took Archer's place behind the wheel, grateful for the heater. He'd almost broken the first rule in his line of work—scout the area, know the enemy. Cold slowed brain function.

He glanced at Shea in the backseat, not surprised to see her eyes closed. A quick scan outside showed how low the heavy cloud cover had dropped. It shrouded the mountains and valley on this eastern side of the range. Nightfall would arrive soon, which could work for them or against them. Despite all Vern's familiarity with the area, he didn't have the training, skills, or combat experience that Jonas and Archer possessed. If anyone could find the fool who'd led them on this wild goose chase, Arch could.

His best friend and long-time partner disappeared in the trees several yards ahead. He would make several widening circuits of the cabin before he deemed it safe.

Under normal circumstances, Jonas would have accompanied him, taking up an overlapping route so they covered three times as much territory as a lone scout. But he wouldn't leave Shea unprotected again.

Every instinct demanded he take action and invoke justice. Instead, he sat here with her, alone in the truck. Vulnerable. Sitting ducks.

He spent his time waiting for Archer's return by listing out what they would need to take with them should they have to walk out. Not the best option, given Shea's condition and lack of shoes. If it came down to that, he'd likely have to carry her. Or construct something she could lie on.

Movement in the rearview mirror caught his attention. Jonas twisted to look out the rear window, Sig Sauer P226 in hand. When he recognized Archer's gait, he lowered the weapon.

Shea didn't move when he opened the door and

stepped out.

"Didn't find a single track. He's either not made it this far or found shelter for the night. The cabin doesn't look like it's been used in months, maybe years."

Nodding, Jonas jerked his head toward the truck. "You drive. Follow me and stay in the truck with Shea until I get a fire going."

Archer didn't argue.

The snow decreased to ankle-depth in the wooded area, making it easier to traverse. The cabin had a simple design—one door with a simple latch and no windows. Inside, he found a single room with a fireplace. A built-in bed with a thin mattress filled one corner. A small, wood-burning stove occupied a niche in another corner along with a small wash tub and an assortment of dented cookware. A rough-hewn table, one rickety chair and an inch of dust were the only other things inside.

Outside he found a stack of firewood. Filling his arms, Jonas carried several loads in to fill the wood bin by the fireplace. Once he had the fire crackling, he dragged the mattress from the bed, flipped it over, and positioned it on the floor in front of the hearth. Shea needed a constant source of warmth. She'd lost too much of her core body heat from the dip in the stream.

Satisfied, he hurried back to the truck, nodding when Archer climbed out. "I'll bring Shea inside and come back to help you with the gear."

Jonas opened the rear door. "Shea, baby, I need you to wake up. Let's get you inside next to the fire."

She stirred but didn't open her eyes. "Jonas?" Her voice came out in a whispery, raspy croak.

"Yeah, it's me, baby. I'm going to pick you up, okay? Snuggle in close. I've got you." He pulled her from the backseat, got an arm under her legs, and carried her to the cabin. Inside, he settled her on the mattress, making sure to keep her well wrapped in the thermal blanket. "Lay here for a bit. I've got to help Archer get our stuff."

She didn't answer but rolled onto her side to face the fire.

It took only one trip to unload what they needed from the truck.

"I'll get a bucket of snow and see about making something warm to drink." Archer grabbed a couple of the larger pots and headed back outside.

Shea had drawn her knees up and curled into a fetal position.

Jonas knelt at the end of the mattress, concerned about her lower extremities. He reached for her feet and peeled away the hand warmers. Still too cold. Her little toes felt like ice cubes, the skin papery white. Not good.

He turned her shoulders and pressed her onto her back with the soles of her feet on the mattress. "Lie flat for me, pretty girl."

Her whole body seemed on the verge of convulsing

with the violence of her shivers.

Stripping his jacket off, he laid it over her torso for added warmth. Next, he yanked his shirt free from his pants and scooted forward until he could tuck her feet against his stomach.

"Shhhheesh." Gritting his teeth, he held her feet in place, branding his abs with their outline. His core heat should kickstart her own body's temperature regulation. Frostbite was nothing to play around with.

When his own discomfort began to subside, he moved his hands to her ankles, chafing the skin with light pressure in slow circles. His hands moved higher, to her calves, her knees, using friction and gentle squeezes to agitate the circulation to her extremities. Up and down, knees to ankles, front and back, squeeze, release, rub.

Little by little, her shivers diminished in intensity until she lay quiet, staring up at him. "Thank you," she whispered again.

Archer knelt by her side. "Let me help you sit up. I've got some hot tea to warm your insides."

Jonas took the moment to examine her feet, fearful he'd find her skin still too-white, a tell-tale indication of circulation problems. He grinned when he found rosy pink toes with red-painted toenails instead. "Very nice. I like the flowers," he remarked on the design adorning the big toes.

"Buddy, you need to stop stroking her like a cat and drink some of this tea." Archer kneed Jonas's shoulder and offered a second battered tin cup, his gruff voice full of amusement.

Jonas stopped mid-stroke and realized his chafing, kneading, circulatory-stimulating massage had turned into a languorous, sensory delight. He set Shea's feet firmly on the mattress and scooted away.

Oblivious, she sat up with Archer's help. "I don't suppose this place has a bathroom, does it?"

Dumbfounded, all Jonas could do was stare at her. Of course, she would need to use facilities. "Uh ...."

"Believe it or not, there's an outhouse about fifteen yards behind the cabin. Let's wrap you up and I'll—"

"I got this," Jonas said.

Later, over a tasty soup Archer concocted from freeze-dried rations, they discussed next steps. Shea no longer shivered, but neither did she stray far from the fire. "Do you think he's still out there?"

Jonas had given a lot of thought to Vern's whereabouts and what actions he might take if he was still breathing. "From the little we learned before we lost cell coverage, Vern grew up in these parts. You said he claimed this was his cabin. If so, he knows his way around the area. It wouldn't surprise me to find him frozen on the hillside, but I'd put my money on him holing up somewhere for the night. A cave, a den, some ground burrow."

"I ... I don't know where we are. We were already in the mountains when I came to."

Jonas's eyes locked on the bruise and the cut over her eye. The left side of her face looked almost black in the firelight. Her words made him rage inside.

"We're over the border of Montana near a little place called Sula," Archer answered. "Tell us what happened, Shea."

She related how Clint had come for her, of seeing Vern on the side of the road, and how he'd dragged her to his truck. "Did you find Clint? I don't know what happened to him."

"Somebody reported his car abandoned on the side of the road with the engine running," Jonas explained. "Kyle found him unconscious in the ditch. Said he looked like he'd been pistol whipped. Last report we had he'd come around but Doc Burdette shipped him off to Pocatello for a CT scan."

Her fingers slid over her injured cheek.

"Vern better hope he freezes to death before I get to him," Jonas grumbled. Part of him hoped he survived, while another side hoped he'd succumbed to the cold.

"Shea, we found two rifles from his truck," Archer interrupted. "Do you know what happened to his handgun? Did he have any other weapons?"

"I found a gun in the jockey box. I thought it might come in handy, so I put it in my backpack."

"Jockey box?" Archer asked.

"Glove compartment," Jonas answered. "Local

vernacular."

Archer nodded and went to the front door where he found her pack in the corner. Sure enough, he found the weapon. "Huh, would you look at this. An old Colt Diamondback .38 special. My dad had one of these. They're ancient."

"We don't know if he has a weapon now or not. Since his tracks didn't return to the crash site, I doubt he's armed." Jonas hoped he'd made the correct assumption.

"If that's the case, it would be stupid for him to come after us." Archer did several fast draw maneuvers, pretending to point the relic of a handgun at a mock target. "Although a desperate rat is the most dangerous enemy."

"I agree. We should be fine for the night. It's too dangerous and too cold for him to move around in the dark, but we'll keep watch anyway. First light, we check out the road conditions. If it's no worse, I say we move out."

"Agreed." Archer emptied the fully-loaded chamber of the Colt and stowed it in his duffel. "How about you, little girl?"

"Whatever you think best. All I want is heat. Please don't let the fire go out." She closed her eyes and pulled the thermal blanket to her chin.

Jonas stared at her profile for the longest time. It was difficult to assess the damage to her beautiful face given the discoloration and swelling, but he thought he could detect a slight indentation along her cheekbone. A possible

fracture. All the more reason to leave this place as soon as possible. She needed medical attention.

Archer slipped out the door without a word. They'd take turns keeping watch throughout the night.

Jonas, who'd taken the dawn watch, stomped his feet at the cabin's door. Sometime during the night, the storm had dissipated. The sun crept over the horizon bringing clear, blue skies and hope for a beautiful day. Still bitter cold, but a real spirit lifter.

Archer had hot water going, enough for tea anyway. Ablutions would have to wait until they got back to civilization. Holding a finger to his lips, he pointed at the still sleeping Shea. If anything, she'd inched closer to the now dying fire.

Jonas tiptoed to her side and tucked the blanket tighter. She rolled over and smiled at him. "Hi."

Her voice heavy with sleep stirred something inside him. His heart ached for the beautiful, broken girl. The damage to her face, all too visible in the morning light, made him sick. Her left eye remained swollen closed, the discoloration darker and more menacing. He'd never understood how a man could take his fists to a woman or a child.

"Good to see you awake, little girl," Archer said. "We've got enough hot water for one round of tea. Drink up while I take a last look around. Fifteen minutes and we hit the road."

Shea gifted him with a lopsided grimace of a smile.

Jonas squatted beside her and held out the battered cup.

Behind him, the door opened and closed as Archer left. A moment later it opened again.

"We got a problem," Archer yelled.

Through the door, a thick, black cloud of smoke rose over the tree line. "What is it?" Shea asked.

"Wildfire."

"Can't be," Jonas said. "It's winter,"

"Oh, it's possible. Winter wildfires don't last long because of the snow and ground moisture, but trust me, they are very real and every bit as deadly as the summer fires you hear about. We have to go. Now."

Jonas slipped Shea's arms into her jacket and secured the thermal blanket around her legs. He didn't take time to put the hand warmers on her feet, just thrust them into her hands. "Put these on in the truck.

He picked her up and ran.

Archer had the truck's rear door open by the time they reached it and now helped load their gear in the back.

With Shea settled, Jonas raced with Archer back to the cabin for the rest of their stuff. Once they'd stowed everything, he dove in behind the wheel and pulled out onto the miserable excuse for a road, spinning the wheels in the process. "We had two feet of snow dumped on us yesterday. And now we have a wildfire? Doesn't make sense." He yelled over the whine of the engine.

"The whole northwest United States went through the worse drought in a hundred years last summer. Timbers are dry. The fire will jump from treetop to treetop. It's how fires like this get out of control. The good news comes when the fire hits a clearing. Unfortunately, I didn't see many clearings on the way up.

"You think Vern set it?" Shea asked.

"Given the weather last night and this morning, I don't think we can blame lightning or careless campers."

"You pegged it right about him still being dangerous." Jonas peered out the driver's side as the smoke grew thicker. "Can we outrun this thing?"

Archer shrugged. "I'd say we got a fifty-fifty shot if you're willing to take a few chances with the speed, my friend."

Chapter Twenty-Three

The snow had stopped overnight, which helped them as they fled the cabin. Following the swath cut by the truck the day before, Jonas pushed for speed, thanking Archer in silence for insisting they stop to put on the tire chains.

As they topped the first curve and turned down again, this time into the face of the fire, he caught glimpses of the flames through the trees. The truck fishtailed toward the drop-off, but Jonas tapped the brakes and maneuvered the truck through the slide.

Archer grabbed hold of the dashboard in front of him. "Would you try and keep this thing on the road? I don't need to be tenderized before I'm barbequed."

Jonas's lips twitched, but Shea's yelp when she slid against a door erased any thought of humor. He and Archer had walked some fine lines in their time together. They'd tempted fate and spit in the eye of the devil, but now ... she changed everything. He wouldn't take chances with her life.

Thinking about Shea brought out emotions. He couldn't afford the touchy-feely stuff right now, not if he intended to get them all out alive. He switched to automaton mode. Cold. A machine. "Frosty it is," he murmured for Archer's ears only.

They passed the spot where Vern and Shea had gone over the side. The gouged earth and broken trees gave it the look of a raw wound.

Loud crackling and another gasp from Shea drew his attention to the outside mirror on his door. Not bothering with the snow-covered brush on the ground, the fire jumped from tree limb to tree limb like a monkey on speed, moving fast and right at them. No snow to impede the spread through here. The western white pine boughs were too skinny to hold much snow weight.

He clicked the button for inside air and checked to ensure all the windows were up.

Tendrils of smoke reached them, curling around the truck. They had to go down around a hairpin turn before making the climb out of the valley, but at least the incline ran straight. He'd need sure hands on the wheel and a steady foot on the accelerator.

The smoke increased. Visibility dropped.

Archer gave him a sharp look. "If we can get through this turn, the road curves north on the other side, out of the path of the fire."

Jonas nodded.

"We're not going to make it," Shea exclaimed.

"Oh, yes, we are," Jonas answered. "Hold on."

The fire raged up the incline off to his left, running like the wild thing it was. Tapping the brake as they descended into the turn, he voiced a prayer. "Please, God. Get us through this. Let me get Shea to safety."

For the span of forty seconds, the fire washed over and around them. Heat seeped in from the windows and floorboard. For those long moments, he couldn't see anything but flames. Had to rely on his memory of the road's curvature. Forty seconds. An eternity where he didn't know if he'd hit the side of the mountain or tumble off the other side and become the barbeque Archer had mentioned.

They burst through the inferno. On the other side, Jonas found he'd centered the truck right smack in the middle of the road. *Thank you, Lord.*

A buzzing sound filled the truck. He and Archer looked at each other.

"It's coming from under the seat," Shea said.

Archer came up with one of the walkie-talkies. Someone had squawked them. He powered it on, pressed the talk button, and said, "Archer. Go ahead."

"Answer your blasted cell phone," came the angry reply.

Jonas lifted one eyebrow, mimicking Archer's expression. "Fowler? How did he break into our walkie-talkie channel?"

Archer dug his cell phone from his pants pocket, both of them surprised to find they had bars. He tapped the speaker button before answering. "Archer."

"I see the fire closing in. What is your status?" Fowler demanded. Jonas would know his growling voice anywhere.

"We're ahead of the flames for the moment. We recovered the girl. She has head injuries and will require medical attention. Suspect is still at large."

"Proceed another 1.4 miles to the road's highest point. We will insert a team and drop a basket for the girl after which you and Cameron will lead the team and acquire the suspect. Under no condition does he escape. Are you clear?"

"Jonas?" Shea asked. "What is he talking about?"

The fear and worry in her voice singed Jonas's soul. He looked over his shoulder at her, looked at Archer. Back to Shea, and back again to Archer. Torn. A much too simple word to describe the rending argument going on inside him. Vernon Beauchamp was his to hunt down. His to bring to justice. His to beat the crap out of.

But Shea was his, too.

Archer didn't need to hear the words. "Negative. Jonas goes with Shea. I will lead the team." Archer's tone allowed no room for argument.

A heavy silence ensued before Fowler spoke again. "Very well. We'll retrieve Miss Townsend and Cameron. You have your orders. Proceed."

"Retrieve me?" Shea asked. "How? Go where?"

"Agent Kevin Fowler is someone we used to work for," Archer told her. "When you went missing, I called in a favor. He sent a helicopter."

"A helicopter can't land in these mountains, can it?"

Archer squirmed in his seat. "Well, no."

"They'll drop a line from the chopper with a basket," Jonas explained. "We strap you in and they haul you up to safety. Simple."

"Have you done this before?" she asked.

Both men nodded yes.

"Well, that explains why you think it's simple."

"Shea, baby, it will take hours by truck to get you to a medical facility. Helicopters are fast, and among the safest forms of travel, and—"

"I can't afford a helicopter. I can't even afford an ER visit. Why can't we go back to Hastings Bluff in your truck? Doc Burdette can fix me up."

Jonas looked at Archer in time to catch him rolling his eyes. Hopefully, Shea didn't see him, too.

"Doc Burdette would take one look at your face and

ship you off to a specialist before you could blink. You're going by helicopter. Deal with it. It won't cost you a penny." Jonas used his most commanding voice, hoping to quell her arguments.

"I know I look awful, Jonas, but I'm not taking your money. I don't need your charity." Shea leaned back with her arms folded over her chest.

"You're the most beautiful person in my life, but you need medical help beyond what Doc can offer. Please."

She didn't agree, but neither did she argue anymore.

Ten minutes later, with some distance between them and the fire, they rounded the curve of the mountain and spotted the helicopter hovering above. Black, unmarked, and with rotor blades beating at a wicked pace, it looked like a malignant blotch against the pristine backdrop of a cloudless blue sky.

Shea leaned forward between the front seats again, her one good eye opened wide. "You're both crazy. I'm not going anywhere near such a monstrosity."

Archer coughed to hide his laugh.

Jonas laughed outright. "Yeah, you are. And I'm going with you."

She withdrew and pulled her blanket tighter around her, all the while mumbling under her breath.

Ahead, four men stood in the road, two with binoculars trained on the forest below, all of them with rifles in hand. Four rappel lines dangled from the helicopter but were now being retrieved.

One of the men broke away and came toward them. "My name is Lopez. Which of you is Mr. Archer?"

Archer raised his hand.

"Right, sir. We'll send Miss Townsend in the basket first. Once she's inside, they'll drop a winch line for you, Mr. Cameron. Ready when you are."

The young soldier turned away and motioned to the rest of his team on the ground.

"Get Shea's backpack." Jonas pointed at the pack lying between Archer's feet before he got out, opened the rear door, and reached in for Shea's hand. When she didn't come right away, he climbed in. "You're safer with these guys than anywhere else. I need you to do this. I need you to be okay. Will you trust me? I promise, I'll be right behind you."

The fear in her eyes didn't lessen, but she nodded and took his hand.

Jonas helped her from the truck and carried her to where a single dangling rope remained. "I'm going to lay you down in the basket. We'll strap you in tight, and they'll lift you to the helicopter. Easy as can be. Okay?"

She didn't look impressed. "It's a wire coffin."

"No, it's a transport basket."

"Don't let them drop me," she pleaded.

"I'll be here to catch you if they do. Come on, Shea. The sooner we get you in the chopper, the sooner I can get out of this cold."

She fixed a look on him reminiscent of the way his mom would look at his dad when he said or did something she didn't approve of. Not knowing what else to do, he grinned. His smile had gotten him out of more than one tight spot with a woman.

Her shoulders slumped in defeat. "Alright. How do I get in this thing?"

"Like this." He knelt and placed her in the basket, taking care to tuck the thermal blanket in around her.

One of the soldiers on the other side of the basket tied multiple straps across her legs, torso, and chest. Another soldier hooked two wide straps, one at the head and one at the foot of the basket, to the center rope.

"Stabilizer ropes," Archer explained as he kneeled at Jonas's side. "You okay, little girl?"

"Thank you for coming for me, John. You and Jonas." A tear leaked from her good eye.

"My pleasure, Shea. I would do anything for him, and he would do anything for you. That makes you and me family. Never doubt I will be there for you if you need me. Now, let's get this rig moving. I've got a kidnapping, woman-hitting, wannabe terrorist to catch."

When Archer stepped away, Jonas took Shea's hand. "Here's another promise, a tidbit of personal information. I hate cold weather, so please close your eyes and go quietly."

He leaned down and kissed her forehead before moving away with a hand signal to the men in the chopper.

"Yeah," she answered. "Well, here's something I haven't shared before. I'm afraid of heights." Her one eye still reflected fear, supporting her statement.

The basket jerked and Shea let out a yip.

Jonas smiled and followed the basket until the airmen above pulled her into the maw of the aircraft.

"Your turn, sir." Lopez handed him a harness. "Winch is coming down."

"Thanks, Lopez. Do us all a favor, make sure you neutralize the target. I don't want to come back out here." Jonas stepped into the harness and snapped the connector. When the winch rope came within reach, he grabbed it, connected the carabiner hook to his harness, and signaled to the men above.

The young soldier gave him a snappy salute and scurried away once Jonas was airborne.

"Don't worry. I got this," his best friend yelled.

"Take care," Jonas called back.

As soon as he stepped into the helicopter, the pilot heeled over and headed southwest.

"What took you so long?" Shea quipped. "The creepy guy over there has been staring at me like I'm a bug and he's the swatter."

Jonas sat on the floor beside Shea and looked across the way to where Fowler sat in a jump seat, staring at them.

"That creepy guy used to be my boss. I can't think of another man I'd want to have my back than him. Now, he's got your back, too."

One of the crew members handed Jonas a helmet. He pulled it over his head and a moment later, a voice spoke in his ear.

"Before you ask ..." Fowler tapped his headset. "This channel is secure. You and I are the only ones on it. ETA into Boise is right at two hours. The Medical Director at the trauma center there owes the department a favor, plus it's a well-regarded facility in the medical field."

Fowler leaned forward to hand over a piece of paper. "Miss Townsend lost her father two years ago. She has been estranged from her three step-brothers and their families ever since. Her mother left many years ago. Whether you reach out to any of them or not is your decision."

Jonas unfolded the paper to find three names: Elijah, Noah, and Benjamin Townsend, along with a Montana address and telephone number. Further down the page, a second address was listed, this one in Denver for a Lydia Farley. Shea's mother. Would she want her family to know of her injury?

"All of Miss Townsend's expenses will be handled through the department."

Jonas nodded and did something he'd never done before. He reached across and shook Kevin Fowler's hand.

The elevator opened with a discreet ping, drawing Shea's attention to the sounds around her. The *shuuursh-ing* sound of wheels rolling over tile. Murmured conversations. The whispered hiss of curtains being drawn. Muted groans. Soft beeps from life-monitoring machines. Subtle squeaks from soft-soled shoes. Even the televisions were turned low.

Why had she not noticed the library-quiet atmosphere of hospitals before? Their feeble attempts to soothe harried visitors didn't work, though. Not with harsh overhead lights, floors polished to an eye-squinting sheen, disinfectant smells to wrinkle your nose, or that underlying uneasiness between life and death.

She'd experienced this feeling before when her father lay at the mercy of the hospital staff in the final days of his life. They'd been wonderful, had worked so hard to save him despite his having waited too long to seek help.

"Here we go," the x-ray tech announced as he pulled the curtain aside on her assigned cubicle.

Jonas sat in the one chair in her room, elbows on his knees, hands clasped between them. He smiled when he saw her and the whole world brightened. "You good?"

"Yeah." She climbed onto the bed, thanked the guy who'd chauffeured her back to the emergency room, and let out a long, frustrated exhale.

"That's a big sigh for okay."

A nurse entered the room. "The doctor is looking at your x-rays. He'll be in to talk with you soon." She fiddled with the I.V. line, checked Shea's blood pressure, typed a few things into the little in-room computer, and left.

Soon turned out to be almost two hours before the ER doc showed his face. "Hi, Ms. Townsend? I'm Dr. Gibson. Sorry to take so long, but I wanted to speak with one of my colleagues first, an ophthalmologist."

Turning to Jonas, he said, "And you are?"

"Jonas Cameron."

The two men shook hands.

"It's good you brought Ms. Townsend in right away." He pulled an x-ray from a folder and slipped it onto a view screen on the wall. "You have three orbital fractures here, here, and here." He pointed to the fracture locations on the film. "Two hairline cracks here and here. We can leave those alone to heal on their own. This one, however ..." He pointed at a place below the eye socket. "It will require surgery."

Shea closed her eye against the spinning sensation.

"I spoke with your brother, Eli, a short time ago and let him know what was going on," the doctor said.

Her one good eye snapped open again. "Wait. What? You spoke to my brother?"

Jonas had eased his chair closer to her bed. "I gave him Eli's number while you were getting x-rayed. He's your family, Shea. He deserves to know."

"No, you don't understand." She shook her head. And winced.

"Try to refrain from unnecessary movement, Miss Townsend. I've scheduled several more tests in the morning to help us understand the extent of involvement to your eye."

"So, I'm staying?"

"You're staying. Someone will be down to admit you and see about getting you a room."

Chapter Twenty-Four

Between getting carted upstairs to a room, stripped of her clothes, dressed in a hospital gown, settled in bed, having more blood drawn, and satisfying the nurses with all the vital signs anyone could want, the time sped by. Eleven o'clock came and went, along with the hospital's visiting hours but no one suggested Jonas leave. Shea was surprised he hadn't ducked out on his own.

He lounged in a recliner-style chair next to her bed, eyes closed, footrest extended. Weariness lined his face. He hadn't gotten much sleep the night before. None of them had.

She smiled at how his long legs hung past the footrest. Bigger than life in so many different ways.

He opened his eyes while she studied him, first darting

around to take in the room before settling on her again. Always the protector. "You okay?"

"You felt me watching you, didn't you?"

He rubbed his chin, fingers raspy against the new growth. Jonas could never achieve the scruffy look so many men strived for, not with such a heavy beard. What would it feel like, the rough bristles against her cheek?

"A knack I picked up along the way."

"Will you ever tell me about some of those journeys?"

His frown deepened the lines around his eyes.

"Never mind. If you ever talk about your past, it has to be on your terms. Not because I badgered you. Perhaps I'll share my past instead."

The frown eased allowing a smile to blink into existence. "Thanks."

"So, are you planning to get a hotel room? Get some rest?"

"Since I don't have a car much less clothes, I hoped you wouldn't mind if I stayed with you tonight." His smile turned wicked, reminding her of the big, bad wolf. "Polly Prescott will never find out."

The laughter escaped before she could temper it. "Ow, ow, ow. Don't make me laugh. It hurts."

"I'm sorry."

"No, you're not. You're still laughing. And I don't care what Polly Prescott or the rest of her cronies think. I hoped you'd want to stay."

"Why?"

Time to put up or shut up, as her brother, Ben used to say. She and Jonas were both so skittish. One of them had to take a chance. "Because I'm afraid of what the doctors are going to say. Because I don't want to be alone in a hospital, with nothing but strangers around. Because I feel safe with you. And you still owe on your promise."

Jonas unfolded from the recliner and came to sit on the side of her bed.

Shea scooted over to make room for him.

He took her hand, the one free of the I.V. tubing, brought her palm to his lips, and pressed a warm kiss to the center of her hand. "I'll stay as long as you want. I'm glad I make you feel safe, because the good Lord knows I'd do anything to keep you that way. And so you know, I always keep my promises."

They talked for a long while. Shea regaled him with stories of her childhood, of the happier times when her mother was still around, of life growing up the only girl on a cattle ranch. They held hands long into the night, even after weariness claimed them both.

∙◌◌◌∙

Jonas slept fitfully, aware when the nurses came to check on Shea and always mindful of the machine whispers monitoring Shea's vital signs.

When her door opened early Saturday morning with a

soft swoosh, he knew the visitor was someone other than the nursing staff. He got to his feet without a sound.

"Shhh," Archer whispered. "It's me."

"I take it you being here means success?" Jonas settled back into the recliner.

"Of course. Did you doubt me? The sucker hadn't gone more than a mile from the cabin when we caught up to him. His toes were frostbitten, and he'd attracted a few wolves. The man blubbered like a baby when we hooked him up to the winch and hauled him aboard the chopper. Couldn't tell if he was relieved or scared."

"So, he's still alive?" Jonas whispered, not wanting to wake Shea.

"Last I saw, he was. Fowler has him now, though. I'd rather take my chances with the wolves."

Jonas nodded, satisfied. Bad guys had a way of not reappearing once Fowler took them into custody.

"Vern is gone?" Shea asked in a sleepy voice.

Archer turned to her with a smile. "The technical answer is the threat has been neutralized. You no longer need worry about Mr. Beauchamp. I can't say anything more."

"All I want to hear." She returned a lopsided smile. The breaking dawn revealed the damage to her face. Swollen. Purple, red, and blue, with greenish tinges at the extreme edges. Healing would take a long time.

A knock on the door interrupted their tête-à-tête. Not

waiting for an invitation to enter, the newcomer pushed the door open and came in.

Archer moved to stand between Shea and the visitor, but her squeak made him pause.

"Eli!"

Elijah Townsend, the oldest of her step-brothers, bumped Archer aside and hurried to his sister's bed. There, he tossed his ten-gallon hat on her legs and, after an awkward hug, he straightened and swiped a hand across suspiciously wet eyes. "When the doctor called last night saying you had a head injury—I can't describe the nightmare images I conjured up. Although seeing you now ...." Eli took her chin in his hand and turned her head side to side to study her injury. "This ain't much better. Look at you, baby girl. You're a mess. What happened?"

Tears spilled from Shea's eyes, both the good one as well as the one swollen shut.

Jonas clenched his fists. What kind of brother would say such a thing to his sister? He ought to—

Archer beat him to it. With a solid shoulder nudge, he bumped Eli aside. "Hey now, no need for insults. Shea might have some bruising and swelling, but nothing the docs can't fix. She's still the prettiest sight I've seen in forever."

Jonas wanted to punch her brother. He'd have to thank Archer later for staying his hand. Estranged or not, Shea wouldn't appreciate him mauling her family.

Another knock on the door had them all turning around. Two men in long, white coats entered, doctor-types straight out of a television show with their name embroidered above the breast pocket and stethoscope slung around the neck.

"Good morning, Miss Townsend. Remember me? I'm Dr. Gibson from the ER. This is Dr. Goldman. He's the ophthalmologist I consulted with."

"Excuse me, would you gentlemen stand over there?" Goldman said to Eli and Archer as he edged to Shea's bedside. "Now, let's have a look."

Archer took the moment to leave. "Going for coffee. Be back later."

Eli joined Jonas on the other side of the bed.

Goldman performed a cursory examination of Shea's soft tissue injuries, all the while making remarks to the ER doctor in the strange language of medicine. At last, he straightened up.

"I've scheduled you for a CT scan and some other tests this morning. I'll return to discuss them with you once I get the results."

"How serious is it, doc?" Eli asked.

Goldman shrugged. "The x-rays revealed a couple of small fractures of the orbital bone. It's serious, but my concern is what damage has been done to the eye itself. A CT will tell us more."

Yet another knock on the door brought a man with a

wheelchair into the room.

"Ah, here's your ride now." Dr. Goldman slipped out.

"You gentlemen can wait right here for Miss Townsend," the orderly said as he helped Shea into the wheelchair, tucked a blanket around her legs, and raised the footrests. "We'll be back in no time."

Shea's brother cleared his throat. "You're Jonas Cameron, right?"

Jonas nodded and stuck his hand out. "And you must be Elijah Townsend."

Eli shook his hand. "Call me Eli. And thanks for giving the doctor my name and number. I'm surprised Shea mentioned me."

And here he stood, not at all prepared to have a man-to-man conversation with Shea's brother and unable to explain how he came by Eli's information. Awkward didn't begin to cover the situation. Best they avoid going there. "I'm surprised to see you here this early. Must be a seven, eight-hour drive from Missoula."

"My brothers and I haven't seen our little sister in two long years, her choice, not ours. When the call came in, well of course, I came. They wanted to tag along, too, but I pulled rank. Somebody has to run the ranch."

Jonas nodded. "Cattle, right?"

"Yeah. Cornerstone Cattle Ranch. We run about two thousand head of beef. What about you?"

"Horses." The less he said, the less he'd end up

explaining.

"Bought a horse from a man named Cameron down in the southern part of Idaho about ten years ago. Any chance you're related to Cody Cameron of the Triple C?"

The world cinched its belt and got a little smaller. What were the ever-loving chances? "Yep. He's my dad."

Eli nodded with a slow up and down motion. "A pretty little brown quarter horse. Got it for Shea's fourteenth birthday. She named her Kit-Kat. Mare is getting fat now without anyone to ride her."

Jonas laughed for want of something to say.

"So, Jonas Cameron of the Triple C Ranch, how do you know my sister?"

And here it came. He could almost see Eli Townsend's chest puff up in his big brother role.

"Shea moved to Hastings Bluff about two years ago. Her Uncle Preston lived there. I guess that makes him your uncle, too."

"Uncle Press. Haven't heard his name in a decade or more. He and our dad didn't get along. You said lived. He not there anymore?"

"Nope. When Shea appeared on his doorstep, he handed his house and catering business over to her and hit the road for Florida. I could find out where if you want."

"We'll see."

"Anyway, he did the catering gig part-time, kind of a hobby for his retirement. She soon learned it wasn't enough to live on, so now she cooks at the local diner. Everybody loves her."

"Not surprised. Shea's easy to love. Always was. Shame me and my brothers were so much older. We never got to spend much time with her while she was growing up."

"Why did she leave?"

Eli gave Jonas a hard look like he could drill through steel. "Shea didn't say?"

Jonas shook his head no.

"Well, it's her story to tell. But you still didn't answer my question. How is it you're here with my baby sister? What does she mean to you?"

A knock on the door saved him from answering. This place had more traffic than Dee Dee's diner on a Monday morning.

Archer walked in carrying a tray of coffees. "Found a donut shop down the street. Got a round of black coffee." He handed one to Jonas, offered a second one to Eli, and kept the third for himself.

Jonas removed the lid and blew on the steaming brew, using the delay to formulate an answer to avoid betraying secrets, but one Eli would buy.

"Shea and I got to know each other while working with some of the local kids. When she was kidnapped, I got involved. Called in a favor from one of my Army contacts. We were able to track her cell phone. The fool tried to go up a mountain in a snowstorm without proper equipment and ran the car down an embankment. We found her. I brought her here. Archer went after him. By the way, this is John Archer. Arch, this is Eli Townsend, Shea's brother."

Eli shook Archer's hand. "Did you get him? Where is he now?"

"Yes," Archer said. "He's in custody. With his terrorist ties, it's doubtful you or I, or anybody else will ever see him again. You can rest assured he no longer poses a threat to Shea or anyone."

The orderly returned Shea to the room, with Dr. Goldman on their heels.

"Okay, here's the scoop. As I mentioned, the x-rays show fractures of the orbital bone—the bony shell around the eyeball. The CT scan revealed another fracture, this one in the base of the orbit. Under normal circumstances, I would keep her for a day to monitor her concussion, send her home until the swelling decreases, and bring her back for an in-depth examination. This new fracture changes things, but with the extensive edema, we can't look inside her eye. I recommend against waiting for the swelling to dissipate."

"What are you saying, Dr. Goldman?" Shea asked.

"I've spoken with a colleague of mine, someone I went to school with, Dr. Richard Eicholmann. His specialty is ophthalmic trauma. He works at the Stein and Doheny Eye

Institute at UCLA. It's one of the finest ophthalmic hospitals in the United States, Shea, and I want to send you there."

Shea's mouth opened and closed, opened and closed, almost like she was gasping for breath.

Eli stood at the foot of her bed, gripping the footboard. "Los Angeles?"

Archer, always the picture of discretion, slipped over to a corner of the room.

"Yes," Dr. Goldman answered. "I know it's a long way from your home, but it's one of the preeminent eye hospitals in the country.

Jonas sat in his chair by the bed and took her hand. "Shea, look at me."

Her one good eye met his, fear the predominant emotion.

"This is a good thing. You'll get the best care at the best hospital."

"Jonas," she whispered. "All these tests ... the transportation ... the specialists ... I can't pay for any of it."

He laughed. "Don't you worry about money. Your creepy man from the helicopter is covering all your expenses. All you have to do is lie there and let me, the doctors, and the nurses take care of you."

A loud cough reminded him of who else was in the room. "And your brother, of course."

"But Los Angeles? It's so far away."

"I'll be there every step of the way."

Dr. Goldman tapped his watch. "I hate to interrupt, but we need a decision right away. I want her there as soon as possible, and it takes time to arrange a medical flight."

Archer tapped Jonas's arm. He leaned in and spoke in a low voice. "I've got Fowler on the horn. The chopper left ten minutes ago for home base in Vegas, but he rerouted it back to us. They can have it refueled and ready to go in two hours, plus he'll put a medic on board. Flight time to UCLA Medical Center is a little over five hours with a thirty-minute refueling stop in Sacramento."

Jonas nodded and returned to Shea's side. "Fowler is sending his helicopter back for you."

"Too fast." She studied him for a long moment, worry obvious in her expression. Before long, though, she nodded assent.

"Dr. Goldman," Jonas said. "Air transport from your hospital here to the UCLA Medical Center has already been arranged. The helicopter will be ready to leave with her in two hours. Please contact your Dr. Eicholmann and whomever else needs to know. ETA is seventeen-hundred Pacific time. Give me the contact information for UCLA and I'll pass it along to our pilot."

If the doctor was surprised, he didn't show it. "Right. I'll get the info right away and order sedation for the trip so she's comfortable." Goldman hurried out of the room.

"I'm going with you, baby girl." Eli came and sat on

the side of her bed.

Shea looked from her brother to Jonas. "Would you mind stepping out for a moment, Eli? I'd like a private word with Jonas."

The man couldn't hide his surprise, but he did as Shea requested. "All right. Five minutes."

Archer followed him out the door.

Jonas leaned down and kissed her forehead. "I like your brother. He's a good man, and he's worried about you."

"I didn't give him or the others a chance to explain. I left them and never looked back. Now, he's here for me." Tears leaked from her poor eyes.

"Shh, baby. Don't cry. It will make your head hurt."

"Jonas, I don't want you to go with me."

The words struck him like a knife to the heart. He sucked in a breath and leaned back. "What?"

"I mean, I do. But ... I can't ask it of you. The ranch, your brothers, the whole breeding and training side of the business—they need you. We don't even know how long this will take."

The pain in his chest didn't go away, but it changed. This selfless, beautiful, generous woman lay here on her hospital bed, injured and in pain, and scared to death of what the future held for her, and she worried about his needs. "Shea—"

"No. Stay with me until the helicopter arrives, but then

you need to go home. I'm right but I'm not strong enough to argue, so don't make me. Besides, I need this time with my brothers to heal the hurt between us."

He would never forget those last bittersweet moments. Shea had refused the sedative the doctor ordered right up until they came with a gurney to transport her to the helipad.

"I don't want to be all dopey. I want to remember this time with you."

They'd laughed and talked about inconsequential things, held hands, and made promises to text, email, and call. Jonas entered his contact info into her cell phone and provided the same to her brother. Noah and Ben would meet her and Eli in Los Angeles.

Letting her go was one of the more difficult choices he'd had to make. Having no idea when, or even if, he'd see her again made it harder still.

He stood outside the rotor wash and watched the proceedings. Helpless. Superfluous. Useless. An unnecessary bystander.

The rotor blades never stopped churning. The skids touched down. Cargo bay doors opened. The hospital staff rolled Shea out to the bird. Crewmen from the aircraft loaded and secured their patient. The orderlies retreated and Shea's brother boarded after her. The chopper doors closed.

The pilot looked over and gave him a sharp salute. Lucky Winscombe. One of the best. Jonas had worked with him many times. None better to deliver the precious cargo aboard his aircraft.

The chopper lifted from the helipad, rose higher, banked left, and sped away. Five heartbeats later, it had disappeared into the vast sky.

The transfer had taken two minutes and fourteen seconds to remove Shea from his life.

Chapter Twenty-Five

One week later

Jonas tugged on the front cinch to tighten it, while Diablo snorted and fidgeted.

He checked the saddle for the proper position behind the horse's shoulders and then ran his fingers under the strap to ensure a snug but not too tight fit. Satisfied, he stroked the stallion's forehead. "Stop it, you big baby. I was gone for a few days this time, not three months."

He'd encountered the same behavior from Diablo when he returned from his stint in Africa. Call it high-strung or temperamental, the stallion made clear his displeasure at Jonas's abandonment.

The horse's bad behavior wasn't all that had recurred. The nightmares had resumed, the same terrible events he'd experienced playing on loop—the concussive blast of the IED, the loss of two of his men with three others maimed, the heart-pounding fear when he'd thrown one of them over his shoulder and carried him to safety, the desperation on little Madenu's face as she ran to warn them. Except it was Shea's face this time, her face he saw in every incident. And lost again and again.

Diablo sidestepped, bumping into him and Jonas realized he'd been standing at the horse's side for who knew how long, lost in his memories. A psychiatrist would have a field day with him.

"Sorry, boy. Let's go for a run, what do you say? I need to work off yesterday's Thanksgiving dinner." He led Diablo out of the barn, closed the oversized sliding door behind them, and swung up onto the horse's back. Nudging Diablo with his heels, they headed out.

Snow still covered the ground, so he wouldn't go far, only enough to take the frisk off the stallion's energy and hopefully clear his head. What he really wanted was to take off and disappear for a while, but that couldn't happen, not with Clint laid up. The kid had come to him still wet behind the ears, his only experience with horses what he'd learned growing up on a potato farm, but he had a work ethic that rivaled any of the Triple C's ranch hands. He'd already made an impact.

Now, with Clint laid up, Jonas had to pick up his slack. On top of all his other responsibilities.

Was this how Rascal and his brothers felt last summer when he'd stayed behind in Nigeria after Mallory's rescue? He'd not given a thought about the burden he'd thoughtlessly dumped on them until now.

Diablo wanted more than a trot and fought Jonas for the bit. "Okay, boy. Let's run." A strong tap with his heels set the big horse flying over the land. He made sure to keep to the familiar trails where the land was level.

Giving the spirited animal his head had a soothing effect on Jonas, too. Freezing cold air in your face. Blinding speed. All his worries disappeared for the moment.

When the horse's speed dwindled, Jonas reined him back to a slow trot before settling into a sedate walk. Lather flecked the great horse's neck. His nostrils flared from the effort.

Using his coat sleeve to wipe sweat from his own face, Jonas studied the wild, untamed land around him. He'd traveled all over the world, but nowhere made him feel more alive than here on the Triple C land. It was ingrained in him, a part of his blood, and he couldn't imagine living anywhere else.

Shea had landed here in Hastings Bluff when she came searching for her uncle. And stayed. Did she feel the same connection with the land? Would she come back here once she'd healed or return to her childhood home now that she'd reconciled with her family?

His thoughts turned anxious. Since getting the call after her surgery three days ago he'd heard nary a peep from Shea or her brothers. The surgeon had expressed cautious optimism according to Eli, so why did his subsequent calls roll to voicemail? Why didn't they return his calls or text him? His fingers itched to try Shea's number—he wanted to hear her voice, needed assurance she was okay.

Diablo jerked and snorted, unhappy with his tightened his grip on the reins. Jonas leaned down and patted the horse's neck. "Sorry, boy."

The urge to go to her, remain by her side while she recovered was strong, but he couldn't. He had responsibilities here. He owed it to his family and Rascal, to the ranch and the horses. Heck, he owed it to himself. Much as he disliked the thought, Shea was not his responsibility. She would call when ready. Or not.

His pocket vibrated interrupting his pity party. He dug the ringing phone out, his pulse racing when saw Eli's name on the display. "Jonas Cameron."

"Hey, Jonas, it's Eli. Sorry I haven't called. It's been a rough couple of days."

Fear invaded his mind. "What's wrong? Is Shea okay?"

"Yeah. Now. She had a bad reaction to the pain medication. It left her wired and crazy with hallucinations. I had to stay by her side 24/7 to keep her from messing with the bandages. Keeping that girl still is a lot like trying to hogtie a squirming heifer for branding."

A morsel of relief calmed the panic. "She's better now?"

Eli chuckled. "Yeah, you could say that. The doc ordered up a new drug that laid her out. She dropped off around midnight and hasn't woken yet. Uh, about that heifer bit, don't tell I said that, okay?"

"I called and called ... why didn't you answer? Or call me back? You scared the crap out of me."

"Sorry about that. My phone died. I left the charger at the hotel and didn't want to leave her to go get it. Noah, my middle brother, got here this morning. He's on Shea-watch now, so I'm back at the hotel. He has your number. Man, I'm beat. I need to grab a few hours of shuteye before I head home."

Jonas shut down a pang of jealousy. He should be the one with her, not her brother. "Wait. When can I talk to her?"

"Try her tomorrow. The nurse said she'll sleep most of today."

"Okay. Thanks, man. I appreciate it. Text me Noah's number, would you?"

Six weeks later

"You heading up the mountain again?"

Jonas draped the saddlebags across the stallion's rump before turning to Rascal. "Yep."

The old foreman stood near Diablo's empty stall. He pushed his hat back on his head "Your mama said they haven't seen much of you at the house since Christmas. You get here before the sun yawns and hightail it back up the mountain at dusk."

Jonas smiled. Rascal wasn't above using guilt, but those tactics wouldn't work on him. He'd left guilt behind weeks ago along with all the pitying looks from his family. All he had left now were regrets.

He gave one more tug on the cinch straps to make sure the saddle sat snug on Diablo's back, looped a sack of oats over the saddle horn and another of apples, and swung into the saddle. "I'm not very good company right now. Get the door for me, would you?"

Outside, the weather had eased its icy grip on the world for the moment. According to the Almanac, they'd have a mild winter this year and spring would come early. Be nice not to chop firewood for the hunting cabin quite so often.

Diablo danced a little on the trail. "I know, boy. I want a good run, too, but it's too dark. We'll head out earlier tomorrow."

It would take twenty minutes to reach the cabin. Twenty minutes to either indulge his thoughts of Shea or try to bury them. He didn't know what he wanted anymore other than for the ache in his soul to go away. With a sigh, he pulled out his phone, found her name in his favorites, and tapped the number. Connecting with Shea had gotten harder, not easier. With the good report from her doctors and the next surgery four months away, she'd signed up at the college in Missoula where she'd taken her culinary courses. This time she intended to finish and earn the degree she wanted so badly. He couldn't blame her, but their schedules never seemed to mesh. Texts and emails worked, but he needed to hear Shea's voice, not read typed words.

"Jonas, hi. I was about to call you."

He almost dropped the phone. "Uh, yeah, hey, how's it going?"

How's it going? They hadn't spoken live in two weeks and *how's it going* was the best he could come up with?

"Good. Eli let me use one of his trucks for school. The drive to Missoula takes about forty minutes one way, so I'm not burning anyone else's time now. This first week has been all about review and getting comfortable again."

"Glad to hear it." He closed his eyes and soaked in the sound of her voice. Shea soothed him like no one else could. And yet, something was missing.

"So, what's new at the Triple C?"

"Tiki Fire had her baby. A colt. His colors and markings are almost identical to hers. Both mama and baby are doing fine. No effects from whatever Vern fed her."

Inane and impersonal. Like strangers. Their connection, that impossible-to-define link he had with Shea was MIA. Did she feel it, too? Did she miss it as he did?

"Good news. Did you ever figure out what it was?"

"The vet did. Some noxious weed I've never heard of. Don't know where Vern got it from. It's not common around here."

"How's Clint?"

"Back at the ranch, but on light duty. Doc Burdette keeps a close eye on him."

Silence. Awkward. Uncomfortable.

"Well, I guess I better let you go."

"Yeah. Talk to you soon. Goodnight."

Four months later

A chime rang out.

Jonas swung once more and wedged the ax in the log on the chopping block. He brushed sweat from his face and reached for his phone. A text message from Eli. About time.

> SURGERY SUCCESSFUL. DR OPTIMISTIC VISION GOOD AS BEFORE. MAYBE BETTER. HEADING HOME TOMORROW.

Relief was sweet. And short-lived. Shea had gotten past her final medical hurdle ... but what now? When she completed her culinary degree would she want to come back to Hastings Bluff? To the diner? A town this small didn't offer much in the way of a career for a professional chef.

A second chime announced the arrival of another text. SHEA HAS BIRTHDAY COMING UP. SHE MISSES YOU. COME FOR HER PARTY?

They'd blown right through Thanksgiving, Christmas, his birthday, New Year's, and Valentine's Day without a mention of any of the holidays, but Eli wanted to celebrate Shea's birthday?

Jonas shook his head in disbelief. If she missed him, she had a funny way of showing it. He'd tried three times now to Facetime with her, but she always declined and called him on his cell instead. How would she react if he showed up on her doorstep unannounced?

The more pertinent question was—did he even want to go?

Time and distance always put things in perspective. Perhaps she no longer cared for him the way he cared about her. Maybe she never had. He closed his eyes and lifted his face to the sky. "Shay-Shay, what are you doing to me?"

"What did you say, son?" his father asked.

In the time it took to snuff out a candle Jonas whipped around, grabbed the rifle from where he'd leaned it again the cabin porch, and in one smooth, continuous movement raised it to his shoulder. In half that amount of time, he registered his father's voice and lowered the barrel of the rifle toward the ground. "Dad," he managed, his voice strained. "You know better than to sneak up on someone in the woods."

"Hard to call it sneaking when Blackjack here sounds like a herd of buffalo."

The horse snorted and shook his head.

"Sorry, boy." His father dismounted, his movements slower than usual. He patted the horse's neck. "Guess we're both getting too old for this."

Mortification settled on Jonas's shoulders. Years of rigorous training, numerous enemy encounters, and way too many life or death situations had fine-tuned his instincts to razor sharpness. He could sense another person's presence, detect whether they were hostile or friendly, and knew within a few feet where they were positioned, but right here, right now, his seventy-year-old father had ridden up the mountain on a lumbering old gelding and caught him unaware. He needed to either get Shea back into his life or out of his system. "Look, I know why you came, but I'm not ready for this conversation."

Truth be told, he was surprised it had taken his father so long.

"Are you at least gonna offer me some water?"

Jonas walked inside the cabin and dipped water from the pail he'd fetched from the stream earlier. Handing the battered tin cup over, he studied the tall, silver-haired man he'd revered his whole life. A little more stooped these days, his fingers gnarled and swollen, but still a legend in these parts. His dad might be a slower, his hearing not as sharp, but he was still full of vigor. Cody Cameron was nobody's fool and no one you wanted to cross.

"I gave you space and time, Jonas. Been waiting for you to make the first move. You're a grown man, but you're still my son, and I can't let you worry your mama like this. You've been home for months now, but you spend more time in this broken down old shack than with your own family. I mean, look at you, sporting whiskers like a mountain man. I never could grow a full beard like that. Looks good but I doubt your mama will like them."

"Yeah, well, I've had a lot on my mind. Shaving's not high on the list."

"I understand, but there comes a point when you have to stop pushing people away and start living again."

"I get it, Dad. Believe me, I know. And I will." Staring at his father was like looking in a mirror at an older version of himself. He and his brothers had always heard how much they looked like their father, but he'd never seen it until now. "Soon as I work through some stuff we'll talk. I promise. Okay?"

"That's all fine and good, but not why I came all the way up here. You've changed since you went to fetch Mallory and then stayed on over there to finish business.

Might be you'll never talk about what happened and that's okay by me. Sometimes a man has to hold his cards close. But you're home now and last I heard still part of this family. Now, today's your mama's birthday. If you miss dinner it will break her heart and you know I can't abide that. I'd have to whup your butt, not to mention she'd never let you or me forget it." He chuckled.

Jonas winced. He raised his arms, clasped his hands behind his head, and turned in a circle, unable to meet his father's gaze. "I ... I forgot."

Birthdays were special to his family. Mom always made a big deal of them—cake, candles, singing ... and presents. Didn't matter if they were big or small, expensive or handmade, presents meant you cared enough to take the time to make a birthday special. Even when he'd been deployed, he'd made a point of sending something. And she'd come through every year with a humongous box of goodies for his birthday.

Jonas glanced at his watch. If he left now, with Dad, they could get down the mountain in time for dinner. But not enough time to get her a gift. That was almost as bad as not showing. He could hear her passive-aggressive rebuke now. *That's okay, son. I don't need a gift.*

He snorted. The reproach in her eyes would gut him.

His mind-reading dad came to the rescue. "Don't worry none about a gift. I keep a stockpile of baubles and doodads for occasions like this. Not like I didn't forget a

time or two. Here's a piece of advice you can tuck away for the future. Women will forgive you once if you forget their birthday, but they don't forget. Do it again and you'll pay till doomsday. Now, unless you got something better to do, how about we get going and I'll let you pick something from my stash. You gotta wrap it, though. That way she'll know it's from you."

Laughter burst from the depths of Jonas's chest. An honest to goodness laugh that blossomed into something more, something liberating. With all the skills he'd cultivated over the years, gift wrapping didn't make the top one thousand. He sucked at it.

His father was the wisest man he knew. Maybe he should give this family thing another shot. Gripping his father's shoulder, Jonas said, "Thanks, Dad. Give me five minutes."

On the ride down the mountain, he broached a question to his father. "Do all women like their birthdays acknowledged?"

With a sideways glance at him, his father answered. "Never met one that didn't."

He led Sheba into the corral. A few laps around would get her used to his touch. Rascal said Clint had been working with the mare for several weeks and that they'd made good progress, but with Clint laid up he couldn't continue her training. It fell to Jonas, otherwise, they'd have to start over at the beginning.

He gave a quick flick of the reins to get Sheba moving.

The birthday dinner last night was a huge success, thanks to Dad's intervention. Now Jonas had to decide whether to go see Shea for her birthday. If he did, he'd need a gift, something special. But not too special.

The horse snorted and tossed her head.

"C'mon, Sheba. Behave." Jonas gave a sharper snap on the rein, but it didn't settle the restless horse. She continued to prance and pull away.

He slid his hand on the rope closer to the bridle and shortened the slack.

Sheba's eyes widened. Her nostrils flared, fighting him every step.

He tugged her forward, running with her to set the pace. At last, she settled into a rhythm. After two full circuits around the corral, Jonas slowed his steps while lengthening the lead rope again.

Sheba continued her pace. Better.

If he left on the Thursday before Shea's birthday party that night, he could spend all day Friday and Saturday with her, leaving Sunday for the six-hour return drive. He would get Rascal or one of his brothers to cover for him—

Sheba shook her head.

Caught off guard, he almost lost his hold on the rope when she reared up on her hind legs.

Patience frayed, he pulled in the slack again. "Fine. No exercise, no apples."

Frustrated, he turned to take the horse back inside the barn and spotted his father leaning against the top rail of the corral.

"Rascal said you were having trouble with this fidgety little filly."

"Hey, Dad." Jonas led the horse over to where his dad stood, frowning when she followed like a docile little lamb. "Sheba's a little out of sorts this morning. Seems she's not interested in training today."

"She's not interested? Or you? Females are sensitive, you know."

Jonas frowned at his father. No one knew horses like Cody Cameron. "Sensitive, huh?"

"Yeah. Don't matter whether two-legged or four-legged, they tune in on emotions better than us men. Take your mama for example. She was over the moon when you showed up for dinner last night. Hasn't stopped talking yet about the nifty leather journal you gave her. Worse wrapping job I've ever seen, but it did the trick. Still, she's worried about you staying up at the cabin. I heard her yammering at you this morning."

"Yeah, well she wouldn't be Mom if she didn't worry about something."

"Could be. Or maybe like Sheba she's annoyed you're not giving her your full attention."

Jonas's frown deepened as he tried to follow his father's drift. "Wait, we're not talking about Mom or Sheba, are we?"

"Your mother, horses, or Shea, it's all the same. Women are sensitive."

Jonas's mouth flattened out. It was one thing to talk about Mom, but no way he was discussing Shea. "You're saying Sheba acts out because I don't pay her enough attention?"

He already knew the answer. Shea owned his thoughts. Knotted his insides. Lately, he had the raging hormones of a teenage boy, up one minute, spiraling down the next. *She loves me, she loves me not.* Grown men don't twist themselves into an emotional pucker like this. Ever.

Dad reached out to stroke Sheba's forehead before turning his all-seeing stare on him. "I'm neither a female nor a horse. I can't sense whether you're distracted or not. I have to rely on what I can see, and right now there's no reason Sheba should like me better than you. She don't know me from Adam's house cat."

Stepping up to the challenge, Jonas lifted his chin and reached out to rub Sheba's neck.

The tetchy, cantankerous little filly bared her teeth at him before moving back to his father.

"Fine. You take her." He handed the lead rope to his father, shoulders slumping when Sheba nuzzled her new handler.

"I let Shea get away. I don't know how to fix it."

"You used to be a ball of fire, son. But for a motor-mouth with a quick smile and a ready laugh, you don't say much anymore, not to your family, your friends, or the horses. You don't go into town, don't chase after the girls no more. That's not a bad thing, mind you, but you haven't even asked after those kids you were so excited about helping. One thing I do know, hibernating up on the mountain won't fix nothing."

Much as he wanted to look his father in the eye, Jonas couldn't stand to see the disappointment there. The ground held infinite interest where the toe of his boot dug circles. "I've had a lot on my mind of late."

"Late being a couple of years now? I been watching you, Jonas. You've spiraled downward for three years, ever since you came home from wherever it was the Army sent you. And this last trip." He shook his head in a slow back and forth motion. "Thought maybe you'd snap out of it on your own, but I guess not."

"I can't talk about it, Dad."

"Can't or won't? Don't matter. I'm not asking. Of all my children, you've always felt more, seen more, and understood more than all the rest together. Heck, son, we've all got demons, ever last one of us. But you had balance. You always landed on your feet ... until now."

Jonas looked up and met the deep blue eyes that matched his own.

His father lifted one eyebrow. "Want to know what I'd do in your shoes?"

Jonas swallowed. Did he? His head bobbed up and down of its own accord.

"I'd have a sit-down, heart to heart talk with the Man upstairs. Tell Him everything wrong and right in my life and ask Him how to fix it."

When the silence grew uncomfortable, Jonas asked, "And then?"

"I'd listen. Hard. Sometimes you have to get out of your own way and trust the good Lord to figure things out for you. And then I'd go get my girl."

Jonas nodded. After he swallowed down the lump in his throat, he said. "What about Mom? I don't want to worry her anymore."

"You leave your mama to me. There's something you might not realize. Every inch of you radiates with a pain everyone around you can feel. Get your head clear, make peace with yourself, and I guarantee your mama will be happy."

"Thanks, Dad. Will you keep an eye on Sheba for me?"

Chapter Twenty-Six

One month later

Six hours and five minutes. The time it took to drive from his home to Shea's home southwest of Great Falls, Montana. How odd to think she'd grown up so close to him and yet so far away.

The last fifteen minutes of the trip after passing through the town of Cascade consisted of nothing but wide-open pastureland. A sign marked the property line of Cornerstone Cattle Ranch. Acreage-wise, it had to be three times bigger than the Triple C.

A gravel road loomed ahead off to the right. Two monstrous red cedar logs marked either side of the drive with a third pole laid across the top of the other two. No gate. Only a metal sign swinging on chains from the crossbeam—CCR.

He turned down the narrow gravel drive between the two fenced pastures on either side. Hundreds of cows roamed the area. In the distance, he saw a curl of smoke.

A sprawling farmstead came into view. More details came into focus with each passing mile. A two-story, white clapboard house, with dark gray shutters and trim. An older design he recognized from the fifties or sixties. A tall, red-brick fireplace rose high above the roof on one end but was not the origin of the smoke.

A campus of outbuildings—grain silos, sheds, two huge barns, what looked like a long carport, and sundry other buildings needed to run an operation this size—stood a short distance from the house. Not so dissimilar to his own home.

As he followed the drive to the front of the house, Jonas caught a glimpse of a spacious backyard. A good-sized group of people had gathered there, around a massive barbeque pit. The smoke he'd seen billowed up from it. With the weather so fine, he wasn't surprised they'd moved the birthday party outside.

Acid burned in his gut. It had been building the entire drive. Had he done the right thing coming here without warning her? No turning back now. Eli had spotted his truck and was coming out to meet him.

CCC

A birthday party.

They meant well, but this was not what Shea wanted. Forty-eight people milled through their house, mingled on the big split-level deck out back, and spilled into the yard. Family, friends, employees, and neighbors, all curious and staring at her scars. At least Trina hadn't gotten her way. Eli's wife, ever the social climber, wanted to invite the entire town.

Shea had never gotten along with Trina, but she'd won this battle. It was her party after all. Why did dear, sweet Eli put up with such a shrew of a wife and her social aspirations?

She knew the answer. Eli had told her a long time ago. "She's my wife, Shea. And the mother of my children. Trina might be shallow, but she's good to me and the kids. I love her enough to look past the warts, the same way she looks past mine."

Shea twirled several long curls and tugged them over the side of her face. Eli might have stumbled onto one of life's great truths. If you love someone enough, you look past their faults. Could she do it, too? Would she find someone who could love her the same way?

And there was Porter again, coming her way. Some warts couldn't be overlooked, no matter how hard she tried. And the Lord knew, she'd worked at it. Since she'd returned from Los Angeles, he'd apologized no less than a dozen times for his bad behavior in Hastings Bluff and went on a tear to prove how much he'd changed. He visited almost every day, brought her gifts, offered to chauffeur her wherever she wanted to go, and asked her out on dates. Persistent fool.

Right. Like anything he could do would change the way she felt about him. He'd lied to her for years, made fun of her behind her back, and cheated on her. With Gina. Her best friend.

No. She had his measure now. Forgive him? Sure. Why not. But she didn't buy his one-hundred-eighty-degree turnaround. No way she'd ever trust him again.

Turning sideways, she slipped between Alfie Durden, the ranch foreman, and Isabelle Foster, the preacher's wife, her course set toward her brothers who stood with several other men around the massive barbecue pit in the yard. A man's refuge, Eli called it. Men and their great slabs of meat on the grill.

Porter wouldn't bother her there. Eli, Noah, and Ben intimidated him.

Sooner or later, she'd have to talk to him tonight, but not yet. Birthdays meant balloons and cake, presents and happiness. Porter brought depression and constant reminders of her unsightly scars. No one would find her attractive with such flaws.

"There you are," Porter caught her arm and pulled her to his side. "I've been trying to catch up with you all night. If I didn't know better, I'd think you were trying to avoid me."

So much for evading him. Shea sighed. Maybe if she gave him his time now, he'd leave her be for the rest of the night. Of course, the rest of her so-called special night would be ruined. "Hello, Porter."

"Your brother Ben says the band will start playing soon. I know you're afraid no one will ask you to dance but your brothers, and how that will embarrass you. But I'm here. I'll always dance with you, Shea. Your scars don't bother me."

"Thank you, Porter." What else could she say? He had a knack for reading her emotions and playing on her vulnerabilities, which meant he knew how difficult this little soiree was for her. Dance, indeed. And draw all those pitying looks? Maybe she could feign a sprained ankle or an upset stomach.

Porter ran his too-soft hand up and down her arm. Ugh. How had she ever thought she might marry this man? Repugnance was the best she could come up with to describe her feelings for him.

Jonas Cameron had ruined her for all other men.

She chided herself. Months had passed since she'd seen him. Sure, they had conversations, more written than speaking, but with each passing week, he'd grown more and more distant. Not that she could blame him. He had a career he loved at the Triple C Ranch working with his horses. His life lay in Hastings Bluff, while she had no idea what the next months and years held for her.

"We should go inside and rest for a while. You look fatigued."

Porter tried to lead her toward the door, but she worked her arm free of his grip. "No, Porter. I'm not the least bit tired. On the contrary, I want to visit with the friends and neighbors I haven't seen in ages. I want to laugh and, yes, dance. You go rest. I'll let you know if I need you."

There. That should put him in his place. For a few minutes anyway, enough to get free of him. Turning, she wandered down the steps to find her brothers.

"Looking fine, Shea." One of their fifty-year-old neighbors raised his cup to her as she passed.

"Darned if you don't get prettier every day," one of the ranch hands said. Of course, he was pushing sixty.

"You sure ain't the snaggle-toothed little darling I remember. When did you go and get so pretty?" Another man of her father's generation stood near the first two.

She looked around, noting the age of those at her party. Other than Porter, none of the guests in attendance came close to her age. They were her brothers' friends and acquaintances. Not hers.

She smiled at all their quips, recognizing the blatant falsehoods, but it was sweet deceit meant in the nicest way. She didn't need their lies, though. The mirror in her bathroom told her the truth.

"Well, lookee there," Eli said. He lifted his can of

Coke and gestured toward the side of the house before starting that way.

A truck had pulled up in their yard. The big, black Ford made her heart quiver. When the door opened and a man stepped out, the setting sun formed a blazing corona around him that cast his features in shadow.

Shea shaded her eyes with one hand and squinted, excitement unfurling in her stomach.

Her brother reached the man's side, grabbed his hand for a hearty pump, and then clapped him on the back.

The new arrival towered over her brother, dwarfing him with his wide shoulders. But then he looked up, his gaze searching until it landed on her.

An electric tingle started down Shea's spine, a feeling she knew well but hadn't felt in a long while. He walked by Eli's side toward the party, through the crowded backyard, his eyes never looking away from hers.

Jonas. He'd come.

All the doubts and uncertainties disappeared as she raced toward him.

Jonas's long strides left Eli behind. His arms opened and reached for her.

Shea flew into his embrace, uncaring of who watched or what they might say. "Jonas."

Heavily muscled arms closed around her, lifted her from the ground, and swung her in a slow circle. "Shea."

Tears pricked her eyes. She wrapped her arms around

his neck and buried her face against his chest. "You came."

"I did," he whispered against her ear. "I couldn't stay away any longer."

His warm breath made her shiver. His touch felt so right. "I'm glad."

CCC

By eight o'clock, most of the guests had left. Country life started early no matter the previous night's festivities. Animals still needed to be fed, cows needed milking, eggs gathered.

One of the nice things about country folk was their appreciation for hard work. Folks who worked the land understood the bone-tired ache of a job well done. This crowd was no different. They were careful to throw their trash in the proper receptacles, take their dirty dishes to the kitchen, and lend a hand wherever it was needed without being asked.

Once the stragglers slipped away, her three brothers cornered her on the patio.

"We've been saving this present for after everyone left," Noah said.

Ben handed her a ... hatbox?

Curiosity burned through her. She took the round box and opened it. Inside, she found six leather-bound journals.

She looked at each of her brothers in turn, a question in her eyes.

Imperfect Lies

"They're your mother's," Eli explained. "We ran across them while converting the back bedroom into the nursery. We didn't know if you'd want them or not, but thought you should decide whether to keep them, not us."

Their thoughtfulness touched her, but the act also left her confused. And maybe a little bit hopeful. "Thank you. I'll save these for another time."

Shea left Jonas with her brothers and joined her sisters-in-law for the remaining clean-up—scraping food scraps into a bin for the pigs, stacking dishes on the counter by the sink where they'd be rinsed for loading into the dishwasher, wrapping leftovers for the refrigerator—all work natural to her because she'd done it her whole life.

By eight-thirty, Porter was the one guest—other than Jonas—who hadn't left. He stood off to one side and followed Shea's every move.

"Well, looks like he's not leaving until you give him the time of day," Lisa, Noah's wife said. "Might as well get it over with so you can spend some alone time with your man."

"He's a looker," Katy, her brother Ben's new bride, said, her eyes roving over Jonas. "The new guy, not Porter. Ugh. What's his name anyway? I didn't get to meet him."

Shea followed Katy's gaze to where Jonas stood with her brothers. Taller than all of the other men here tonight, he'd drawn all the women's eyes, married or not. "Jonas. His name is Jonas Cameron."

"Mmm," Lisa hummed.

Trina, Eli's wife sniffed and lifted her nose in disapproval.

Shea turned away to hide her smile. The woman would find fault with the angels.

"Um, Shea?"

She looked up to find Porter at the kitchen door.

"Shea, please come outside. I'd like to talk to you." Porter knew enough to stay out of Katy and Lisa's way. They disliked him almost as much as their husbands did. None of Shea's brothers cared a fig for Porter. Trina, on the other hand, could care less whether he came or went seeing as how Porter had no social status and therefore no value in her world.

Using one of the dish towels to dry her hands, Shea opened the back door, stepped out onto the patio, and headed for a chair near the railing. "Five minutes, Porter. No more."

"Not here," he said.

"Yes, here. We have nothing to say my family can't hear."

Porter stepped closer, crowding her space, looming over her. Not drop-dead handsome like Jonas, but still far from ugly. His gray-green eyes were his best feature with their long lashes. She couldn't miss the hardness glinting in their depths right now.

"Walk with me ... unless you want your family to hear

how you're making a fool of yourself. I wouldn't want to add to your embarrassment."

She ignored him and sat in the chair. "No."

Her refusal surprised him. She could see his discomfiture as he turned to pace a few steps.

"Very well," he said facing her again, drawing himself up to his full height. "In this non-receptive mood, I already know you won't like what I'm about to say, but you need to hear it anyway. I didn't mention anything before because I thought he ..." Porter nodded toward where Jonas stood with her brothers, staring at them. "Was out of the picture. I mean, for all his professions about caring, he hasn't shown his face once since you returned home."

"How do you know any of this?" she demanded, angry now. Who would talk about her behind her back like this?

Shea turned her head and looked through the kitchen window. Lisa and Katy were laughing as they put the dishes away, but Trina's face was plastered to the window. Watching them. Trina. She should have known.

Porter was still talking. "Jonas Cameron is not who you think he is. Stop acting so cow-eyed around him and wise up. He has an unsavory past, a sordid reputation, and as the youngest son, little to no hope of inheriting anything substantial from the ranch. It's why he's sniffing around you. He wants the money your brothers gave you."

Cow-eyed? Unsavory past? The reputation she couldn't dispute, but the comment about him inheriting nothing from the Triple C was so ludicrous she laughed in Porter's face. "You're sad, pathetic, desperate, jealous, and delusional. If I want to make a fool of myself with Jonas Cameron, it's none of your business. Never will be. Now, I'm going to spell it out for you like I should have done when I first came home. I don't love you, Porter. I don't even like you, and I will never marry you. Now, I want you to leave. And don't come back. You're no longer welcome here."

She stood, forcing him to take a step back.

"Bout time, little sis." Ben, the youngest of her three brothers, approached the patio steps. "You heard the lady, Porter. Need help finding your car?"

Porter glared at Ben and then her. His eyes darkened, filled with daggers, broken bottles, guns, and rusty chains as he stared—the same look he had the last time she saw him in Hastings Bluff. Wild, crazed, angry, ticked off. His parting words whispered through her mind. *You'll be sorry.*

Porter turned on his heel and stormed off.

"Good riddance," Noah said, coming over to put an arm around her shoulders.

"Never did understand why you tolerated Porter. I never could stand him, even as a pup." Eli clapped her on the back none too gently. "Baby girl, we put Jonas in your old room. Why don't you have him walk you back to your cabin and let's call it a night? It's past my bedtime."

Jonas walked up, a small duffel bag over his shoulder.

Shea dipped her chin to her chest. No doubt her face glowed like the neon beer sign at Sidewinders. How much had he heard?

"I like your family." Jonas dropped his duffel on the porch by the door, took her elbow, and guided her toward her cabin. "But I didn't come here to see them. Why don't you show me this little one-room cabin Eli is so proud of? He said he remodeled it so you could have your space from Trina and the kids."

He took her hand, his much larger one engulfing hers. Warmth seeped into her, a warmth she'd missed for too long.

She didn't know whether to be pleased or disappointed when he insisted on them sitting on the front steps instead of going inside.

"I have to leave Sunday morning to get back, so I want to spend every waking moment with you tomorrow. Tonight, we're both tired, so I'm going to leave you here. Sweet dreams."

Shea nodded, both relieved and disappointed that he wouldn't stay for a while. Still, she needed to show him how he affected her, this six-foot-three, walking, talking hormone-whisperer with a heart of fire and ice.

Reaching up, she pressed her hands on either side of his face and pulled him down for one chaste kiss. "I am tired, Jonas, but I'm also beyond thrilled to see you. This long-distance stuff is hard."

His lips, firm but soft, brushed her cheek, both eyes, and her forehead before he pulled away. "Best I head back to the house now. You okay staying here in the cabin? Alone?"

She smiled and nodded. "Yeah, I've been here since I came home. Don't get me wrong, I love my nieces and nephews, but they can be a bit overwhelming. And Trina is ... well, we get along much better when we're not around each other."

He chuckled. "She's a handful."

"You have no idea."

After one more lingering kiss, he stepped away. "Don't you think for a minute this fulfills my promise."

"Oh, I hope not." Shea's fingers touched her lips.

He walked away then, stopping to look over his shoulder after a few paces.

She waved before slipping inside and closing the door behind her. Her dreams would be sweet tonight.

She moved through the darkness, not needing the light to find her way. Tomorrow she would join the family for breakfast. Afterward, she wanted to take Jonas for a ride around *her* ranch. Show him all the similarities in their lives, how—

An arm slipped around her waist. A hand clamped over her mouth. "Shhh, now," Porter said. "We didn't finish our little talk."

Chapter Twenty-Seven

The bright outdoor floodlights still shone around the farmhouse illuminating the way. A shadow stood at the front window. Eli. Waiting up for him.

Jonas smirked. Protective big brother. With as much as Shea had been through, he couldn't blame him. He felt the same way about Mallory and Cassidy, and goodness knows how much trouble his sisters had gotten into over the years. He and his brothers had busted the chops of more than one lusty teenage boy.

Eli opened the door for him, but before either one could say anything, a scream ruptured the night's silence.

Jonas never stopped. He turned mid-step and was off the porch in one giant leap, running flat out back toward Shea's cottage.

His training and years in the field kicked in after three steps. He angled his course toward the side of her house and slowed his pace for silence. With his back to the cabin's wall, he inched closer and closer to the window. The dimness of the interior and the night's shadows made it difficult to determine details, but he saw enough to know Shea was fighting off an attacker. In a matter of seconds as Jonas sized up the situation, the assailant backhanded her across the face. She fell to the floor where he now leaned over her.

"Drink it or I'll force it down your throat!" The man ordered, one hand gripping her face.

Throwing caution to the wind, Jonas ran to the front of the cabin and with one mighty shoulder slam, broke the door in. The next second, he grabbed Shea's attacker by the shirt and threw him across the room.

"Oooof!" He hit the wall face-first and collapsed to the floor, moaning.

Not enough. Not nearly enough. Fury flowed through Jonas's veins like a spring runoff. He flipped the guy onto his back, ready to pummel him.

Porter Townsend.

How dare he assault her like this. Enraged and more than a little out of control, Jonas grabbed Porter's shirt, pulled him to his feet, and drew back and slugged him.

Porter dropped like the spineless weasel he was, this time without the moaning. Without any sound or movement.

Pain zinged through Jonas's knuckles, but the solid crunch of Porter's nose disintegrating added fuel to an all-consuming fire. That a man, any man would lay hands on a woman intent on harm infuriated him. That it was Shea unleashed murder in his heart.

He reached for Porter again but had to haul the man's dead weight upright. As he drew his fist back to hit him again, Eli grabbed Porter, swung him out of Jonas's grasp, and dumped him on the floor.

"He's not worth going to jail for. I got this. See to Shea."

The blood haze took a second to clear enough for Jonas to comprehend what Eli said. When the words sank in, he wheeled around to find Shea on the floor, her back against the small love seat and holding a hand to her cheek. His heart, already pounding from the adrenalin rush, doubled its pace, beating so hard he wondered if a heart attack was imminent.

Her right cheek. She held her right cheek. Thank goodness. Had Porter hit the side she'd had surgery on, he would have killed him for sure. Might still.

Jonas fell to his knees in relief, crawled to her side, and pulled her hand away. Unable to see much in the dark, he kissed her hand. "Don't move. I need to turn on the light."

"I got it," Eli told him.

With the light came reality. The busted door hung

lopsided on its hinges. A table lay overturned in a corner. Furniture in disarray. Splinters of glass littered the floor. Did Shea break the lamp while struggling with Porter?

Jonas tamped down his bull-charging, red cape impersonation again.

Shea sat with legs outstretched. Her head wobbled like a bobble-head doll's. "Jonas?"

She slurred his name.

"It's okay, baby. I'm here. You're safe." What had Porter done?

"Drug," she mumbled.

"What?" It took a second for him to decipher the meaning, but then he searched the floor around her. A vial peeked out from under the sofa. Mostly empty, but with a small amount of fluid still in it.

He collected the bottle and carefully set it on the table in the kitchen. If Porter wouldn't talk, at least they had something to analyze.

He grabbed a towel, held it under cold water, and returned to Shea's side to wipe her face.

Her eyes had a dull, dazed look, her pupils big and unfocused.

"Shea's been drugged. We need to get her to a hospital."

Porter lay on the floor unconscious. Not a problem for now.

Eli whipped out his cell phone. "Let me make a few

calls."

Jonas lifted Shea's chin with care and stared into her cinnamon-brown eyes. "Shea, baby. Nod if you understand what I'm saying."

She never made eye contact, but she did grab his wrist and held on.

"Stay with me, Shea. Fight this."

Whether she understood or not he couldn't tell because her head never stopped nodding and bouncing.

"Ben's on his way."

He didn't remember lifting Shea in his arms or carrying her out the door. When Ben opened the rear door of the truck, Jonas climbed in with Shea cradled on his lap.

Eli held the door. "Ben will drive. He knows the shortcuts, but it will still take half an hour to get there. Wade's on his way here. We'll stay and wait for the police."

"Shea said Porter drugged her. I found the vial and put it on the kitchen table. Can you get it?"

Eli nodded and raced back inside. He returned in less than thirty seconds. "Here. Be careful. I couldn't find the lid."

The engine raced, the door slammed, and then they were flying through the night.

They made it to the ER in Great Falls in twenty-one

minutes, a record according to Ben. He took the vial, jumped out, and ran ahead to get help.

Jonas slid out of the truck and carried Shea inside. She'd lost consciousness a few minutes before and her breathing had slowed to a scary rate.

A doctor and one of the ER staff met them at the registration desk with a stretcher. "I'm Dr. Greene. Put her down and tell me what happened." He slipped the stethoscope bell under Shea's shirt and listened.

"I saw her assailant hit her across the face. She fell. I don't know if she hit her head or not, but he was trying to force a liquid down her throat when I got to him. I have the bottle, but I don't know how much she ingested."

"Wanda, have the lab guys run an analysis on the contents stat."

The nurse took the vial and raced off.

The doctor turned to Jonas and Ben. "What is your relationship to the patient?"

"I'm her brother," Ben said. "Jonas is her fiancée."

Jonas hid his surprise, grateful when Ben's phone rang and he stepped away to answer it.

"Grab the foot of the gurney. Help me roll her into room twelve." The doctor didn't wait for an orderly. He yanked on the head of the gurney and steered it down the hall.

Jonas jumped into action.

Ben found them a few minutes later. "That was Eli.

Porter talked. He said he got the stuff from a guy he knows. Called it 'salty water.' He bought 2.5 grams of the stuff."

"That's the street name for GHB," the doctor responded without looking away from Shea.

Two nurses entered the room.

The doctor directed them to strip Shea and get her hooked up to an IV and various monitoring machines. Next, he ordered blood work, a urinalysis, and x-rays before taking Jonas and Ben aside. "The nurse needs to catheterize her. Let's give them some privacy."

He motioned Jonas and Ben into the hallway, closed the curtains of the room behind him, and continued explaining. "GHB is one of many date-rape drugs. It's fast-acting and leaves a nasty headache, but it wears off within six-to-eight hours with no lingering effects. Now, this is the tough part. Should I order a rape kit? Have you notified the police?"

Ben looked horrified. "My brother called the police. It was the Cascade County sheriff who got the attacker to identify the drug."

"No rape kit," Jonas said. "It was only two, maybe three minutes from the time I left Shea to when I heard her scream. I got to her in less than thirty seconds and pulled that animal off her. Her clothes were intact."

The reasons for ending Porter Townsend's existence continued to mount.

CCC

Jonas sat by Shea's bedside, counting the freckles that danced across her nose. Sixteen. Seventeen if you counted the tiniest dot on her right cheek. He admired her thick lashes, golden brown, long, and curling, framing the delicate lilac shadows beneath her eyes. High cheekbones and the soft curve of her jaw gave Shea an aristocratic look.

He would never tire of looking at this woman.

The word 'never' carried a forever connotation which startled him. Jonas didn't do forever stuff, at least not with the ladies.

He could with this one.

Shea stirred. Her breathing changed. She turned her head toward him. Her lashes fluttered but her eyes didn't open. This new position offered an unhampered view of the new bruise forming to mar her porcelain skin.

His anger, never quenched, flared again. The police would come to question her—and him—after they finished with Porter. She would have to recount what had transpired last night, although the doctor intimated she may or may not remember much, a characteristic of the drug Porter had used.

The brunt of the storytelling would fall to him. Never had his control been tested so fiercely, but he couldn't let his fury loose. For Shea, he had to do this the right way. She deserved justice, and he would see she got it. One way or another. Porter Townsend needed to go to jail for a very long time.

Soft murmurs crept into her subconscious, one familiar voice in particular. Shea smiled despite the ache in her head and opened her eyes.

Jonas sat on a nearby chair, watching over her as she knew he would. Everything about him screamed protector. His blue eyes held a softness, but storm clouds lurked in their depths. He stared at her unblinking. His intensity both thrilled and terrified her scrambled brain.

She looked away, took a long, steadying breath, and met his eyes again. "You're here."

Crinkles appeared around his eyes, but rather than softening his effect on her, the smile amplified the buzz between them. "Someone has to scare the monsters away."

"And who's going to scare you away?"

Perfect, even, white teeth gleamed in response. He stood with the grace and lethality of a lion stalking its prey as he moved to sit on the side of her bed. "No one."

Despite the drums clanging in her head, an intoxicating mix of excitement, comfort, desire, and trepidation skittered through her. In one of the biggest quirks of her life, she'd found a boyfriend who sat at the top of the food chain.

Boyfriend. She smiled. To call Jonas a boyfriend was

like labeling a jaguar a kitty.

A knock on her door preceded the entry of a man and a woman, both of whom flashed a shiny badge. "I'm Detective Evan Balboa." He motioned to a woman who'd come in behind him. "And this is my partner, Detective Anna Kramer. We're with the Cascade County Police. We need to ask you some questions about last night."

Jonas motioned them in and slid the single chair in the room over for Detective Kramer. "Please. Have a seat."

After ascertaining both she and Jonas were involved in the altercation with Porter, as well as her brother, Eli, Detective Balboa led Jonas from the room to question him separately.

Detective Kramer edged her chair closer to Shea's bed. "Miss Townsend, can you tell me what you remember of the altercation?"

Shea remembered everything—right up until she didn't. The recall stopped like a door being slammed shut. One moment Jonas tackled Porter, leaving her sprawled on the floor, and the next she woke up here, in yet another hospital bed.

The detective asked Shea several intimate details. "Porter Townsend has been arrested. With his confession, the accounts of your brother and Mr. Cameron, and your testimony, I believe we have everything we need to put this guy away. When you're released from the hospital, I'll need you to come to the station and press charges. That is, if you want to."

Jonas and Eli walked in. "Yes, she does," they both said in unison.

The two detectives looked at each other before turning to her again. "Miss Cameron? Is this your wish?" Detective Kramer asked.

Shea took a moment to think the question through. She had no desire to hurt Porter, even though he'd hurt her. But letting him go free, without any consequences for his actions wouldn't solve his problems. He needed help. Counseling. And yes, he deserved prison time. She didn't bother looking at Jonas or Eli. She met Detective Kramer's unflinching stare and asked, "You said he admitted attacking me. Why did he drug me?"

"Porter had an Idaho-issued marriage license in his pocket. Idaho laws do not require a blood test or waiting period before a marriage ceremony. His intent was to drug you into compliance and drive back over the state line where he had a justice of the peace waiting to perform the marriage."

Jonas slammed his fist against the far wall. "He had to know she would have it annulled. And what kind of person would perform a marriage for someone so obviously out of it?"

"Happens all the time in Las Vegas. A little money slipped into the right hands ...." Detective Balboa opened his hands and shrugged.

"Desperation often results in foolish behavior," Detective Kramer went on. "Porter owes a substantial amount of money to a loan shark who threatened to carve him into little pieces if he doesn't repay his debt by the end of the month. In his panic, Porter saw Ms. Townsend's inheritance as his only way out. He planned to coerce her into marriage and then hold her captive until he got his hands on the money."

Eli threw his hands in the air. "Pathetic."

Sickened by the revelation, Shea closed her eyes. "Yes, I want to press charges against Porter."

The doctor released her from the hospital in the afternoon. After losing a battle of wills to Jonas, Eli agreed to leave his truck for them and called Ben to come pick him up.

"We planned to spend today together," Jonas told Shea after settling her in the passenger seat. "It's already half gone. The rest belongs to me and I'm not sharing."

"I wanted to take you horseback riding, show you my ranch, but I'm not sure I'm up to it."

"I'd love to see your home from horseback, but we'll do it another time."

"Okay. What do you think about a picnic instead? We could stop and pick up a few things, maybe go to the lake."

Jonas glanced at her. "Or we can go back to your place

and hang out there. Lounge on the sofa. Watch movies. Eat popcorn. Or sit and talk. Doesn't take much to make me happy. Time with you is enough."

Her heart melted. "Home it is. You can help me cook supper."

"Grilled cheese is my specialty," he chuckled. "In fact, it's the one edible thing I make, but I'm good at following directions, too."

Somehow, she doubted that, but it didn't bother her.

Cooking turned out to be a non-issue because her sisters-in-law left a lasagna and a salad in the fridge for them along with a note to call when they arrived.

After they ate, Shea showered and changed into yoga pants and a baggy t-shirt before turning the television to the classic movies channel.

One movie turned into a marathon, the chatter becoming white noise after a while. Content to sit beside him and luxuriate in the heat he generated, she turned the volume low while they spoke of what they liked and disliked—foods, movies, colors, hopes, and dreams. Casual topics depleted, their conversation turned to more serious subjects.

"Eli mentioned one more surgery. I thought you were done. What is this one for?" Jonas asked.

"All the serious stuff is over. My vision is getting better and better, and the doctors are pleased enough, I don't have to go back to LA. The next surgery—if I have it—is merely cosmetic." She dipped her head, her hair forming a curtain over her face. "For the scars."

"What do you mean if you have it? Why wouldn't you?"

She'd gone back and forth on her reasons too many times to count, never reaching a decision. "I don't know. I guess I'm tired of all the hospitals, doctors, and pain. I'm tired of putting my life on hold."

"So, the scars don't bother you?"

"Me, no," she answered. "It's more that they bother everybody else. I don't like it when people stare the first time they see my scars. Some of them still stare."

"I think you should have the surgery. You've come this far, why not finish it?"

His words surprised her. And hurt a little, too. "Do they look so bad?"

"What? Your scars? No. Not to me. I know they're there, but I don't see them anymore. But if people staring upsets you, get rid of them. The scars, not the people." His lips twitched.

"Mm." A novel thought. So simple. Why hadn't she thought of it? "Maybe I will."

"When?"

"Dr. Eicholmann said to wait three months from the last surgery, which would put it late May, but I haven't consulted with the surgeon he recommended. I guess when depends on his schedule."

"Call on Monday and make an appointment."

She'd struggled with this decision for weeks and he'd reduced it to a simple, cut and dried conclusion. A weight lifted from her shoulders.

"Now, what about school?" he asked.

She beamed. "I have one more course to go. The new class starts next week, which means with a little bit of luck, I can graduate before having this last surgery."

"What comes after that?"

Her smile slipped. "I don't know. I haven't thought beyond school and the surgeries. The future is kind of out there somewhere."

"Why do I hear a 'but' in that statement?"

She searched his eyes for a clue of how he felt. Would the truth scare him off? That she wanted to return to Hastings Bluff because of him? Jonas had made it clear he wasn't into relationships. Any hint of clinginess would no doubt send him running.

"It's not uncommon for culinary school graduates to do post-graduate internships with chefs at big-name restaurants in the city. Kind of on the job training. I suppose I could get one of those."

"Doesn't sound like you."

No, it didn't. "Well, I've always wanted my own restaurant, but it's not very realistic. I don't have the start-up capital—"

She stopped when he quirked an eyebrow. Her

ELIZABETH NOYES

brothers had made good on their promise to include her in their father's inheritance. "Okay, money no longer poses a problem, but lack of experience does. I don't know how to run a restaurant."

That questioning eyebrow remained arched, prompting her to question her excuses. She'd worked for Dee Dee the last two years, cooking, waiting tables, ordering supplies, and managing the books as often as not. She could run a small business if she wanted.

"Okay," she said. "I'll think about it. Now, what about you? What's on your calendar while I'm going to school, playing hospital, and dabbling in the entrepreneurial world?"

"First, I didn't get a chance to give you your birthday present last night." He dug in his pants pocket and handed her a small box wrapped in plain white paper and secured with a ribbon that had seen better days. "I've been carrying this around in my pocket, waiting for the right time."

She took the box from him, her insides fluttering. Jewelry. But too small to be a bracelet, and too shallow for a ring, thank goodness. She unwrapped it with care, savoring each moment. When she lifted the lid, relief and delight flooded her. Earrings. In a beautiful, but curious design.

"These aren't just earrings. They have a tracking device embedded in the design. My brother Wade made a pair for Lucy when she had a stalker trying to abduct her.

Garrett, James, and Derek all ordered them for their better halves. I want you to have a pair, too. Not that I would stalk you or anything. I just want to know I can always find you ... in case ..." His voice trailed off. He looked away.

From anyone else, the idea of a tracking device sounded creepy. With Jonas though, the gesture was thoughtful, caring, indicative of his protective ways. If she hadn't already given him her heart, he had it now. She touched his face. "Hey, look at me."

Those amazing eyes turned her way, blazing with intensity.

"Thank you. I'll wear them and treasure them."

He reached into his shirt pocket and pulled out a folded piece of paper. "There's something else. I debated about giving you this, but after Eli and the boys handed over your mother's diary, I realized they were right. It's your decision, not mine." He handed her the piece of paper.

She opened it and found a name, an address in Colorado, and a phone number. Tears misted over her vision. The name, Lydia Farley, brought bittersweet memories from the past. Her mother. In Denver, Colorado. "She's alive?" she choked out.

He nodded.

She refolded the paper and crushed it in her fist. Did she want to talk to her? See her, a mother who left her child without a goodbye or a backward glance? First, the diaries. Now this. "I don't know if I can."

"You can," Jonas reassured her. "You're stronger than you think, but only if that's what you want. Don't make the decision now."

He was right again. It was too much to digest right now.

Chapter Twenty-Eight

Jonas had no intention of returning to Eli's house before daybreak. He'd left Shea twice before, once at the hospital in Boise and again last night. He regretted both actions. He also knew he'd make the same decisions again given the circumstances. What's wanted and what's right don't always mesh. Shea had needed time with her brothers and he'd had responsibilities waiting at home. Still did.

Tonight, he intended to protect and comfort her, but nothing more. Not yet.

When the current movie ended—he had no idea what it was—Shea turned to him, her expression serious. "What is this thing between us, Jonas? Where do you see it leading?"

The same thoughts had nagged him for weeks, but it

came as a surprise that she would have the same concerns. "I don't know. This is uncharted territory for me. I don't have a roadmap."

She frowned and caught her bottom lip between her teeth. Several moments passed before she spoke again. "Look, I don't know how to play games so I'm going to just say this. I care about you, probably more than I should. I want to see where whatever this ..." She waved a hand between them. "Takes us."

He leaned in with every intention of kissing her senseless, but her hand came up and pressed against his chest.

"But slow. Is that okay?"

He smiled and continued to press forward until only a breath separated them. "I can handle slow. It's the distance that's killing me."

He kissed her then, a simple, feathery brush across her lips, and then he pulled away. "Goodnight, Shay-Shay. Sweet dreams. Be sure to lock the door behind me."

When the sound of the lock clicked behind him, he released a frustrated sigh and walked away. The night would be long for him, outside, under the stars, keeping watch over her. Alone with his thoughts.

Jonas swabbed the last bite of waffle through the puddle of maple syrup on his plate, stuffed it in his mouth

and nodded when Trina offered him a refill on his coffee. "Thanks," he said between swallows. "This is delicious."

Shea sat beside him at the big dining table and sipped her coffee with a contented smile.

The whole family had gathered here this morning, although the kids had long ago finished and taken off to parts unknown. It amused him to think of Garrett and Wade with their rug rats running wild like this in another year or so.

"Well, your visit turned out a mite more eventful than I expected." Eli leaned back in his chair and patted his lean, non-existent belly. "Any idea when you might get up this way again? I'd love to give you a tour of the property, show you how a cattle ranch operates. Bet it's not so different from horse ranching."

"I'd like to, but the next few months might be difficult. Shea has her classes, tests, and graduation, and then the final surgery and recuperation. I've got two brothers with pregnant wives due to pop at any moment, twin sisters trying to plan a double wedding around the babies' arrival, and two brand new houses they're building on the property. Plus, we're doing a remodel of our main barn, have our semi-annual round-up scheduled, and three out-of-state auctions we're showing in. Add in a long overdue vacation Mom and Dad are taking, well ... it might be the fall before everything shakes out."

He and Shea had discussed all of this the night before,

but when he put it out there all at once it seemed a bit overwhelming, like maybe this long-distance relationship might go on for longer than he anticipated. Which sucked. Still, despite the ruckus with Porter, Jonas wouldn't trade this time with Shea for anything.

One month later

Shea took her apron off and dropped it in the laundry hamper outside the ladies' locker room. She'd finished her last class the day before and had aced her cooking demonstration in front of no less than five well-known local chefs.

She packed up all her stuff, took one last look around the school's culinary kitchen, and left for the last time with mixed emotions. On the one hand, she was thrilled with her work and the chef instructors' remarks. High praise indeed from two of the best known for their dismissive attitudes. One had even offered her an internship with him in Las Vegas. She hadn't yet declined, but she would. A big city was the last place she wanted to go.

On the other hand, life had set her adrift. She had her surgery date in two more weeks with a short recovery time and a long healing period, and afterward, she could get on with her life—if she only knew what to get on with.

Like before when Jonas left her at the Boise hospital, their communication dwindled to sporadic texts, infrequent

emails, and a short call once every week or so. Her head understood the conflicts in their schedules but her heart ached with the fear of the distance growing between them. Which was why she finally got up enough courage to contact Dee Dee.

Her friend, boss, and soon-to-be partner had embraced her idea and asked her to send a proposal with a business plan, suggested changes, ROI, and proposed terms. They had a call tonight to discuss it in more detail. Shea slid into the Ford truck Eli had given her to use for school. It didn't look like much but was in better condition under the hood than most brand new cars.

Back at the apartment—the one Eli and her brothers kept for when they came to Missoula for the Cattlemen's Association meetings and events, for the auctions they attended throughout the year, and now for her to use while in school—Shea grabbed the suitcases she'd already packed and headed home to the Cornerstone Ranch.

She stopped at a burger takeout and ate as she drove. The thought of eating dinner with Eli, Trina, and the kids seemed like too much effort. Maybe she could catch Jonas tonight, tell him about her talks with Dee Dee and get his perspective.

By the time eleven o'clock rolled around, she'd tried his cell phone three times with no answer.

"This is Jonas. Leave me a message."

Disappointment crushed her. "Hi, Jonas. It's Shea. I

was ... uh ...hoping to talk to you tonight. I finished up with school today. Had my kitchen test and aced it. Now it's hurry up and wait ... and, uh ... I haven't heard from you for a while. I'll try you another time. Bye."

She grabbed a carton of ice cream from the freezer and a spoon and flopped down on the sofa in the dark. Loneliness ranked right up there with rejection, failing confidence, heartache, and a good dose of the stomach flu.

Jonas dumped his gear in a heap on the barn floor, stripped Diablo of the tack, and led him outside for a wash. The roundup had been dusty and tiring, and longer than the four days he'd planned on thanks to downed fences, one ornery stallion, and the fact both his brothers had stayed behind on baby-watch.

He'd dreamed of a long, hot shower while lying on the cold, hard ground last night. Now, it was within reach. A shave wouldn't hurt either. And some hot food. First, though, he had to get Diablo washed and fed, the tact cleaned, and his gear stowed.

An hour later, with clean skin and fresh clothes, and feeling human once again, Jonas grabbed his cell phone. After six days of neglect, his mailbox was bound to be full. He never took the phone with him on the roundups. No coverage out in the far pasture and foothills.

He picked it up, thumbed the power button and ...

nothing. Dead. He'd forgotten to put it on the charger before he left.

No matter. It was late anyway. Messages could wait until tomorrow. He plugged the phone in and trudged back downstairs to heat up the plate his mom had left him.

The next morning brought more delays. A sick horse, a morning delivery, a missed order leaving them short of feed, a limb through the barn roof, and a new customer who decided to drop in without notice kept him from his messages until evening. By the time he saw Shea's missed calls and listened to her voice mail, the night was too far gone. Tomorrow. First thing. He'd make her his first priority.

At 9:05 A.M. he pressed her name on his favorites list. Three rings later, her voice mail picked up. Same thing at 10:10, 11:30, 12:16, and 2:00. He gave up at 4:40 and left his own voice mail.

"Shea, I'm so sorry. It's roundup time. I've been out on the range for a week without cell coverage. I didn't pick up your voicemail until late last night and played catch up all day today. Hey, I miss you, baby. Call me."

Later, as he undressed for a shower, he knocked his phone into the toilet.

Shea spent the day at the Park City Grill in Great Falls, an experience that proved both eye-opening and exhausting. Chef Luis Saldona, one of her final evaluators, had taken a liking to her and one other student and invited them both to spend a day in his kitchen to see how a real commercial restaurant operated. A great honor, but at the end of the day, he had only one internship to give.

Shea didn't wait for Chef Luis to make his choice. Her future lay in a different direction, one well south of here. She thanked him for his mentoring and consideration, for letting her see his operation firsthand, explained her plans for the future, and walked away with a feeling akin to relief.

The euphoria of the day's experience carried her out of the city and part of the way home before her mind to turn to Jonas again. Had he returned her call?

At a red light, she saw the missed calls and a lone voicemail from him. Smiling, she started to thumb the speaker button—but laid the phone on the passenger seat instead. Weary and distracted did not make good companions while driving at night.

The anticipation built all the way home. She pulled up outside her cabin and parked, anxious to listen to his message.

In person, nothing matched the way Jonas Cameron turned her inside out and upside down. Hearing his voice came in a close second, though. Even in the brief, hi, how are you message he left. Grinning like a crazy woman, she raced to the door of her cabin.

Her first attempt to call him back went to voice mail.

As did the second. And the third. Shoulders slumping, she finally left a voice message. "Hi, it's Shea. I'm home. Call me back as soon as you can no matter how late. I have so much to tell you. I miss you, too."

Midnight came and went with still no answer. At 2:20 A.M. she gave up and went to bed, but sleep didn't come until the dark sky lightened to gray.

At twenty past noon, resignation set in. She and Eli would leave shortly. The surgeon who would perform her cosmetic procedure, the last surgery she hoped, had had a cancellation and wanted her in his office today for pre-op. Surgery tomorrow meant she'd have bandages on her face for graduation. She didn't care about attending the ceremony, only the diploma that would give her credence in the culinary world. That and putting this last surgery behind her so she could get on with her life. But now Jonas wouldn't be a part of this either.

"Ready to go?" Eli asked.

She looked up at her brother, grateful for his big heart. Eli had been her champion from the moment he stepped into the Boise ER. After the shabby way she'd treated him and the others, leaving them the same way her mother had run out on her, she wouldn't have blamed him if he'd turned his back on her. But he didn't.

It was Eli who'd deposited her portion of the inheritance in a separate bank account after their father's funeral. His suggestion to let the addendum in the will expire, which forfeited her share of the estate to her three brothers. His action that transferred ownership of the original funds back to her as a gift, thereby eliminating the huge expense of disputing the will. And it was Eli who arranged for the DNA testing that proved once and for all Wallace Townsend did indeed father her. And now Eli had set aside his own needs once again to ensure she had someone with her for the next round of medical visits.

Maybe she should focus more on her brother than on Jonas. Eli never failed her. She couldn't even reach Jonas by phone.

Guilt hit her with a rush. This separation was no more Jonas's fault than her own. She had suggested he return home to his responsibilities there. She had wanted the time apart to reconnect with her brothers. If the trials of a long-distance relationship bogged them down before they even got started, they had no chance of enduring.

She needed to make a decision regarding Jonas because Dee Dee wanted to move forward with their deal. She'd found her future.

Chapter Twenty-Nine

Two weeks later

"Okay, let's sign and make it official. When do we start, what's the timeline, and what's our first step?"

Shea stared at the woman across from her. She hadn't understood until seeing the excitement in Dee Dee eyes just how much the other woman wanted to do this deal. The fact she'd taken off from the diner and driven six hours to come here on a Monday should have been an indicator.

For the first time since hatching this crazy, wild scheme, Shea believed it might actually happen. She would provide the capital to buy the property next to the Calico Diner, combine the two buildings, remodel the diner, add a bakery section, enlarge and upgrade the kitchen, and renovate the new building into a dining room where they would serve dinner by reservation two nights a week to start. The dining hall would also serve as an event hall for receptions and other occasions, and if its popularity grew as she suspected it would, they might expand the dining room service to three or even four dinner nights. The last part of the renovation included the upstairs apartment. It would be enlarged and updated, with the access moved to the front of the building for safety but remain separate from the diner.

In return for the investment, Dee Dee agreed to give her fifty percent of the business making them co-owners. They would also change the name of the diner. To what, she had no idea yet, but they needed a new name to signify their new start.

"I've already gotten proposals from three construction crews—one in Pocatello, one in Idaho Falls, and ..." Shea smiled and crossed her fingers under the table. "The third one is not a construction company per se. He's a local handyman. I know firsthand the quality of his work, so if you agree I'd like to keep our business as local as possible. Of course, you'll need to review all these proposals and decide."

"Let me guess. Edward Spencer and his four sons?"

Shea slid a stack of file folders across the table. "Right on the first guess. Here are the three construction bids. Edward's farm was hit hard by the drought last year. He and the boys need the cash, which means they'll move a lot faster than the out-of-town crews."

Dee Dee glanced at the bottom line of all three proposals and handed the folder right back to Shea. "Their price is within our budget and beats the others. I've known Edward for years and I trust him. Let's do it."

Grinning, Shea took the folders and returned it to her bag. "Meaning with him local and you in on all his secrets, you can bully poor Edward into working faster."

Dee Dee's laughter filled Shea's little cottage. "He estimates twelve-weeks from start to finish. Let's see if I can motivate him to finish in ten."

With the contract signed and the construction crew selected, they decided Dee Dee would engage Spencer and Sons, meet with Edward to select suppliers, and oversee the actual construction project.

Shea would handle the administration and financial side and would work with local banks and services. She liked the thought of giving back to the community. They're the ones who made the diner a success.

They had a short celebration filled with tears and hugs before her new partner made the return trip to Hastings Bluff.

"One more thing," Shea added as Dee Dee walked out the door. "I want to keep my part in this on the down-low for as long as possible, okay?"

Dee Dee tilted her head to one side and gave her a considering look. "In other words, you don't want a certain

Cameron to know what you're up to."

Right on time, Shea's face caught fire. How to explain the complicated relationship she had with Jonas when she didn't understand it herself? She squared her shoulders instead. "Correct. We have some things to work out, and I don't want to scare him away or make him feel trapped. Hastings Bluff is my home, my future. If things work out for us, he'll be happy for me. If they don't ...." She shrugged. "I'll move on with my dream, with or without him."

Nodding, Dee Dee pulled her in for one last, fierce hug. "I can't tell you how much I admire and love you, girl. And I can't wait to get you back home where you belong."

Alone now, Shea thought about her timeline again and looked in the mirror.

Her face had grown thinner, almost gaunt like the rest of her. According to her sisters-in-law, she had the classic cheekbones of a Hollywood starlet. Even Trina had agreed.

Two weeks since her surgery and the swelling had dissipated. Some bruising remained, but the awful greenish color faded with each day.

Shea laughed, thankful the surgeon had worked his magic on both sides of her face. Looking closer, she could see the red scar lines in front of her ears. They could take up to a year to fade like any scar. One day, though, the thin lines would turn silvery white, too faint for casual notice.

Tears filled her eyes. The journey from the fateful day

when Vern had abducted her to this present time had been filled with more emotional ups and downs than any one person should bear, but she'd come through it all, come out on top.

Now, she wanted Jonas with all her heart, but not if he didn't have the same deep longing for her. It would be difficult to live in the same town, seeing him out and about, and she couldn't even consider the thought of him with someone else, but a survivor survived. And the good Lord hadn't spared her from the clutches of a monster, hadn't brought her through all these trials for nothing. There was a reason for her life, one which may or may not include Jonas.

❦❦❦

Six weeks later

Life had become impersonal, boring, and a burden. Jonas loved his work, loved working with the horses, but it no longer filled the emptiness inside him.

He loved his family, but his brothers were always laughing and bragging about their new babies. Forget going out after work like they used to, Garrett and Wade couldn't wait to go home.

Derek and James were much the same way, wrapped up with his sisters, sans the baby pictures. He'd never seen two more besotted, adoring men. Of course, he was happy for all of them, but every conversation on the ranch seemed to center around the new babies or the joint wedding next month.

Dad watched him but didn't say much these days. He frowned a lot instead, sometimes shaking his head before he walked away. Waiting to see if his words had taken root, no doubt. Whether his boneheaded youngest son would pull himself together enough to go get the girl. At least Mom had gotten off his back. Between working herself into a tizzy with all the wedding plans and wanting to spend every possible moment with her grandbabies, there was no time left for him other than a snappish, "Stop moping around, Jonas."

Perhaps Dad had the right of it. Maybe he should go get his girl. He talked and texted with Shea most every day, but two long months had passed since he'd seen her, touched her soft skin, or smelled the sweet fragrance of her hair. Thinking of her lately left an ache in his chest.

Or maybe he just needed to cut loose with the boys for a change.

The thought repulsed him. All the guys he'd hung with before joining the Army and after he returned home had never quite grown up. They still drank too much on Friday nights, got themselves tossed in jail to sleep it off, and did it all over again the next week. Thirty-somethings now, those boys had no clue what they wanted from life.

That lifestyle no longer appealed to him. Sometimes he wondered whether he'd done the right thing leaving the service.

His phone vibrated in his pocket and jerked him out the reverie. He pulled it out, looked at the screen, and smiled. *Shea.* Perfect timing.

"Why, hello, beautiful. How did you know I needed to hear your voice?"

Her tinkling laugh filled him with delight. "I guess the vibes you were sending got through. Good morning, I miss you, too."

"So, how was your last appointment with the doctor? Did he release you?"

"Yes, he did. The bruises and swelling are gone. I'm through with the surgeries and finished with school. Yay!"

"That's wonderful. So, what's next?"

It was hard to nourish a long-distance relationship via airways. He found it more and more difficult to find meaningful topics to discuss. This last month their conversations had grown short and stilted. The last thing he wanted to do was invite more shadows in, but he had to know. Did they have a future?

"That's why I called. I'm moving back to Hastings Bluff, Jonas."

The awful loneliness he'd been fighting exploded in a burst of rainbows. Joy surged through him. She was coming *home.* "Thank you, Jesus! When, baby? Tell me the day and I'll be on your doorstep with my truck to load whatever you want to bring."

She laughed again, the sound bubbly and carefree. "That's so sweet, but not necessary. I've got everything arranged. As for when ... how about tomorrow?"

The world burst into color. He heard the birds singing, felt the sun's warmth on his face, and stared up at the clear, blue heaven with a prayer of thanks on his lips. He didn't have to go get his woman after all. She was coming home to him. He cleared his suddenly tight throat.

"Jonas?" She sounded worried. "Is that okay?"

"Oh, baby, nothing has ever been more okay. I've been out of my mind with wanting to see you again. What time will you get here? Is one of your brothers bringing you? Are you coming out to the ranch? My mom will be thrilled."

"No, I'm coming alone. Eli signed over the truck I've been using, so I've got good, reliable transportation now. Dee Dee's letting me stay in the apartment above the diner. She had it remodeled. I expect to roll into town late afternoon."

"You're going back to work at the diner?"

"Something like that."

Evasive little minx. What did she have up her sleeve? No matter. There'd be plenty of time to ferret out her secrets with her back in town. All the time in the world. "Promise you'll call me when you leave your brother's. In fact, call me every hour on the hour so I can track your progress. I'll be the one in front of the diner waiting with open arms."

Jonas pulled double-duty through the rest of the day, intent on getting ahead of the workload so he could take time off tomorrow. Even so, the hours passed with agonizing slowness. When his phone rang again with Archer's name in the window, he answered the call with eagerness. "Yo, buddy. What's up?"

Archer's booming laugh had Jonas yanking the phone away from his ear.

"I heard through the grapevine that something had sugared up your attitude. Does that mean your girl is finally coming home?"

Shaking his head, Jonas groaned. What was so fascinating about his love life that everybody in this town needed to discuss it? "Is there a point you want to make, or did you call just to harass me?"

"I'm heading over to the steakhouse in Challis tonight. The mighty Sheriff Evers has given me a rare night off and I hoped we could maybe shoot the bull like old times. If your honey really is coming back, this might be the only free night you get for a long while."

"Har-har-har, very funny. What time?" Jonas rolled his eyes but couldn't stop a smile forming. He'd take Shea over Archer any day.

"Meet you there at six?"

"See you then."

CCC

Jonas spotted the Ford Bronco with the HBPD emblem on the side, pulled in beside it, and strolled down the sidewalk to the steakhouse. Inside, he spotted his old friend at a table near the back.

Archer gripped his hand. "Good to see you, man."

"You, too."

After they ordered and offered each other a few good-natured insults, Archer posed an unexpected question. "I've been meaning to ask you about something, the name of this town. Hastings Bluff. It's not like there are any steep cliffs overlooking the rivers in the area. I haven't run across any Hastings either. So, what gives?"

Jonas leaned back in his chair with a laugh. "The town wasn't named for a physical bluff. Legend has it back in the mid-1800s a man from Chicago by the name of Hastings was making his way west to Seattle when his wagon broke down near here. The homesteaders in the area wanted to help him, but they had crops to gather and needed every available hand for harvest. They told him he'd have to wait.

"Unhappy with their response because the delays would put him at risk with the approaching winter, he conned one of the farmers into a poker game. Hastings wagered his broken wagon and all of his supplies against the farmer's parcel of land. Smelling a windfall, the farmer agreed. The tale goes that the cards Hastings dealt himself were awful. He had nothing, not even a pair of deuces, but he kept raising the pot until the farmer folded despite having three of a kind."

Archer grinned. "I can see where this is leading."

Jonas ignored him and continued. "Instead of taking the farmer's land, though, Hastings asked again for his help fixing the wagon's axle. Grateful not to lose his land, the farmed helped him repair the axle. After the traveler went on his way, the farmer harvested his crops and decided to name his land after the man. That, my friend, was how Hastings Bluff was born."

Archer laughed and knocked over his glass, spilling water and splattering the waitress as she arrived to deliver their food. "I'm sorry, ma'am," he managed to say between chuckles.

After she sopped up the mess with a towel and departed, he asked another question. "Remember when we left Fowler's compound this last time?"

The too-innocent look on his friend's face made Jonas wary. "Yeah,"

"And the talk we had about settling down. You meant it when you said you had someone in mind."

Rather than respond, Jonas raised one eyebrow.

"It's Shea, huh? She's the reason you've been ornerier than an angry badger for so long, and now that she's coming back, you're all smiles and joy-joy. I'm right, aren't I?"

"Joy-joy?"

Archer slapped the table, his mouth curved in a lopsided smile big as a crescent moon. "My, how the mighty have fallen. Don't get me wrong, man. I'm happy for you. A little jealous, too, truth be told."

"Mmm," Jonas mumbled. He couldn't bring himself to be angry with his best friend for digging out the truth.

"What's the timeline here. When do you plan to propose?"

Jonas choked on the bite of steak as panic surged through him. He'd barely admitted his feelings to himself. Propose? "I, uh, haven't thought ... haven't gotten that far," he stuttered and wiped imaginary beads of sweat from his forehead.

Archer reached across the table and gripped Jonas's wrist, his expression serious. "Don't worry, Jo. I've got your back. It's not every day a man clamps a ball and chain to his ankle."

"What?"

That's when the cackles started, deep, belly laughs that left Archer wiping tears from his eyes. A moment more and he faceplanted on the table, drumming on it with his fists.

"Some friend you are." Hard as he tried for a scathing tone, Jonas couldn't pull it off, not with the smile tugging at his own mouth. Funny how the initial idea of proposing

had scared the bejeebers out of him, but now that he considered it .... Yeah, he liked it of locking Shea down. He liked it a lot.

The next morning, Jonas awoke to a perfect August day. A great start for the beginning of his future with Shea.

He'd only thought the hours dragged by yesterday. Today the wait was excruciating and reminded him of one of his father's old sayings—*days are long, but years are short.* Hard to believe an entire year had passed since he returned from Nigeria.

Unable to wait any longer, he left work at two o'clock and headed home to shower and shave. Again. He wanted to look his best for Shea.

By three o'clock, he'd driven into town and parked in front of the diner. He sat there trying to decide whether to go in or wait for her there.

A rap on his window made him groan.

"You going to sit out here all afternoon?" James grinned at him. "C'mon inside and have some coffee with me."

Jonas opened the door and slid out. "You're the sheriff. Can't you find somebody to arrest instead of harassing me?"

"I hear you're having difficulty getting through the day. Thought I'd help you pass the time. Now, if you'd rather I give you a citation for loitering and haul you off to jail, I can do that."

"No, thanks. Coffee it is."

The sheriff of Hastings Bluff and his soon-to-be brother-in-law laughed, but then his eyes shifted to look over Jonas's shoulder. "Well, maybe not."

Jonas turned and spotted the truck Shea's brother had given her. She sat in the driver's seat, barely tall enough to see over the wheel, coming down Main Street.

His heart rate kicked into high gear, his eyes latched onto her like a lifeline. Everything around him faded away.

She pulled into a parking space at the end of the row, but he was already there before she could open her door.

"Hi," she whispered, eyes shining up at him.

"Hi yourself." He wrapped her in a bearhug and carried her to the sidewalk where he swung her around in circles. "Woman, you are a sight for my sore eyes."

Chapter Thirty

One week later

Jonas stared at his reflection in the mirror, turned his head side to side, and removed the bit of toilet paper from his chin. Satisfied the bleeding had stopped where he'd nicked himself, he tossed the bit of tissue into the trash. Cleft chins made shaving difficult, but he couldn't remember the last time he'd cut himself. Of course, shaky hands might have something to do with it.

He held his hands out in front, palms down, and watched them in the mirror. Yep. Trembles. The one other time he recalled this fluttery feeling in his belly was the first time he took a girl on a date. Susie Mueller. Ninth grade. Homecoming dance. He'd almost run off the road on the way to her house and could still remember the fear clawing at him after her father had a come-to-Jesus talk with him about getting her home on time.

Back in his bedroom, he donned the fancy silk shirt, looped the bolo tie under his collar, and pulled the string tight. A quick buff of his dress boots against his calves, and he was ready.

"What in blazes is keeping you, son?" Dad stood in the doorway, dressed to kill in the blue-gray Armani suit Mom had insisted on buying for him. He could still hear her arguing. "A suit can make a man, but sometimes it's the man who makes the suit, and you own this one all the way, Cody Cameron."

Jonas studied him for a moment. He did indeed wear it well.

Of course, his mother had followed up with similar suits for each of her three sons. His was a dark charcoal gray. He'd worn it twice before—for Garrett's wedding and then Wade's. And now tonight, for Shea and Dee Dee's *By Invitation Only Pre-Grand Opening* event—a dinner party for their special friends which included the entire Cameron family.

Pride bubbled up inside him, exacerbating his already nervous stomach. In another week, Shea and Dee Dee would host the real grand opening of the newly expanded and remodeled diner which now included a bakery café and new dining room. Due to some great marketing strategy and keeping most of the work and buying in town, their reservation list for the first four weeks had filled up on the first day. It didn't hurt that everyone was thrilled to have Shea back—as a co-owner this time.

"I'm almost ready, Dad."

"You got your shirt and pants on, what else is left to do? You buff any harder on those boots and you'll rub a hole in the legs of your pants. Now, let's go. You know how your mother feels about being on time for dinner."

Jonas put on his suit coat, patted his pants pocket for the twentieth time, and started down the stairs. With another quick look in the foyer mirror, he caught himself brushing a hand over the sides of his hair. Funny. He'd relaxed the 'high and tight' cut he'd worn in service to the somewhat longer 'high regulation' length, but there was still nothing to brush.

"My, don't you look handsome, dear." His mother reached up and patted his cheek.

Somehow, he managed to hold back a groan.

"Your brothers are taking one truck and your sisters are going with Derek and James in another. You're welcome to ride with us." His father said, helping Mom into her coat. Nights in June were often too cool for bare arms.

"Thanks, Dad, but I'll drive my own truck."

"But—"

Mom's jab to his ribs cut him off. "Hush, Cody. He might not want to come home when we do." She gave

Jonas a knowing smile and winked at him.

Heat rose up his neck and flooded his cheeks. He'd need a miracle to survive tonight.

Not waiting for the others, Jonas fast-walked to his truck, cranked it up, and pressed the gas a little too hard on his way down the drive.

Too nervous to go in alone, he pulled into a parking space in front of the diner and waited for the others. The big drop cloth over the diner's sign flared in the evening breeze. Hung four days before, it hid the new name. The big reveal would happen tonight.

Soon, the other members of his family arrived and got out.

Jonas noticed the crowd gathered across the street. Though not included in tonight's festivities, they waited for the unveiling. Small town residents knew everything about everybody, and all this secrecy about the diner's new name was driving them nuts.

One of the ladies of the hour opened the diner's front door and stepped outside. "Hello everyone," Dee Dee called in a loud voice. "Tonight, Shea and I want to share the diner's makeover, the new bakery and introduce a new style of dining here in Hastings Bluff. Be sure and come back for the grand opening next week. Now, it's time to share our new name. Are you ready?"

A cheer went up.

She motioned to two guys, high schoolers from the

looks of them. They stood on either side of Dee Dee holding a rope that would pull the tarp down. At their nod, Dee Dee began the countdown. "On the count of three ..."

The crowd joined in. "One ... two ... three!"

The boys gave a mighty yank and the drop cloth released in a slow flutter to the ground.

"Welcome to Shady's." Dee Dee lifted both hands.

The sign lit up in fancy, neon-blue script letters a foot tall.

"Shady's. Get it? It's a play on both our names, Shea and Dee Dee. Here's to new beginnings."

The cheers grew to a roar with lots of clapping and a few ear-piercing whistles.

"Thank you, thank you," Dee Dee said over and over. She waved to the people, a huge smile revealing every one of her pearly whites. Once the clamor died down, she turned to Jonas and the rest of his family with open arms. "Ready?"

Jonas was beyond ready. He wanted to see Shea.

Dee Dee led them into the new dining room where the tables had been arranged in one long line. The places were set with new dinnerware, flatware, and cut-glass goblets. Nothing too frou-frou or intimidating. Simple fare. But so much better than the scuffed, scarred, cracked, and stained plates and glasses used in the diner.

"Find your name and have a seat. The waitresses will get your drink orders."

Three waitresses dressed in black slacks and white, starched, button-down, shirts stood off to one side. They wore short black aprons around their waists and a white dishcloth draped over one arm, notepads in hand.

Jonas looked for Shea while he found his seat at the far end of the table next to his mother. A place setting had been laid on his other side but had no name card. He didn't give it much thought as he held his mother's chair for her before taking his own.

Once they were all seated, Dee Dee clanged a teaspoon against one of the glasses. "Thank you all for coming. As you know, this is our trial run with the new dining room service, so I guess you could say you're our guinea pigs. Now, the other half of this operation, Miss Shea Townsend will tell you about our menu."

When Shea walked into the room, Jonas's mouth dropped and his stomach did that crazy, fluttery thing again. He devoured her with his eyes.

She wore a form-fitting black cocktail dress with a scooped neck and a hemline that rode a good four-inches above her knees. Long, lean legs led down to delicate feet encased in shiny black heels. A goddess.

He tried to swallow and found all his spit had dried up. He'd never seen her in anything but jeans and baggy shirts. Shea in a dress stopped hearts.

He completely missed the first part of her speech.

"So, while the recipes are mine, the food tonight is

prepared by our own Chef Cecil. Thank you for coming, and I hope you enjoy the meal."

He continued to ogle her as she made her way toward him. Realizing at the last moment she planned to sit next to him, he jumped from his chair to pull hers out. Her smile and a murmured thank-you were angelic. Sheesh, this woman *owned* him, and he loved it.

The dinner seemed interminable. Everyone wanted to offer an opinion. They wanted details, reasons for the reconfigurations, how the idea for the partnership came about, why they chose to give their business to the locals, and on and on.

When the waitresses started to clear away the dirty dishes, Jonas got to his feet. "I think our hardworking waitresses deserve a break. I think it's time we clear out of here, so they can too."

The others grumbled but got to their feet and gathered their things. After many more profuse congratulations, the diners finally cleared out.

"Come with me, Shea." Jonas tried to steer her to a quiet corner.

"But, I need to help Dee Dee clear things—"

"Go on, girl. We've got this." Dee Dee made a shooing motion with her hands.

He took Shea's hand and led her across to the diner

section, choosing a table well away from prying ears. "You know I love you, right?"

Shea ducked her chin, but a beautiful smile curled her lips even while her long lashes hid her eyes. "I suspected you did, but you never told me."

"Well, let me correct that mistake here and now. Shea Townsend, I love and adore you. I also know how much you value truth and honesty, but there are things in my past I can never tell you. Not because I don't want to, but because I'm sworn to secrecy by the government upon penalty of imprisonment. Do you understand? Can you accept that?"

"Yes, Jonas. I understand and I accept it."

"There are other reasons, too. I've seen some wicked things I don't ever want you to know about. Can you accept that, too?"

"May I ask a few questions first? Not about your missions or what you can't talk about. General questions. About you?"

He gave her a cautious nod, ready to shut her off if she veered down the wrong path.

"Did you choose your missions or were they assigned to you?"

"The mission last summer was my choice. All the others were assignments."

"Did you ever doubt the veracity of your assignments?"

He didn't hesitate with his answer. "No. I had complete faith and trust in my chain of command and my decisions."

"Okay, if you could go back to the beginning and make new choices given what you know now, would you make the same choices?"

Again, no hesitation. "Yes."

"It's because you believe in what you do, Jonas. Don't you see? You're a good, honest, moral man. You saw your duty. You did your duty. Without question or doubt. You stood on the front line against the evil in the world and protected your country, your homeland, your family. You protected me." She reached up and captured his face between her hands. "Thank you for your service, soldier. Thank you for your sacrifices."

He tried to shake his head no, but she wouldn't let him. "I didn't sacrifice anything, Shea. I had men on my team, friends who lost limbs, lost their health, and some who lost their lives. They sacrificed."

"No, Jonas. You sacrificed everything. You gave up your innocence, your future, and your joy. Not seeing the scars doesn't mean they're not there. You'll carry them the rest of your life, on your heart and soul, and in your memories. Don't denigrate what you've done. Be proud of it. You stared at the face of evil and stood tall doing it. I cannot tell you how proud I am to be loved by you. Know this if you know nothing else. I love you but I also respect and admire you more than any man I've ever known."

His heartfelt near to bursting from her outpouring. The fancy speech he'd concocted flew right out of his head. "Shea, baby." Even his voice had choked up on him. Him. Mr. Control.

Jonas fumbled in his pants pocket for the little box he'd stashed there. He pulled it out and after three attempts to get the top open, he sank to one knee. "I want to be the man who changes your name, Shea Marie Townsend. You see me, the real me, and you don't run away. Will you marry me? Love me forever and have my babies? Will you stay by my side?"

Both hands covered her mouth while tears pooled in her eyes. Her head moved in a slow up and down motion as she stared at the ring in the box.

"I need to hear you say it, Shea."

A perfect teardrop trickled from each eye. No ugly crying for his girl. She nodded more vigorously, drug her gaze from the ring in the box, and met his eyes. "Yes, Jonas. I will marry you."

She stretched her left hand toward him, fingers spread.

Somehow, he got the ring out of the box and slid it onto her ring finger. A perfect fit. A beautiful fit. His heart hurt with the amount of joy it tried to contain. Shea was his. Almost. "How soon?"

"Wha ... what?" she stuttered.

"I don't want a long engagement. Waiting has almost

done us in too many times."

She beamed. "Okay. How about next week?"

"Yes!" He got to his feet in a rush, grabbed her around the waist, and twirled her round and round.

Her laughter and his shout brought Dee Dee, Cecil, and two of the waitress running into the room.

"What on earth?" Dee Dee exclaimed.

Jonas set Shea back on her feet, his eyes on the meat cleaver in the chef's hands ... the mallet one of the girls held ... and the can of mace the other girl had aimed at him. He'd had one encounter with mace once upon a time when his sister-in-law, Lucy, had sprayed him. He had no desire for another.

Shea didn't say a word, but she held her left hand out to display the three-carat diamond he'd picked for her. It sparkled under the pendant lights.

Dee Dee screamed then.

Cecil tossed his cleaver onto a table and grabbed Dee Dee's hands. Together they danced in a circle, bouncing up and down.

The two waitresses joined hands with them and danced, giggling all the while.

One month later

Jonas stood on the back deck of the Triple C with his arm around his wife's waist and surveyed the sweeping vista before him. Once again, the backdrop of the ranch played host to a Cameron wedding reception. Two, this time. Mallory had become Mrs. James Evers and Cassidy had become Mrs. Derek Naughton earlier today. According to their mother, he and Shea were included in this celebration, too.

He sighed and squeezed her. Mrs. Shea Cameron. Friend. Wife. Lover. And one day, mother of his children. Contentment filled him. He was in love with the most beautiful woman in the world and anxious to take this journey through life with her by his side.

She'd summoned her brothers and they'd come but without their families. A ranch didn't run well for long without someone at the helm, and a six-hour trip down and back in the same day wasn't good for the little ones. Still, they'd come, reluctant at first and hesitant, but Eli, Noah, and Ben loved their little sister and would give her the stars if they could.

His mother wandered over. "Jonas, dear. You do remember we're leaving on our vacation tomorrow, right? You won't forget to water my roses or the vegetable garden, will you? And check the mail, and—"

"My house now, Mom. My responsibility."

When he told his parents he and Shea didn't want to build a new house on the property, they wanted to live here in the home he'd grown up in, Mom had broken down and cried. Even Dad had a suspicious piece of lint get into his eye. They'd been so worried about what to do with the house. With his dad's health becoming more and more problematic, Mom wanted them to spend more time in milder climates. This way they could come and go with peace of mind all was taken care of on the home front.

"Of course, you're right. It's my lot in life to worry though, so indulge me." She patted his face and traipsed off to visit with the guests.

Guests. Three-hundred-plus. Trampling his lawn. It would take weeks for the grass to recover. His smile widened, liking this new focus on life.

The nightmares had stopped, and he gave Shea all the credit. Wrapped around her at night, enveloped in her love, the shadows of his former life had abated. The memories still haunted him, probably always would, but with Shea, he had a formidable weapon. Her light no longer allowed the demons of the past to taint his happiness.

Shea nudged his ribs. "Look over there."

"Where?"

"Archer, Kyle, and Wes ... there." She pointed across the way.

He looked for and found the three now close friends and laughed. They were circling a group of Cassie's friends from her college days.

"Oh my gosh, Clint's joining them?" Her laugh contained a trace of fairy dust, so magical a substance it had the ability to raise his smile no matter the circumstances.

"Life in the west. Wolves always stalk the pretty little deer."

"Yeah, but which ones are the predators and which the prey? From what Cassie says about her friends, those boys might ought to run."

"Speaking of predators, take a gander at Dee Dee dancing with the old dude. Who is he anyway?"

Shea searched for her friend and partner in the dance crowd. "Ahh, Bert Hickman, Wes's boss. He's quite dashing, don't you think? And not much older than Dee Dee. When Wes explained he was coming to town this weekend to finalize the property deal, your mother invited him to the reception. She didn't like to think how everybody in town would be here at the ranch, leaving him in a ghost town with nowhere to eat. He seems ... friendly, don't you think?" She had a speculative look in her eye.

"Is this how it's going to be? Are we going to grow old together, watching over and matchmaking for all the poor deprived singles?"

"Whatever rocks your world, Jonas."

He turned her around and pointed at the window behind them. "There."

With a little effort, she lifted a single eyebrow, something she'd been working on for months.

He grinned when it quirked upward a fraction more. "The dining room, that's where I first saw you."

"When I catered Cate's party."

Jonas found himself nodding and remembering. "Garrett was talking to you and I thought to myself, 'No way. She's mine.' The table was full of luscious things you'd made, but none of them looked as good as you. I knew at that moment my life would change."

"And did it?"

"Oh yeah. Despite all the imperfections of this world, Mrs. Cameron, my life couldn't be more perfect."

To My Readers

Imperfect Promises touches on the issue of Homegrown Terrorism, but this is not a new phenomenon in our country. One early recorded incident was the assassination of President Abraham Lincoln in 1865, a political act motivated by the outcome of the Civil War. Sadly, domestic terrorism has continued through the years.

The al-Queda international terrorist attack on the United States on September 11, 2001, prompted the Patriot Act, which was signed into law by sitting President George W. Bush on October 21, 2001. This Act defines Domestic Terrorism as an attempt to intimidate or coerce a civilian population as a way to influence the policy of a government by intimidation or coercion; or to affect the conduct of a government by mass destruction, assassination, or kidnapping.

Since then, other of our government agencies have further delineated such violent acts as Homegrown Terrorism—violence perpetrated by U.S. residents against U.S. residents while on U.S. soil with the intent to injure, maim, or kill said victims. Such attacks are almost always premeditated and typically stem from a political or religious motivation to draw attention to a perceived injustice, as revenge, to influence an audience, or incite further violence.

Homegrown terrorists are made in the United States, they are not imported. Nearly half of the terrorists who carried out or plotted terror attacks on our country were born here, while many of those born abroad arrived in the U.S. as children. They typically operate alone or in small cells, and target innocents who are unprotected and unaware. Some of these homegrown terrorists plot their attacks and stockpile deadly weaponry for greatest effect. Others are opportunists who act on whim and use whatever is at hand as a weapon.

Be assured, our government works tirelessly to prevent such atrocities, and with a great deal of success, I might add. (The media seldom reports on thwarted attempts.) But the simple truth is the authorities cannot stop them all, so the question arises— With the randomness and unpredictability of such acts, what can we as private citizens do?

The most important thing you can do is educate yourself. Know what is happening in and around your community. Maintain situational awareness at all times. Stay alert and watchful. Find the exits for all venues as soon as you enter, whether inside a building or at an outside event.

Take time to know the psychology behind such violent acts and learn the telltale signs of a potential attacker. If you see something, say something. Report suspicious behavior to the authorities, whether seen firsthand or observed through posts on social media.

Trauma can paralyze a victim's ability to think clearly and cause them to panic. Knowing what to do in a life-threatening situation is imperative. Sign up for safety classes offered by many local communities and train yourself on how to respond in the event of a homegrown terrorist attack. The few moments you save, by not having to decide what to do, can save your life ... and the lives of others.

Imperfect Lies

Acknowledgments

Writing a book is easy. Getting it reader-ready is not.

I am both blessed and honored to have one of the finest support groups in this industry. They analyze, question, refine, critique, offer quality suggestions and encouragement, and give feedback line by line, page by page, chapter by chapter. Without them, I'd never make it to print.

My heartfelt appreciation goes out to: Emily Gray, Brenda Curtis, Shari Nardello, Vicki Mobley, Barry Thomason, and, of course, to my soulmate, Paul Noyes without whose vast experience and knowledge of all things military these books would not be possible. And then there's my publisher, Marji Laine Clubine, and her team of editors, particularly Shirley Crowder, whose expectations elevate everything to a higher level. Thank you all from the bottom of my heart.

Collect the Imperfect Series!

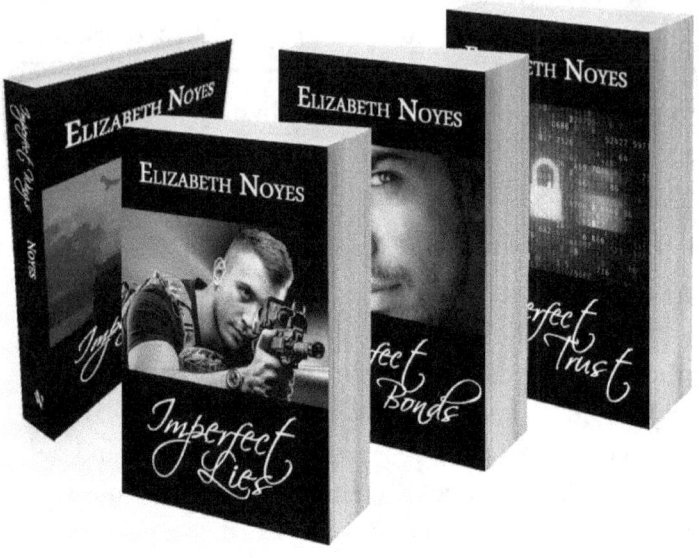

Follow the Cameron family through each of the books and learn how these siblings fight together and sometimes even against each other. You've met the couples through this final book, but if you haven't experienced their stories, you don't want to miss out!

Suspense from Write Integrity

The Amazing Grace series by freelance editor and multi-published author Fay Lamb.

Heath's Point Suspense by Write Integrity's executive director, Marji Laine Clubine.

Award-winning Rogues series, a dystopian with heart and hope, by Kristen Hogrefe.

Stalker action & adventure set against the rugged nature of the Northwest by Dena Netherton.

**Thank you
for reading our books!**

**Look for other books
published by**

Write Integrity Press
www.WriteIntegrity.com

www.ingramcontent.com/pod-product-compliance
Lightning Source LLC
Chambersburg PA
CBHW051436260626
47162CB00001B/120